CLASHING HEARTS

HAVEN CROSSROADS
BOOK 1

EVEY LYON

HAVEN CROSSROADS SERIES

Clashing Hearts

Hidden Hearts

Bound Hearts

Tangled Hearts

Copyright © 2026 by Evey Lyon, Lost Compass Press

Written and published by: Evey Lyon, Lost Compass Press

Edited by: Contagious Edits

Proofreading: Rachel Rumble

Cover design illustrated paperback and illustrated e-book: Concepts by Canea

Cover design hardback and e-book: Lost Compass Press

All rights reserved.

No part of this book may be reproduced in any form or by any electronic or mechanical means. including information storage and retrieval systems, without written permission from the author, except for the use of brief quotations in a book review.

This book is a work of fiction. The names, characters, places, and incidents are products of the writer's imagination and used fictitiously and are not to be perceived as real. Any resemblance to persons, venues, events, or businesses is entirely coincidental.

The author acknowledges the trademark status and trademark owners of various products referenced in this work of fiction, which have been used without permission. The publication/use of these trademarks is not authorized, associated with, or sponsored by the trademark owner.

The author expressly prohibits using this work in any manner for purposes of training artificial intelligence technologies to generate text, including, without limitation, technologies that are capable of generating works in the same style or genre as this work. The author reserves all rights to license uses of this work for generative AI training and development of machine learning language models.

Author's Note: No artificial intelligence (A.I.) or predictive language software was used in any part of the creation of this book.

This book is U.S. copy registered and further protected under international copyright laws.

ABOUT

I was hired to survive him—not to fall for him.

Six assistants didn't survive Julian Haven—billionaire, business shark, and a walking storm cloud. Now, I'm lucky number seven on the assistant list. The one who's supposed to run screaming before the ink on my contract dries.

Except I'm not like the others, and he isn't impressed that I'm the sunshine he never saw coming. His grumpy scowls? Don't scare me. His impossible demands? Don't faze me. The twisted little games he plays? I'll be his match. His habit of peeling off those crisp white shirts in his office like sin? Not. Even. Blinking... really, totally... okay, a little.

But then came my solid choice of evening dress.

His eyes possessively on me.

The first crack in his icy armor. And my eagerly awaiting lips.

Somehow, I become his—kept close, kept hidden.

But Julian uncovers a secret he never knew he was keeping—one that will make him fight for me, even when I promise that he'll never have me.

Then came a relationship where I'm the secret we want to keep. He isn't just my boss—he's the man determined to keep me, even if it means following me back to my tiny hometown and staying until he makes me his again.

1

SAVANNAH

Coffee dribbles down the side of my hand, but it isn't a code red. Not even a code orange. Luckily, I've never spilled an entire cup all over myself, though I probably just jinxed it. I adjust the lid on my to-go cup. My usual, oat milk cappuccino, and I grab a napkin to wipe my hands.

"What's on the docket today?" Elodie asks as we head to the elevators. We fall into step in our usual rhythm, side by side. We grew up together on Everhope Road and somehow landed at the same logistics company in Chicago.

"The usual. Meeting planning, checking slides. At least the workload is light, so no late nights," I say, taking a sip, with the patter of my low heels in the background; I paired them with a flowy dark green dress today.

I don't take for granted that I'm paid more than the average 25-year-old assistant. But Haven Crossroads treats its employees well.

Almost well.

The elevator doors open, and a crying Jill quickly exits, mascara running down her face. She's young, but I thought she was responsible and handling her role as assistant to the CEO well. She glances at us, then sobs and continues to the exit, and I'm sure that's the last we've seen of her.

Elodie and I wince at one another when we enter the elevator. "For fuck's sake, that's assistant number six in the span of six weeks," she comments as she pulls her caramel-colored hair to the side. "My two-year-old daughter has tantrums less often than that." That's not a fair comparison, as her daughter, Lola, is a little angel, which is lucky, as Elodie is also a single mom handling so much on her plate.

I jab the button for the seventeenth floor. "Julian's really been in a mood lately."

Julian Haven is anything but a haven. His name is the biggest con, to be honest. He isn't the easiest to work with. He's edgy, demanding, and it's his way only and nobody else's. Despite being younger than your average CEO, he's still ten years older than me. The expensive suits accompanying his scowl sometimes cause me to do a double-take and make my thoughts drift for a mere second. Maybe it's his hair that matches his brown eyes that slice through people that completes his appeal. Some say his eyes are mesmerizing, and I say they lure you into the gates of hell—a hell of his own making.

"I've never seen anything like it. He goes through assistants faster than a revolving door."

I give her a pointed look. "Very true." My smile turns taunting. Elodie rolls her eyes. "You owe me."

Because we put wagers on how long the new assistants last. This time, I bet four days, and I was oh-so right.

Elodie sighs. "You drive a hard bet, Savannah."

"I know."

Elodie smiles at me as the doors open on the floor with the finance department. One floor up is me. I'm so grateful that I work with Charles, our Chief of Operations. He's older, with grandkids, and it brings out a softer side in him, making him a breeze to work with. He also respects my ideas and knows that I envision working my way up if the opportunity arises. Outside of the office, I'm working on my master's in business, and he is a big supporter of that. I'm almost done, too. One more paper to go.

Arriving at my desk, I set my coffee down and slip off my winter coat because Chicago is giving us winter in March. The door to Charles's office is ajar, and I hear him on a call. It gives me my usual five minutes to set up my desk for the morning and double-check the calendar and the notes I made for the upcoming day. A few minutes later, after tidying my desk and finishing my coffee, I toss the empty cup into the trash. I stand, smooth my dress, gather my laptop, and plaster a smile on as I inhale a deep, excited breath, ready for the hours ahead.

I love mornings and new days. It brings new possibilities.

Charles greets me with a cheery hello when I enter. He's always in a good mood, and if he isn't, then he never directs it at me. He's in his typical polo shirt, which takes the focus off his hair, which is more gray than dark these days.

"Good morning. Have you eaten? Or do I need to get you a bagel from the break room?"

His lips twist. "Keeping me in line. Does my wife phone you at ten or something?"

I go silent and quirk my lips out because she actually does. "I mean, blood sugar levels and all. There's research on that, should you feel inclined to read it."

He grins to himself at my reply. "Have a seat, Savannah." I take my usual seat across from his glass desk, the cloudy Chicago skyline behind him, and open my laptop.

"That won't be needed today." The way he says it is different. Serious. Firm.

Oh... Strange.

He must see the bewilderment etched on my face.

"Relax, I'm not going to fire you," he assures me as he leans back in his chair.

My eyes widen. "Didn't know I was on the chopping block."

Charles chuckles under his breath. "You're not. I'm the one with news."

Phew.

"What might that be?"

"As you know, my schedule has been lighter. More time for golf, the grandkids, the things in life that are not in the office. I've also had more meetings with Julian. I'm not getting any younger. I've invested wisely through the years and made some great stock choices, which means I can retire early."

My stomach sinks because I know where our conversation is going. He's been subtly dropping hints about his future over recent months, and deep down, I anticipated this happening at some point.

"I'm retiring," he says at last.

I force a smile, wanting to be happy for him. "That's... wonderful."

Selfishly, I can't help but wonder what this means for me.

His head lolls to the side gently, and he examines me. "Say that with a little more conviction, will ya?" he jokes.

I straighten my posture. "Sorry. I'm not surprised, it's merely that I thought it would be another year, perhaps."

He shrugs. "I'm ready. I have a house in Hilton Head to enjoy when I'm not here in Illinois."

I nod, listening, unsure what to say. My intuition told me this moment would come.

After a stiff silence, he grins. "Wondering what'll happen to your role?"

A long exhale leaves me, and I'm thankful he can read my mind and bring it up. "Yes," I admit.

He claps, eyes shining. "You're one of the best—bright, high-energy, tough. You keep me moving. You're essential. That's why I'm promoting you."

Suddenly, my mood perks up. My drooping shoulders straighten; my neck elongates. I ask, "Really?"

"Yep. My role as COO is to ensure we run a tight ship, including staff. I need to be confident that whatever we do will improve and ensure the strategy is met. Day-to-day operations need to run smoothly. I see a significant risk if I don't act, as we urgently need to fill a role. Should have thought of this solution sooner, since it's so obvious. Not many people can handle him, but I know you can."

No. Oh no. Why does worry now hit me?

"Assistant to the CEO is perfect for you, and you will do great."

My face sours. I force composure. "Julian? You want me to be his assistant?"

Charles's face falls with understanding, and he holds his hands up to calm me. "I'm aware that he may not have the… *best* record with assistants. All the more reason I need to be assured that he has someone who won't quit, especially during the transition of somebody new in my role." I'm not impressed with this turn of events, and it's apparent. "You're great with challenges, and you're the only one I can think of to handle the job. You always update your in-case-of-emergency handover sheet, so I can easily get a temp in to fill your current role. Julian? Well, he needs someone as soon as possible. Someone who can jump in. He needs organization more than me, as I'm going to slowly transition out with fewer days in the office."

Professional. Remain professional. "Uh…" That's all I can croak out.

His face turns to stone, so unlike Charles. "It means a pay raise," he says bluntly.

Ah, he's desperate.

It's tempting. Or miserable. "Trying to sweeten the deal for dealing with Satan?" I joke. With Charles, I can be direct.

He lets go of the flattery. His face relaxes. "The company

will cover all tuition loans for your master's degree if you stay with us, and you will be debt-free. Of course, should you quit within a certain amount of time, then you would need to pay it back. But you are not a quitter," he says, expression flat.

"W-What?" I stammer. It's a profound offer, with major implications for my financial future. "You're very desperate, it seems. That's a big offer." It's more than immense. I managed to get a scholarship, but it didn't cover everything, and as much as I'm paid well here, paying the remaining tuition does make me check my savings more often than I would like.

He snaps his fingers. "It is. But it makes sense, too. Your degree fits with your work here. Plus, I hope this emphasizes this big change. Your contract states that we can move you to a different role, provided your salary and benefits remain unchanged. You will now be getting paid more, a degree paid for as long as you don't quit, and the experience of a lifetime. I know you can't run from that."

"Well, your bribery game is strong," I deadpan.

"I've made up my mind."

My jaw drops slightly. "*So, I'm* his new assistant?"

"Yep." He shuffles papers, eyes a drawer, as casual as someone bringing birthday cake to the staff room. "He's simply misunderstood. You'll be fine." I just blink at him. He looks up. "You two know each other. You've been in plenty of meetings with him."

That is probably one of the problems in this new situation. I've witnessed the way he pretends to fix his expensive cufflinks right after he turns the conversation in his favor without giving anyone a mere glance, including me. Despite my tenure of two years here, he has rarely had to speak to me in relation to work. The few times his eyes have set on me, they felt challenging, dangerous even. I've always had a tiny piece of curiosity about what he was thinking about on the rare occasion when he decided I should grace his vision.

The workday will be like talking to a wall. I'm sure his conversations outside of work probably wouldn't be thrilling, either. More straight to the point and an undressed kind of soul... Why did that even come to mind?

Get it together, Savannah.

Charles seems overly confident right now about the news he just delivered.

I frown in defeat. "Of course. I'll miss being your PA, but better sooner than later to change positions before you leave."

He sticks his thumb into the air. "Exactly. That's the mindset you should have. But really, you are the one I trust, and we need to get someone in now to help Julian. He'll drown, otherwise. The man is pure strategy and only measures outcomes in terms of 100% success. The problem is that he needs someone to keep him in check and ensure all departments use his time wisely. Schedules, reviewing presentations, all that stuff."

"I understand."

"Good." He studies me for a few ticks with his head tipping to the side, studying me, and he softens after a deep breath. "You have wit, and more importantly, backbone. I doubt you will be scared away like the others. Not to mention, it will be a great experience for your resume. People would envy you. I want to leave comfortably, believing that Julian has calmed and has a stable workday that doesn't involve a lack of an assistant."

Simply, I nod my head in agreement and attempt to smile. He isn't wrong about all those things, and I don't want to let him down. Challenges are part of professional development, right?

Still, when I leave his office with my shoulders sagging, I dread what my future employment looks like.

Dropping into my desk chair, I reach for my jar filled with fruit snack gummies. I don't care if it's the food choice of a kindergartener; they're good, and the box says they're made with real fruit juice. I rip open the little packet and throw a purple grape-flavored gummy into my mouth.

I do my best to let go of the feelings of my career demise, because nobody survives him.

But in that moment, it takes over. My confidence.

I have zero tolerance for arrogance, and there was even that time we got stuck in an elevator together for a minute. I didn't fawn over his presence as other women do, even if it was a tiny bit tempting. That feeling is always ruined, anyhow, when he does something borderline despicable.

I will focus forward, remain calm with a smile the sun would be jealous of, and take no prisoners on my insistence that I will survive him. That backbone that Charles has seen is very true.

I accept this experiment, and it isn't because my student debt will be paid off.

I'm doing this because I'm not a quitter.

Instead, I'll challenge him.

I won't falter.

2
JULIAN

I slam my laptop screen down, completely frustrated. I don't understand how to read the calendar; the assistant had some color-coding system that gives a freaking rainbow a run for its money.

This is the last thing I need. We are restructuring, with many internal changes on the horizon, and I need everyone on their A-game. The previous assistant was too slow, and I didn't appreciate her inability to make a proper espresso, nor did I need to tell her what to order for my lunches. She should have been ahead of the curve.

I twirl on my office chair so I can soak in the view of the skyline. This company is important to me. I didn't break away from my father's claws only to fail. Succeeding is the only option. My thoughts drift briefly to him. We don't speak anymore, his lacking qualities as a father and husband made sure of that. Before I can dwell on it, I shove the memory aside. Now isn't the time to dig up old wounds. Let's just say he gave me one more reason to start my own company and excel. My sister follows the same policy. We both cut ties with him. Never looked back. Now, I focus on what really matters: running my billion-dollar empire.

Hence, I have limited tolerance for assistants who do not meet expectations.

A sudden knock interrupts my train of thought, snapping me back to the office.

"You look like you could use a break." Charles smiles as he strides into my office. The man doesn't have a single ounce of stress in his body, and that alone is irritating as hell, but he's a good guy, so I can't fault him for it.

"Nah, simply not caffeinated enough."

He sits on my dark leather couch. I leave my desk, cross the room, and head to the coffee machine on a side table by the wall.

"Could that be because you lost another assistant?" He crosses his arms and gives me a stern look.

I shrug. "Jess wasn't doing well on her trial, and I don't have time to show her things."

"You mean Jill? Her name was Jill," he corrects me with a bit of disapproval in his tone.

I hold up a cup to see if he wants a drink, but he declines with a gentle shake of his head. "Jess, Jill, they're all the same."

He rubs his face with his palms, and he appears exasperated, which often happens around me. "They're not, and now you're without an assistant."

"I'll just have HR send me another." They have a few agencies on their speed dial for temps if needed. Although they mentioned that one agency is no longer willing to collaborate.

"My retirement is upon us," he reminds me.

We talked about it the other week and set a plan in motion for the transition. There will be a battle over who will be granted his role, but I'm good at sensing snakes and vipers.

I hit the button on my machine to drown out my sigh. In truth, I'll miss him. He is more of a father figure than my own.

But as much as I breathe work, I understand why he wants to enjoy life beyond the office. He deserves it.

Coordinating a smooth transition is leaving me with a headache.

"Listen, I've accepted that you're leaving, but let's not throw it in my face every time we see one another. Especially with some of the deals we have in the pipeline. Unless this is your way of telling me that you'll name your new sailboat after me." My mouth twitches, wanting to smirk due to my satisfying effort at humor.

"I only brought it up because I have had a few meetings today, as we agreed. Slowly trickling the information to our key players." He snaps his fingers and grins from ear to ear. "Let's talk about your assistant."

I bring my small Italian-sized cup of espresso to my lips and take a quick sip, then approach the couch across from him. "I don't have one. I'm waiting for Linda to return." I settle in opposite Charles, crossing one leg over the other and leaning into the leather, getting comfortable. Our talks are always smooth and casual. Probably because he's damn good at his job—there's no need to chase or question his decisions. He's been with me from the start.

He rolls his eyes. "Linda? The assistant from four months ago?"

I lift a shoulder. "She was actually good at her job. What happened to her, anyhow? I don't remember firing her."

"She went on maternity leave, and since our company has great benefits for our employees, it means she won't be coming back for at least another six months, and she already expressed that she would only come back if she had a different role… away from you."

I set my cup on the coffee table as I flex my neck side to side. "Someone is being a little honest today."

"I need to keep you in check. As I was saying, I've been having meetings to inform everyone, and today I spoke with Savannah."

My fixed expression almost falters. I don't enjoy that woman. She's too young, sassy, good at her job, and always tucks a honey-brown tendril behind her ear. I shouldn't notice that. Her name is Savannah May; that chimes like a bell. Chiming melodies are for happy people. I'm not a fan of those.

"How did she take the news?" I play it cool, return to my position, and extend my arm across the back of the sofa.

"Okay. I'll miss having her as my extra eyes to keep me in order."

I scoff. "Tell me about it. If we hired real talent on the assistant front, someone would've brought me my 10 AM power bar by now. This morning's treadmill run was tough." I always get up early to exercise before conquering the day.

"Well, that will be solved soon. As Chief of Operations, I'm ensuring you have an assistant who will stick around after I'm gone."

I wait patiently. He's building up to something, I can feel it.

"That's why I told Savannah that she is your new assistant."

My brows immediately rise from being zapped by shocking news. "What now?" I grit out.

"Effective tomorrow, she's your new assistant. She set up a strong system so I can have someone else. You? Well, you will drown if we don't get you help. I'm not sure why I didn't think of this earlier. You've seen her, she's sharp."

Yes, I've fucking seen her. That's the whole damn problem with his solution that he feels is wise.

I scratch my cheek, weighing my thoughts. There are a dozen other options in the company for her. Finance, import & export, legal, clients from every industry, and I'm the winner on the list? "As CEO, I do have final say. What if I have concerns about her fit as my assistant?"

He gives me an unimpressed look for my hypotheticals. "Well, her contract states we can assign her to a new role. Letting her go would be a bad move because she's talented, and also, it would be an unlawful termination. Of course, you are well aware of that."

I am. Now I need to try another angle. "I mean, surely, she doesn't want to travel more or work late nights?"

Late nights in my office, in case my body needs the reminder.

"She's up to the challenge."

"No other solutions?" I volley back.

"Nope." His smile is wide. "I'm sure you'll both figure out a rhythm for working together."

A rhythm together... My mind is too dirty for 10 AM.

I pinch the bridge of my nose. "Right. Tomorrow it is then." I exhale audibly.

Charles claps his hands and stands. "Great. You'll have an assistant who is committed and won't back down. Julian, I want to leave the company feeling truly at ease. You always respect my opinions, and I respect yours. It would bring me joy to know that, day to day, everything is running as it should. You deserve that peace."

Pausing for a long beat, I soak in the genuine regard and esteem that we have for one another. On a professional level, the man is my mentor and easily took me under his wing when I was young and decided to branch away from any business related to my family, and he left that company, too. He stayed with me even when I became a powerhouse that couldn't be tamed.

"Thank you. I respect you, which means if you're convinced, I'll humor you."

He grimaces as he reaches the door. "Good. See you later at the 1 PM meeting on quarterly numbers."

I give a little nod, and as soon as he exits, I scrub my face in frustration. Savannah has always been Charles's assistant, and we rarely cross paths. But that's about to change, leaving me uneasy. There is only one way to ensure my safety.

Ensure Savannah isn't closer in my orbit.

I'll just have to push her buttons until she quits.

3
SAVANNAH

The loud click of my finger pressing the enter key comes only from frustration at my situation. I didn't even get a day to process. I've already been thrown into his majesty's kingdom. Charles was adamant that Julian needed help immediately. Fine. I'm a professional.

I will not be fired. I will stand my ground to the point that he knows he needs me to keep his days in order. He won't even remember how to fire someone once I'm through with him.

I check the time on the corner of the screen. I'm surprised Julian isn't here already. It's 7:30 in the morning, and I assumed he would be in before anybody else. Normally, I don't get in until 8:00, but I wanted to be ahead of the curve, and I'm assuming these are my new hours anyway.

The ding of the elevator draws my attention, and I can already feel his presence. How can I not? Julian is a dominating force that radiates confidence and success. And why, oh why must he be wearing the dark gray suit with no tie today, and his face clean-shaven?

I stand behind my desk, perpendicular to his door. He walks

from the elevator to his office. I smooth my maroon suit dress as if it matters. His eyes, cold yet burning, land on me.

"Good morning, Julian." I smile politely, with extra pep in my tone.

"Savannah," he responds curtly and doesn't bother stopping; instead, he heads straight into his office and shuts the door behind him with force.

Blinking, I try to adjust to what happened seconds ago—a wave of irritation mingles with confusion. He really isn't one for a bright start to the day that usually entails a friendly greeting, leaving me feeling a bit unsettled.

I blow out a breath and sit down. I opt to continue researching his calendar while nibbling on a bagel from the break room, which is for our floor only. I chose blueberry because I didn't want to risk smelling of onion; not that it matters around him, except somewhere inside me cares.

There is a very slim chance I'll be able to leave on time today, and I'll need to study late into the night. The deadline for my final paper is looming around the corner. Most of my degree is online, but I'm approaching the end. I don't want to just pass, I want *cum laude*. It's for me more than anything, because my family is already proud of my efforts.

Before I know it, it's 8 AM, and since he didn't ask for an earlier meeting, I'll assume this will be the time for our daily meeting to discuss the day ahead.

My heart hammers in my chest as I stand, grab my laptop, and head toward Satan's cave.

One gentle knock is all it takes for Julian to say, "Enter."

He doesn't even look up when I approach his desk. "Would you like a rundown of your agenda for the day?" At least I sound measured and not at all apprehensive.

"That is your job," he responds mundanely, still focusing on his cell phone while I sit down on the chair in front of his desk.

I stay composed, flip open my laptop, and list his morning meetings. He doesn't respond. When I glance up, he's staring at me with an unreadable expression.

"Everything okay?"

"You left a protein bar on my desk?" I could swear there is a hint of being impressed in his voice.

One point for me.

I shrug. "Yeah, I saw a note about that. I assumed you were at the gym or something."

He inspects me warily. "Huh, the other assistant never thought of that."

"I think you mean assistants, plural." I smile tightly at him.

His jaw pulses. "Next time, make it peanut butter. I hate berries."

Point down for me.

He wants to make it difficult for me. I sense it. "Sure," I say. "Great weather. The bagels in the break room are excellent. I can bring you one, unless that disrupts your protein regimen. There'll be cake later—someone has a birthday."

"Are you always cheery this early?"

"Yes. Have to start your morning right. Plus, my hockey team won last night against Buffalo, so I'm naturally in a good mood."

Julian sinks back in his chair, and his eyes probe into me as he stretches his fingers. "Tell me, anything I need to know about you that Charles hasn't mentioned? He sings your praises."

"Well, you've seen me in meetings, so my work should speak for itself," I justify.

"I mean outside of the office."

His sentence catches me off guard. My mind scrambles—what does he mean? "Uh, I'm finishing my master's degree?" My drawn-out voice betrays confusion and anxiety, unsure if that's what I should say.

"What else?"

I smirk as my snark slips out, though I meant to keep it in today. "Oh gee, you want to play the get-to-know-you game?"

The corner of his mouth lifts, and he splays his hands out while his elbows rest on the chair arms. "You are the one handling my day."

"Fine." I square my shoulders and close my laptop, unsure how long this will last. "Small town background. Close-knit family. Hate sushi. Anything else relevant for my job?"

"Nope. Now, continue with the meeting schedule."

"Don't you want to share any tidbits of your life? I'm sure your life is oh so festive outside of these walls," I challenge with a fake smile.

His jaw sweeps side to side as his gaze pierces me. "No need. It's my company."

I study him for a second before a sound vibrates under my breath. "Well... let's continue. You have a call at 10 AM with London. Keep the time difference in mind, so there is no pushing back meetings today. At 11 AM, you have a marketing meeting, they want to give a presentation, but I told them to cut it to ten minutes so you don't have to sit through the thirty minutes they had planned."

He interrupts. "Don't you need your laptop for this?"

With purpose, I thrum my fingers on the closed laptop. "Or I know your schedule, and we are good to go." I throw him a contrite smirk.

Julian seems surprised by me. Maybe he expected an assistant to be nervous or to make mistakes, but I'm calm and precise around him. I notice his brows lift slightly, a flicker of curiosity in his gaze.

He clears his throat and adjusts in his seat. "That's, uh, refreshing." There is a struggle in giving the compliment.

"Shall we continue?" I say, not waiting for his answer. "I've cleaned up your inbox that sat unattended for *a while*. Assistants are helpful for that. I'm sure you get it."

His eyes grow wider, probably due to my boldness. "How intuitive of you. Now, Savannah, let's get something a little clear."

He stands and circles his desk. Every step tightens my body, anticipation tingling beneath my skin. I try not to stare but fail when he perches on the desk at my side, closing the distance between us.

"Eyes up here," he orders, and I draw a line up with my gaze to see him, arms and ankles crossed, his gaze set on me. "You shall listen to me. Beck n' call and all that." He rasps the last sentence, and the words float and wrap around me. It's his intention, it's written all over his face. His normal tone returns. "The plus side of this arrangement is you're not new to the company, and I'm well aware of your experience in your role. I run things a little differently. I request more, demand is a better word. I hope you can handle that."

He peers down, and I lift my chin. If not for the chair, I'd be on my knees at his mercy. "Easily," I answer, my voice confident, not weak.

"Don't be too eager, Savannah. You don't know what you've signed up for. I started a logistics company because I enjoy moving things like a game of chess. Chess pieces sometimes need to be sacrificed when you make risky moves. Don't become a pawn in a game when I don't always play fair, Ms. May. So let me be very clear. I have no problem doing things for my business that would turn heads—legal, of course, but questionable to some. Not many assistants grasp that. I need somebody who isn't afraid. I speak my thoughts. I won't sugarcoat or filter them. Not many people can handle that. Can you?" Maybe it's a threat, or maybe I'm intrigued. The way he speaks has an ounce of swelter that stabs me deep, all the way to my spine.

"Of course."

"Great. Because I expect all of my meeting agendas for next week, up until Thursday, to be ready by noon."

I chuff a laugh. "Why next week Thursday?"

He shrugs, a sinful smile spreading. "Because I feel like it. You, Savannah May, must obey your new boss."

Are you fucking kidding me? He's testing me.

I swallow my retort and keep my face neutral. "Of course. It'll be ready. Anything else?"

He propels himself off the desk. "No. You're dismissed."

Julian isn't looking at me when I stand; otherwise, he would see me biting my lip in complete disgust for his attempt to make me break with the audacity of his choice of words.

I walk to the door and pause, hand on the handle. "Your coffee tastes like crap," I say. I inhale, turn on my heel, and watch him. "I've ordered you a new machine."

His fingers brush along the glass of his desk as he stands behind it. "Did you now?"

"Don't worry. I already had HR approve the expense since it involves the welfare of their staff. One staff member in particular. They need to increase the happiness scale for the next employee survey."

Julian fights back an amused smirk. "Enlighten me on how *my* coffee machine will increase the scale?"

"Because you will be in a better mood," I say bluntly and turn to leave.

"Savannah," he says. I'll have to get used to how he says my name. It's not playful, nor serious. His own melody entwines command and entertainment. "Please book a hotel room at the usual spot for 2 PM. I'm meeting someone. You can clear my schedule for the rest of the day."

I freeze, anxiety fluttering in my chest, and give myself a second longer than I would like to gather composure.

"Of course." I force the words out, my voice tight with revulsion, before I flee, overwhelmed by absolute disgust. He is one of *those* CEOs who has weekday-afternoon hotel rendezvous.

Why do I really hate every word in his request? I shouldn't care at all. Not even a morsel. But there is a crumb of something. Jealousy that I need to find a cure for.

4
JULIAN

Pausing with my lips on the rim of my whiskey glass, I realize that I'm toying with Savannah. I shouldn't be. She's my new assistant, and I have to deal with it. That also means that her brazen attitude and the way a dress clings to her body shouldn't bother me. Yet, I was vague on the details of my afternoon and simply let her assume the worst.

She probably thinks I get my kicks from random hookups with the array of women who have made it known they're available. Yet that is not what I'm doing at all.

"Earth to Julian." My friend, Hayes, waves his hand in my face as we sit at a small, low table in the bar of my favorite hotel in the city.

I shake my head slightly. "Sorry. Got sidetracked on a work issue."

Hayes is my buddy from college on the east coast. It's a shame he lives down in Texas, but still, we are in constant contact. It was a no-brainer to catch up while he was in the city.

"Anything in particular?" he wonders as he knocks back a swig of his whiskey. "You seem a little distant. How's work?

Must be going well if you managed to sneak away to see me while I have a break from my conference."

"I have a new assistant." She's as horrible as my past assistants who had no skill. Savannah's problem is that she has skill; it's everything else that is testing my patience.

"Oh yeah?" He grins from ear to ear.

"You find that funny? Explain," I say, peering into my empty glass. I signal the bartender for another.

He shrugs. "I feel like every time I see you, you have a new assistant. You were holding steady for a while. What happened to that assistant?"

"She went off and decided to procreate and add a human to the world. I've had one or two temps, but nothing stuck." Maybe more than two, but I lost count of the number of times HR couldn't find me someone worth keeping. "Well... Charles's assistant has now been thrown upon me. Happened this week."

"That's promising. I bet she'll stick around for a while if she worked for Charles."

"Delightful," I mutter under my breath, and I don't mean it at all. Focus is what I need. Sure, I was missing someone who actually knows my calendar and keeps an eye on the small details. She'll keep me sharp in energy but completely fuck up my concentration purely by her presence.

"Don't be grumpy. Are you still playing pickleball or something?"

My eyes bulge. "Whoa, whoa, whoa, I am not supporting the pickleball trend in order to be relevant. Classic racquetball will do. And no, it's been a while."

"Okay, enlighten me, why are you so tense?"

I scoff. "Don't be silly." He catches my eye. "Really." I drum my fingers. "Work's slammed. These deals are finally closing."

Hayes leans back in his chair, his arm extends, and he points his glass in my direction. "I've known you long enough. That was a lie. Now is the time to share while I'm gracing your city for a few days."

The barman sets a small bowl of nuts and my new drink on our burgundy table in passing. Quickly, I grab hold of my whiskey.

Continuing to study Hayes for a few seconds, I debate whether I should admit my insanity—I'm desperate for someone to talk to. Hell, I've escaped the office at 2 PM on a workday. That's gotta raise alarms for many.

I set my glass tumbler down on the square napkin. "I told my assistant to book a room here to make her think I'm meeting a woman for an afternoon fuck fest." I string the sentence together with speed. I also wince from admitting that out loud.

His jaw drops. "You what?" He grins, clearly entertained.

"You heard me," I mutter and avoid looking at him because I don't want to see his face.

"Testing her discretion or... is there another reason?"

"She has worked for my company for a while. Discretion is second nature to her. Plus, she had to sign an NDA."

"Okay, which means you did it because..." He encourages me to continue.

I bite inside my cheek because I'm trying to keep the reason locked inside. Admittance is dangerous.

"Wait. Is she good-looking?"

My head wobbles side to side. "I mean, if tight dresses and a gentle face with a snarky yet ridiculously peppy attitude is your thing."

Hayes keeps grinning. "Right, so she's attractive. I get it."

I scoff at his accusation. "Please, I have many options to pick from."

"But she's forbidden, right? Your company must have no-fraternizing rules or something like that. But wait, you own the company, so you can change that rule in a flash."

"Forget I said anything. We should talk about how I can persuade you to join my company."

"No rule against employee entanglements? Maybe I'd consider it," he jokes.

I shake my head and raise two fingers in the air to indicate to the bartender that we need another round. "Let's move on."

His palm flies up. "Sure… for today. You went to great lengths to test jealousy and her reaction."

I should really defend the accusation, but I might struggle in the debate because the truth would trickle in.

"Really. It's no big deal. Conversation closed."

I told Savannah to clear my calendar for the rest of the day, but I want to return only after she's gone. I can't risk running into her. I don't want to see her today. That's another problem. She has a strong work ethic for her age and isn't a 9-to-5 worker; she'll stay until the job is done.

I admit I need to fine-tune my avoidance tactic around her.

THE NEXT MORNING, I arrive late at the office. I wanted to take a call from home to discuss a few new personal stock options. It seemed easier to take the 8 AM call when at home to be on time for the day's stock market opening.

Maybe I should've braced myself. When I step off the elevator and see red roses and a gift box on Savannah's desk, I dread our meeting ahead.

"Good morning, Julian." She smiles brightly as she welcomes me. She even stands up as if there is some protocol and I'm the royal highness… which, for this building, maybe isn't far off.

I don't return her look and simply keep my face stoic, even when I stop in front of her desk. "Savannah," I say simply while my eyes attempt to inspect the gift. "Humor me. Who sent me flowers?"

Her shoulders puff out, and her elated look doesn't melt even a tad. "They're not for you. Someone sent them to me."

My body clenches. Instantly. I don't do jealousy, but fury fills me that some man dared to send *my* assistant gifts after a date, or maybe it's her boyfriend. Does she have a boyfriend? No. She has never once mentioned one nor brought anyone to the office holiday party, which should have been a warning sign that I was paying too much attention.

"You can throw them away. I hate flowers and don't want them on your desk or as the first thing people see when they walk onto my floor."

Now her smile wilts. "Right." Her T is tight. "We are going straight for the devil's den aesthetic."

My jaw slides to the side because I want to hide that I might actually find that quip funny.

"They better be gone," I firmly reiterate before I storm into my office, slam the door behind me, and zip to my desk to fall into my seat.

Ah shit, not the best way to start my day. She's probably in the staff room poisoning my power bar, but then my eyes drop—she already left me one. The correct flavor, too.

A few minutes later, I hear her soft knock and tell her to come in. I'm a professional, so I will treat the day normally. One deep breath in and… fail.

Savannah opens the door, takes a few steps, with her hip out and her hand finding a home on her green satin dress. "The flowers are in the break room. Perhaps somebody will appreciate beautiful roses and a carrot cake that says congratulations."

I fold my arms across my chest. "Perfect."

"Now I have to tell Elodie that her present nearly found a home in the trash."

A woman's name eases me slightly, and I know Elodie works for me. "Humor me. Is it your birthday?"

She shakes her head and walks farther into my office before sitting in front of my desk and elegantly crossing one knee over the other to ensure no skin gets to taunt me.

"I won a bet on how many assistants you would fire this month, and she sent me condolence flowers for my new role within the organization." She smiles contritely at me.

I roll my eyes because I need to find a way to knock the sass out of her. "Won't she have a fun performance review." I'm joking, yet no humor finds my voice.

Savannah sighs and looks down at her notebook. "Anyhow, your new coffee machine is up and running, and you have a big day of afternoon meetings since yesterday you decided to play hooky." She pretends to write, but her paper remains blank.

Got her.

It did bother her.

A winning smirk stretches on my face. "Tell me, what do you think I did yesterday that involves your complete discretion?"

Her mouth parts open, but no words follow.

"Hmm." I stand and stride in the direction of my coffee machine on the table against the wall. "You know, sometimes we meet friends from out of town. For example, one who is staying in a hotel, and the room wasn't even needed, instead requested just for kicks."

I glance over my shoulder to see that her face falls and her beautiful berry-colored lips form an O. Perfect form. A gift to look at. Should I throw logic out the door?

She swallows and straightens her spine. "Okay."

I grab a small espresso cup and immediately try to figure out the new machine, then look at her. "I'm curious. Would it bother you if I asked you to book rooms for me when I might have someone, plural or not, who might relax my day?"

She turns her head sharply and daggers my eyes with her

own. "Who am I to be a moral judge? It's my job, isn't it? I signed an NDA." She walks to me with heavy steps, snatches the cup from my hand, and takes over my coffee pursuit.

I tut. "You didn't answer my question." I scoot a few inches closer to her from behind, and it would be so easy to reach out and touch her shoulder.

"It's probably not appropriate to ask me such things." Her voice is weak.

Poking her right now to gauge her thoughts is how I want to play. "For your reference, I had a serious girlfriend in college, which made both our families happy. It didn't make me happy, however. I'm not a relationship guy. My 20s were a time of naivety and afternoon fun. But call it experience with age, but I have a strict policy to keep my mutually beneficial indiscretions out of the office."

Her body stills from my bluntness. After a second, she juts her chin out, and I feel her body shift into a confidence that I recognize in her. She glances over her shoulder at me. "Have you always been this open with your assistants? Or do I get that honor and misery?"

I choke out a low laugh. "Do you mean the way you have a mouth and speak to me, ignoring rank?"

She scoffs. "Wow. You really are a piece of work."

"Should I be proud of that? And to answer your question, no. Congratulations on being special."

"Oh joy," she responds unenthusiastically.

"Let's simply establish that you and I don't have any lines or boundaries. You and I can speak freely, and I won't feel the need to chastise you for your snark. As for appropriate? I don't think you and I understand the word, so I'll let your mind run wild on that one. Should we agree on the new policy established?"

Her intrigue is written all over her face, and her nose lifts slightly; she doesn't seem to be debating with herself, though. "Fine. Agreed."

Miracle of the day.

A shame everything I just spewed out could be a lie, because all I want to ask her is if she will be a problem and cause an actual indiscretion in the office. Savannah threatens every policy I have. I'm not sure if it's a game I am eager to play or something else altogether.

She looks forward and focuses on the coffee, but a micro step on my part and her body stills, and I'm positive her dirty little mind telepathically met mine somewhere.

I do something risky, but I'm far too curious to stop myself. My fingers float without touching her, trailing down her arms to near her hands, which hold the cup under the machine spout.

"So, this is the new machine?"

Almost magnetically, her body gravitates toward mine. Our distance closes, but not enough to touch. I sense a hitch in her breath, and I'm not letting this moment go, either. The feeling of her so close fills my lungs with a heavy breath that in a different setting would be sensual.

"It is. A new type of bean, too." She fills the portafilter and screws it into the drip. She struggles to tighten it into place, and it isn't the machine's fault. My fingers gently skim her wrist before I take over the machine, and her hands fall away. Yet her floral smell is still intoxicating because she hasn't stepped away from me. I wonder if she senses it, too. A dangerous line that we're balancing on.

But I have an empire to run, and I haven't checked the calendar for today, but I'm positive I have a meeting in five.

The sound of the coffee machine grinding fills our ears, breaking the heaviness of our bubble. Savannah steps away, clearly affected, and her eyes avoid me at what seems to be all costs.

"Right. So, uhm, yeah, I sent you the project deck for the two o'clock meeting to have a skim through to ensure you're aware of what the social media team wants to present. Also, your travel is all booked for Boston in a few weeks."

She's flustered, and it's all my doing. That can make a man proud, and I'm no exception.

"Okay."

Our eyes meet and remain self-assured, pretending all is normal. It really isn't, but I'm taking the lead on this. I even slide the freshly brewed espresso out from under the machine and bring it to my lips for a sip. I don't blink even once. Instead, I keep my eyes locked on her.

"Anything else?"

She shakes her head and clearly thinks for a long beat. "No. All fine. Let me know if you need something."

Her on her knees would be one thing. But that idea has to leave my head.

She sashays past me, and I smirk to myself, but she doesn't see because she doesn't look back, only closes the door behind her.

Good girl.

Keep a door between us that shall remain shut for our well-being.

5
SAVANNAH

I rest my head back against the hot wood of the dim sauna. It's been a long few days. Yet, I survived my first week with a new boss. I'm thankful Julian was away on a work trip at the end of the week, though his constant emails and calls were enough to give me a migraine. Even in writing, he's grumpy and impossible. One email had nearly twenty exclamation marks because he thought I'd changed a meeting location, though he simply missed the right room down the hall. It's growing on me, at least. I'm now immune to him and his ways at the office.

Closing my eyes, I attempt to find peace. I was in the office until 9 PM today. Not only because of work, but also because I was in the zone, I figured I would work on my paper. By the time I looked at the clock, I realized how late it was. It also made me think that the company gym and sauna would be empty. Actually, I knew it would be. It closes at nine, but I managed to convince them to keep it open just for me. The perk of being Julian's PA. Everyone bows at my feet—or maybe it's because they realize I need every bit of relaxation I can get.

Wrapping the towel tighter around my naked body, I reach to

the side to flip the hourglass timer. Fifteen minutes will be perfect. I scoot over, lie down, and my body begins to loosen, but after a minute, the sound of the door cracking opening causes me to shoot up because I thought I was alone.

It only takes one look, and dread fills me to the brim.

"Should I even ask?" Julian says, not waiting for my answer as he walks over to the other bench.

I do my best not to let my eyes drift to where the white towel is hanging low on his hips, but it's hard not to notice due to the taut lines on his stomach and the V leading south.

Running through the options in my head, I can either flee or knot my towel strongly. But I don't want either of those options. Instead, I get back into my comfortable position because I've already survived him—well, past the average success rate.

"I could say the same. Don't you have your own sauna in your little castle in the sky?"

I'm not even sure if he has looked at me longer than he should while I'm in a towel, so maybe he *can* be a gentleman. He adjusts his spare towel around his shoulders and sits on the upper bench. "I do. But my flight got in early, and traffic is a bitch due to a baseball game. Normally, when I come this late, they lock it so nobody else can join. Imagine my surprise when they told me tonight that they would have to kick you out so I could enjoy my relaxing time. Lucky for you, I said there was no need."

I stare up at the ceiling, already feeling that familiar urge that always comes when we're together. We volley retorts and jabs back and forth. I sigh and say, "Such a kind soul you are," my voice lacking authenticity.

"I should point out it's wildly inappropriate for us to be here naked except for a towel." He sounds utterly unconcerned. "Company policies. Harassment risks."

"We abolished the boundaries policy, remember?" I counter.

He lets out a brief chuckle, and out of the corner of my eye, I see him adjust the towel draped over his waist, moved to leave little to the imagination.

"Oh yeah, I can ditch this and use the sauna properly. You really only need the towel to sit on—not for anything else. It's better for your body." Now I hear him yank his towel off, and I divert my gaze even further away.

"I'll take that under consideration."

The entire last few minutes have me questioning what world I'm in. This isn't me, is it? I'm not completely on edge or having a meltdown; I'm actually ready to level with him because I need to prove to him that I'm not fazed and to myself that I have the power to hold the upper hand. This scene was nowhere on my professional list, but I've quickly learned that Julian doesn't fit the mold, and we already established our lack of rules.

One tilt of my head and I'll see if reality matches his ego.

"But I could counter, Savannah. Either one of us could willingly leave, yet we don't. Besides, it's a sauna. There are rules for the sauna. You know what you signed up for. There's even a sign that states to enter at your own risk." His tone is a little too patronizing for my taste.

I cross my thighs, his taunting making the pining worse. "Boundaries. We have none," I say, a little too loudly.

The room grows quiet; at least he gives me that—a moment of solitude. But the silence shatters as something in me snaps. I shoot upright, clutching the towel around me so loosely that it reveals more cleavage than I intend. His heavy gaze lingers, and I can feel my pulse quicken under his stare.

"Is this my initiation? Is that why you're here?"

That curl of his lip only displays his arrogance. "No. But that is a great suggestion."

"Do I get under your skin, Julian?"

A tiny smirk plays on his lips. "I don't know, Savannah. Tell me what that must feel like, as I know I'm under yours."

I huff and check my hourglass—only halfway. Nothing is keeping me here. I could leave, but I stay. My feet won't move.

"I knew I should have gone home when I had the chance," I grumble as sweat greases my skin.

"Why did you stay?" he asks, genuinely curious.

"Why do I normally stay late? You know the answer. I haven't quit yet because I can handle the work. I sure as hell am not going to quit because we're trapped in a sauna and you're naked as can be."

His low, devilish chuckle sends a ripple of chills straight to my nipples, despite my body being covered in sweat. "Yet you haven't fully looked."

Does he really want me to look? This is twisted—and still, I'm drawn in. My sense of right and wrong collides with an urge I can't completely deny.

My eyes betray me, and he catches my glance. Sweat sheens our faces; the light glows on our skin, intensifying everything. The sensual setting heightens our senses.

The first word that comes to my mind is long. And hard. And is it because of me?

My eyes meet his with purpose as I falter. "Hmm, I thought I'd need a tape measure, but I guess not."

His lips twist before he wryly half-smiles. "What a wicked little mouth you have."

I shrug my shoulders and sigh. "But clearly one part of your body loves it."

"You're in a towel with nothing underneath in front of me. I'm a hot-blooded man." With intent, I slide my fingers along the edge of my towel, lowering it slightly over my breasts, taunting him as his eyes roam my body. "Don't toy with me, or you won't like the consequences." His voice is firm, making the threat clear.

My brows rise. "Lucky you, my time is up." I remain locked in his gaze, even when I stand in the middle of the sauna to leave. I pause for a second and begin to adjust my towel. "You are so wise with all of your years. You're right. I should follow sauna etiquette better." I rip away the towel to be completely naked in front of him. I'm not shy, and he can't hide that he is taking a photograph in his head.

I'm not going to deny myself that I wonder what he's thinking. Is my body the way he imagined? How would he touch me if I let him? This is me with the power to lead the scene.

That's why I give him a few more seconds—just to taunt him —before turning to leave.

Feeling a heavy set of eyes on me the entire time.

I DON'T INTEND to break the keyboard on my laptop, but my natural instinct is to jab each one with intense frustration. It's not because of the unacknowledged, highly inappropriate moment I had with my boss after seeing him naked. I'm aggravated because some tasks in my role are interesting, but my new boss is draining. No wonder everyone quit. Yet, I still have the drive to succeed and go down in history as the one who broke Julian Haven... *except* being so close to his orbit shakes my confidence; he makes my body buzz.

Sighing, I abandon the email, grab a packet of fruit snacks from my jar, and sink into my chair. Based on the agenda, I might actually leave on time and meet Elodie for drinks, since she has a sitter tonight. I need a moment to unwind. Last weekend, I worked nonstop fixing mistakes left by past assistants during their brief stints at the company.

I eat another red gummy, acutely aware that drinking cocktails on fruit snacks means doom. Hopefully, the place Elodie chooses has solid appetizers.

The elevator dings, and I groan inside because Julian must be back from a meeting.

His stare is sharp as he slows his swagger past my desk, creases forming as he pauses.

"What the hell are those?"

I follow his gaze to my jar. "Uh, fruit snacks."

"Yes, I can see that. Enlighten me why a child's snack choice is on display on *my personal* assistant's desk?"

Every time he says *my personal* assistant, my body is not pleased. Especially now that I've seen him naked, and I imagine him saying it in a different setting. My thoughts could reach a meltdown if I'm not careful.

"Sometimes I need a pick-me-up that isn't candy," I say, tossing a grape-shaped snack into my mouth.

"Well, it isn't the pick-me-up choice that represents Julian Haven, so let's find a new home for that crap, or better yet, give it to the tiny terrors down in the company daycare."

He must see the annoyance that I feel. "Forgive me, dear highness," I bring my hand to my heart, "for not aligning my snack choice with your brand. Let me guess, your family chef growing up wouldn't allow fruit snacks as part of your refined palate."

A subtle shake of his head and his brief check of the ceiling relay that the feeling of annoyance has returned in full. "I don't have time for this. Messages?"

"Yes, Dale Jones from Davenport Group phoned, said he can't reach your cell but needs to talk to you. Wouldn't say why."

Julian's jaw sets as a new irritation has been found. "There is a list somewhere, or ask Charles. The list has the name of every board member from Davenport, and I'll be damned if I give them a second of my day. Learn it, use it, and never let me hear you bother me about it again."

His insistence possesses a different kind of emotion that can't be pinpointed. However, it's in relation to his father's company, which always releases a different sort of cold from Julian, and I have no intention of poking that sensitivity.

"Of course."

"Where are my notes for the Stevens meeting in twenty?"

"On the drive that is linked to your calendar appointment, which I have only told you a gazillion times since last week, that is where notes are kept."

"Fine. My dry cleaning?"

Yeah, I wasn't so impressed with that demanded task he added to my list, and he is probably expecting me to make a snide remark about it. Instead... I smile. "Of course, at lunchtime. I hung it on the hook behind the door. I also adjusted the temperature in your office to ensure your suit remained in pristine condition, free of wrinkles. The man at the laundromat found a paper with a number in the pocket and saved it for you. I thanked him and said he could throw it in the garbage, unless..." I bring my finger to my chin and pretend to contemplate. "You really needed Stephanie's number, who left lipstick stains on the paper." His jaw clenches while I bring my hand to my mouth for theatrics. "Oops, my bad."

He snickers. "Cute."

To be honest, other than the second that I chose to forget to be jealous of a woman with Julian, I assumed it was another number of some doll who slipped him a piece of paper that he forgot he had... I hope. Wait, no, I don't.

"Anyhow, your meetings have been shuffled around for tomorrow. I've ensured that none are too early."

"Good."

"And I told the tech team to take another look at their meeting points for Monday because it would have been a waste of your time otherwise."

"Fine."

Why are his eyes locked onto me as though it's the start of an entrapment?

I don't let him unnerve me. "Anything else?"

"Did you do the report for Tuesday's 11:30 meeting?"

Wait, what? "No."

He doesn't seem impressed. "And why not? You should be on top of it."

I stand and set my hands on my desk, with fury bubbling inside me. "Well, if you had actually said that you wanted me to come up with some report for a measly meeting about the company's spring party, even though the events team are making a proposal, by all means, I would have ensured you received your *War and Peace*-length report by 4:59 PM. Alas…" I splay my hands out. "My boss did not communicate such a thing, probably because he himself didn't even think of it until now, purely because he despises me."

Julian attempts to hide his sly smirk, and I know because his cheek twitches. "Could be. Who knows. You can add it to your list. You can finish your day, then run along," he tells me and walks away.

"Oh golly, how lucky I am," I call out at the same time he shuts the door behind him.

"Things not going swell?" I hear Charles. I had no clue he'd arrived on the floor or how long he was watching us.

I grumble, but at least my body becomes less tense. "He is…"

Charles smiles, and when he arrives at my desk, he's a normal human and actually takes a pack of fruit snacks from my jar. "If anyone can keep him in line, it's you," he reminds me.

"Sure. Doesn't mean it's a joy to do."

He shrugs and glances at the closed door. "He'll lighten up. Give it time. There is something worthy of understanding underneath his exterior." It piques my interest what he meant by that. Julian does have a mysterious aura. "So far, you have lasted longer than most."

I pinch the bridge of my nose and remind myself of that fact while I shake the negative energy away and change the topic. "How are you? Already adding more golf outings to your schedule, I hear."

"Yeah. I'm not going to miss coming to the office every day, but so far, the two days a week that I do go to the office, I'm thankful. Being home more means my wife got the idea that my new career is running all of her errands for her." He beams a smile when he says that, and it makes me smile too. Charles affects people that way.

"Good to hear. Now, what brings you here? Something I can do, or are you here to talk with Julian?"

"My part-time assistant is doing great since you left her a detailed handover. Which means that I'm here for the latter. I was hoping to discuss a client contract."

I glance quickly at my screensaver to see the time. "If you're quick, he has one last meeting for the day."

"Okay. Do you have any plans tonight, or is it a study evening?"

I appreciate that he asks. "I decided that I'm going to meet Elodie for drinks at a place called Jupiter. I deserve a break."

His grin grows wide. "You do. If I don't see you, have a good time."

"Thanks."

How refreshing to have a man who lacks a glare and is genuinely curious if my day is going well. I'm going to miss having Charles around the office. Maybe he's right, maybe Julian will mellow out when he has to accept that I'm not going anywhere.

What a shame that I probably won't be meeting Julian halfway on the calming-down line.

I let the thought go for now, as I want to wrap up a few things before escaping.

A drink is most needed to escape my boss from hell.

6

SAVANNAH

Jupiter is a hot spot. It has an industrial feel, with hanging exposed lightbulbs, inventive cocktails, and a menu that changes with the seasons. I'm relieved when the bar menu presents a few options that are heavy on carbs. The place is bustling, but the acoustics in the place mean that I can still have a conversation with Elodie where we sit at the bar.

She eyes the bartender, and I smirk, since she's so obvious. I nudge her leg under the table with my heeled shoe. She yelps.

"Hey, what was that for?"

"To stop you before you drool." I pick up my espresso martini for a sip.

"Thanks. I should probably watch myself, but the guy has tattoos on muscly forearms, and it's my weakness. Plus, I'm a single mom who hasn't had sex in a long time."

I laugh in understanding. "You'll find a guy to sweep you off your feet in life and the bedroom. Anyway, I'm happy to be out for a drink."

"Oh yeah?" She lifts her wine glass. "Everything okay, other than your favorite boss?"

"I guess so. I'm almost done with my degree, the weather is

warming up, and my family is hanging in there. That reminds me, I need to check the calendar and use some of my vacation days. I want to head back to Everhope and take a few days off to relax with them." The city is great, but I grew up in a small town, and it always feels cozy and relaxed when I visit.

"That would be great. You deserve it since you work your ass off in everything you do. I'm curious if your boss is checking out your ass in the process." She grins and gives me a knowing look.

For some reason, I chose not to tell her that he has already seen my ass. Relaying the event will make it too real, admitting joy.

"Stop it." I smile. "Maybe he does, or maybe he doesn't." I use my hand to display myself, but I believe that I have the answer.

She bursts out with a laugh. "Oh, please, you've really stepped up your work outfits lately. Don't get me wrong, you've always had a great sense of fashion, but now? I don't know, it's the little things. A new shade of lipstick or something."

I shake my head. "Absolutely not." Or maybe. Attraction does things to people, and I'm not blind; I'm positive it's mutual, but I still think he's despicable. "I want to get to work and do my job."

"Is that at least exciting?"

Tipping my head to the side, I quirk my lips out because it doesn't take much thought to admit the truth. "Actually, the work itself is more interesting. I loved working with Charles, but Julian's workday is more fast-paced; his insight is needed on so many things, and when he's on calls with people, then the ruthless asshole persona kind of makes sense."

"That's good, at least."

"Yeah." I brush past the subject and raise my hand to catch the attention of the other barman, who lacks tattoos, much to Elodie's dismay. "I need food. Otherwise, this drink will hit me hard, especially if we do another round." As he approaches, I slide the menu closer and scan it. I'm dying for fried mozzarella sticks, but this place is more sophisticated than that. Hell, my drink alone costs the same as buying new lingerie… Why is that even my point of reference? Quickly, I turn to the barman and flash a wide grin.

"What can I get you ladies?"

"Yeah, uh, let's do the stuffed mushrooms for now, but we'll be back for round two. Thanks." I set the menu down and return my full attention to my friend, giving her a bright smile.

"At least, you're entertained. My team is kind of boring. I have a cat lady, a guy who plays some medieval game all night, and another guy who is barely awake thanks to a new baby. Not to mention that out of the office, my life is attached to a kid who hates carrots and wants to play educational cartoons on a loop."

"They're educational, luckily." I sip my drink and set down my glass, twisting the stem. "I might be entertained, but unlike Charles, who has a doting wife, I'm sent on pointless errands: dry cleaning, power bar restocking." Elodie smirks at my list, then gulps down the rest of her drink. "He hates bagels, so at least I don't have to remember that. I swear, if he could, he'd probably ask me to get on my knees and shine his shoes."

Elodie nearly spits out the last of her wine, and her eyes drift over my shoulder.

"Well, you are *my personal* assistant." The familiar smooth voice has a hint of swelter, and everything inside of me sinks.

A long moment of stiff silence casts over us before Elodie croaks as she stands. "This is probably my cue to leave and wish you both happy tidings. Bye." She swipes her jacket off the back of the chair. "Mr. Haven," she greets him politely before fleeing.

I can't protest or say goodbye—she leaves too quickly. I feel embarrassed and uneasy knowing Julian won't let this go. When he takes Elodie's seat, his smug look confirms it.

"On your knees? Hmm, highly inappropriate, Ms. May." He indicates to the barman, and I'm not sure why.

My eyes set on him, doing my best to show that I'm unaffected by whatever taunt he is about to throw my way. "And what brings you here, dear boss?"

"You're a smart cookie. Many people from the office come here after hours."

I raise my brows at him. "You mean for happy hour? That's what normal people call it. I'm not sure happy is in your vocabulary, though. And you most certainly are not like us normal people."

He leans his elbow on the bar. I notice he ditched his suit, blazer, and cufflinks at the office. The casual style suits him too well. My body instantly reacts—which is a damn problem.

"Happy is very much part of my vocab. I'm just waiting for the moment to use it. And to answer your question, I'm here because I ordered food to take home."

"Didn't want me to do that for you?" I flippantly wonder.

A whiskey is set before him. I might ask how the barman knew, but it's Julian—he's likely friends with the owner, or a regular, brooding in his corner, plotting how to scorch the earth.

"What? Place the order or cook for me?"

We are going to go in circles with our tit-for-tat, it seems, and I accept that, which is why I grab my drink and lift it to my mouth. "I'm positive my cooking wouldn't be up to your standards."

"Why? You're a bad cook?"

I swallow, pleased by the perfect vodka-to-coffee ratio. "No. I prefer family-style meals, right down to the meatloaf and mashed potatoes."

He leans back and doesn't hide that he appraises me up and down. "You don't seem like someone who lives off of meatloaf."

My face warms; that was his way of giving a compliment. It's not so bad that it's about my looks, especially when he could have any model on his arm—and, more importantly, has already seen me naked.

"No, I don't." Right on cue to dodge the past indiscretion, the universe delivers my appetizer. Crap, with Elodie gone, how will I eat all this? "Instead, I eat vegetables covered in a cheese nobody knows."

"You're going to eat all of that alone?" He appears skeptical.

"I was sharing, but my boss scared away my friend."

Julian leans back on the stool, taking his drink with him. "I'll help you finish that."

I freeze, and my eyes meet the dare in his. "That would mean you have to stay and be blessed with my company."

He shrugs. "And? I promise not to bring up work."

I slam my hand on the counter and pretend to search. "Who is this? What have you done with my boss?"

A natural smirk hits a little different on the sexy front. It's... soft and honest. "Give me a break. I'm starving, and I was forced to look at photos of a baby's birthday party when I was done with a meeting."

"Yeah, that is rough," I reply dryly and stab a mushroom with my fork before moving the plate in his direction.

"I knew you were studying, but Charles mentioned once that you're almost done with your degree in business administration."

I'm surprised he's bringing it up, actually astonished. Mostly because he sounds genuinely interested. "Uh, yeah." Suddenly, it dawns on me. "I guess you know that Charles, in his desperation, told me that the company will pay off any of my student debt."

"He did. Desperate is a little harsh, but kudos for the sentiment."

I gawk at him. "It's an incentive not to quit or get fired."

He shakes his head gingerly. "Nah, you don't want either because you are a perfectionist."

I fan myself. "My goodness, Julian Haven just gave someone a compliment." He only stares at me, his face stoic. "I just need to hand in my last paper to finish my master's. Hopefully, I'll put it to good use. I'm still figuring out what that means for my career." I tuck a lock of hair behind my ear, shyly. Talking about non-work things with him feels odd, but it makes him seem more down to earth.

"That's good. Not going back to your hometown to marry a farmer and cook meatloaf every day?"

I chuckle. "No, that's not my calling, but I'll visit Everhope. It's special—everyone knows each other, and the coffee shop on Main Street is to die for. There are always weekend events: markets, music, town barbecues." I point at him. "We don't eat meatloaf, just amazing chicken burgers or rib eyes." Talking about Everhope, I can't help but beam. "As much as I love it, I wanted to spread my wings, and I feel I'm in the right place on my journey now. Still, I won't rule out returning for good."

"Your parents visit?"

My body subdues, and my smile disperses, causing me to grab my martini for a sip to brace myself. Clearing my throat, I look at him. "Uh, my parents aren't in the picture." I nibble the corner of my lip for a second or two. "Dad passed when I was a baby, and my mom wasn't meant to be one, hence why she left when I was six."

His face sours slightly with sympathy, but there is also a shade of something else... almost like he can relate.

"I was raised by my aunt Bea from my dad's side. Never any hesitation, she welcomed me home. I love her so much. She always ensures everyone has a place at the table, and love is shown among the family. She's an amazing human. I'm truly lucky."

Julian scratches his cheek and appears remorseful that he brought up the topic. "Sorry. I didn't realize about your parents."

Out of instinct, my hand lands on his knee to ease him. "Don't worry. You didn't know. I'm over it."

He squints his eyes to examine me for a second. "Are you?" I've never heard him show concern for someone's feelings, or rather, dare to ask the question that people avoid. It strikes a chord in me because it softens him.

"Yeah," I say honestly. "My mom doesn't cross my mind. Why should she? She made her point clear, and if she ever reached out, I've already had it set in my mind for years that I wouldn't accept that." I'm not even numb about the cards dealt to me in life. Probably because I was handed an even better hand.

Julian seems slightly skeptical but accepts my answer either way. "If you say so."

"My aunt, I'm surprised I haven't mentioned her more in the office. Then again, you and I don't really talk... in this way... outside of work. Anyhow, I'm protective of her. I'm kind of angry that the town wants to rezone lines, and that will affect her business. She owns a restaurant on a riverboat." When I look down, I realize I'm still touching his thigh, and I struggle to abandon the feeling of his hard thickness underneath my palm. Another thing to add to our inappropriate-boundaries list, but in this moment, it doesn't feel like that. Maybe that's why I take an extra second before I remove my hand. "Sorry. I didn't mean to..."

"Touch me?" His eyes are pulling me in. "You're fine." He breezes past it. "A riverboat?"

I nod my head. "Yeah, the Riverbell. The boat doesn't actually move, though. It's an old steamboat. She doesn't cook, either. Only owns it and ensures the tiny details are right and hospitality is perfection."

"Your story took a turn. I wasn't expecting the steamboat." I don't want to enjoy his current light mood, but I've already begun. "That's great you have her." He helps himself to the appetizer. "That department might have been lacking for me growing up. The nannies weren't exactly family worthy, but that's years ago and long forgotten." He references himself, which is surprising given his notoriously private nature.

"Is it?" I press.

I don't know the finer details, but it's well known that Julian has zero relationship with his father, and it is a silent rule among the company never to speak his name, even.

It suddenly hits Julian that he shared something personal with me. "Yes," he replies firmly with a warning searing into me not to push on.

"Okay."

He rolls a shoulder back and eases only slightly. "I mean, I have my older sister, Caroline. We don't talk frequently, though. We're on different paths in life."

I'm surprised he's sharing anything at all. "It can happen. I don't have any siblings. Only cousins and best friends."

"Elodie, you mean?"

I nod. "We were neighbors on our street growing up. I'm even a godmother to her little girl. The dad isn't in the picture, but luckily, your company has great daycare to help her out. Do you remember everyone's names who works for you? It's a couple hundred people."

A thin line appears on his mouth. "Almost. Why? Does that shock you?"

"Yes," I say bluntly.

"I can be full of surprises." He smirks sheepishly to himself.

I'm doubtful. "I'm sure your surprises are not earth-shattering."

His intense gaze returns. "You'll be amazed."

Actually... I won't be.

It's always been apparent to me that he has secrets about himself that he keeps guarded. Maybe one day something will be revealed, and I will be prepared to listen.

I tap my fingers on the bar top and aimlessly look around, letting the awkwardness float between us. "The new menu is tasty." Small talk could be a cure.

"We talk about food a lot, but yes. Piano?"

"Huh?"

"Do you play piano?"

My eyes squinch at him. "No. Was that part of the requirements for my job or something?"

He shakes his head with an almost boyish grin. "Nah. Merely wondering. I used to play."

"Really?" He nods. "As in a secret classical pianist or a do-re-mi forced lessons pianist?"

"My secret that you may never find out."

"I used to dance ballet. I would often come into the city when my aunt would take me to see a show."

"You don't dance anymore?"

I stammer a laugh. "No. Probably because I don't have the body for it."

He looks off into the distance behind me, yet the corner of his mouth lifts. "I would highly

disagree." His vision zips and arrows right into me. "I've seen, remember?"

My face warms, and everything he says makes my body sing. "Right." My T is sharp. "That incident."

He takes a sip of his drink while he chuckles low. "We've been good all day at ignoring it. Thanks for actually wearing clothes instead of a towel today, though." He lifts his glass to me in a toast before taking another sip.

"You're welcome."

I'm melting in this chair, and if I'm not careful, the alcohol will cause a slip of my tongue. The only way to be saved is by diversion. "The dancing got me as far as being voted Miss Everhope when I was seventeen, but that's it."

"Miss Everhope? Is that like Homecoming Queen or something?"

I giggle quietly. "I think better. The entire town votes. It's for the summer festival."

His smile is new to me. It's different, it's warm, it's honest. "That's… well… a little too wholesome for me."

"Yeah, you don't do wholesome."

The glint of his eyes grabs me. Perhaps, there was a warning in his words, and I missed it. A hint that he has a dark side. We kept eye contact even though our conversation cooled. I notice a woman on the other side of the bar eyeing him, and I bubble a laugh.

"You have a fan. I'll find her number on a piece of paper during my next dry cleaning pick-up," I tease him.

He doesn't even glance over his shoulder; he stares at me with such concentration and swelter that I'm overwhelmed by his alluring pull. Even when he finishes off his whiskey, he doesn't let go of our eye contact.

In my peripheral vision, I notice a woman behind the bar set down a brown bag, which I assume is his order.

Julian at last releases me from his gaze. Except when he stands, his body brushes against me to grab the handles of the bag. I can't be imagining it. He is doing it on purpose. I have a stronger whiff of his woodsy cologne, and his arm drifts far too close to mine. My breath catches, and my body tightens, and it betrays me, too. My nipples react as a result of him being only inches from me. This man has power in and out of the boardroom. I try not to imagine what he would be like in bed. Or is he a table guy?

His body sweeps back. "Ricky, you can put her bill on mine," he tells the barman.

"Oh, you don't have to do—" I try to protest.

He is quick to interrupt. "Don't disobey me. My rules, since you're my assistant, even if you have to get on your knees, remember?"

I wince at the reminder, and at the same time, I appreciate that we are actually having a casual conversation, though an innuendo is part of the formula to make the evening run smoothly.

"You wish," I volley back, not even registering what I accused my boss of.

He scans the room before he leans down, and his mouth comes close to my ear, his hot breath radiating on my skin, and my pulse is speeding. "Have fun with my next dry-clean run, but you won't find a paper with a number. I have a feeling you won't be finding those anymore," he whispers.

He leaves without any notice to me. It wouldn't matter because I'm sitting here speechless.

Probably to cope with the loss of his near touch, which leaves me cold, because talking to him brought his body close.

Or he probably left me without words to process my thoughts.

The one where I am doubting myself about whether I interpreted everything right.

Because maybe his new no-number policy is because he has no interest, and maybe it has to do with me.

7
JULIAN

Watching the view of the Chicago skyline out of the corner window, it's a shame the clouds hang low today. Gray fits my mood, however. I sit on my chair behind the desk with my feet propped up on the glass and my hands behind my head. It doesn't exactly scream professional, but I don't particularly care. I'm trying to regain focus because I've been stewing in thoughts of my assistant.

Not going to lie, I'm walking myself straight down a road where I shouldn't be going. I've seen Savannah's taut and smooth body naked, I've talked to her outside of the office, and I've learned to notice when she's about to snipe out an answer directed at me. Yet, this all feels oddly right. But today, I need to go back to being a pain in her fine ass. Otherwise, I'm going to fall down a rollercoaster, and I actually do need her work ethic.

I timed my entrance to the office this morning in the hope that it was her usual 7:50 staff room coffee-and-chat routine.

It was a success, minus the twenty seconds when I noticed she restocked her fruit snack jar, and she left her phone, with a background picture of an older woman with faded blonde hair, whom I would assume is her aunt. They're hugging at what appears to be a festival. I wasn't nosy, simply ensuring my assistant is aboveboard. But avoiding her will only get me so far.

I have a potential-client lunch meeting here in my office at eleven, and Savannah might need to take notes. Clark wouldn't be a significant addition to our portfolio, but still, a big enough fish to consider. He purchased a new minor hockey team in Wisconsin and is looking for someone to handle the logistics for games. Usually, our sports and entertainment division would handle this. I prefer to meet with the big fish, and mostly with our import and export division, but this is a favor to Charles.

My chest lunges when I hear a knock at my door, and I remind my body to get it together.

"Come in," I say as I swing my feet off my desk and get into serious "man with power behind a $20,000-desk" mode. Quickly, I pretend to be using my laptop and avoid looking up, only for it to fail when I hear the click of her heels.

"Well, well, well... don't think I didn't catch you," she taunts, and my eyes set on her as she sashays my way in her gray pencil skirt with a matching top.

"Enlighten me."

One arm holds her notebook and folder close, and her other hand, with her perfectly manicured fingers with dark red nail polish, ticks back and forth in scolding, and I want to bite them. "Don't think I didn't see you. Giving the nightly cleaner extra work with your dirty shoes."

I smirk subtly. "Well, well, well, I do remember a certain assistant once mentioning getting down on her knees to shine my shoes." *Great.* Only thirty seconds in, and I'm making a sexual innuendo.

Her face drops. "Funny. Now, shall we focus on your meeting with Clark Gabes? You said you didn't need any notes or an agenda for preparation since you plan to schmooze with your powerful cursed charm over people, whatever that may be. I did, however, contact his assistant to figure out his favorite lunch choices, and I went ahead and ordered from that sandwich place down on Wicker. Apparently, he really has a soft spot for spinach, a triple shot of ginger smoothie, and a buckwheat-bread sandwich with sprouts and some other rabbit food like that. So, congratulations, you're going to pretend to love sprouts and tomatoes plucked from the restaurant roof garden that I'm sure has plenty of Chicago pollution raining down on it."

Ah, damn. I should have known. The man runs marathons and lets it get to his head, both in image and bragging rights.

"Thanks," I say as she grabs something from her folder, darts her arm out, and tosses a paper onto my desk. "What's this?"

"I know you believe that you're the genius in your field, but I did a little extra research for you."

Of course she did. Efficiency, she always gets points for it. Her elegantly tight dresses are where she loses points on the scorecard, all because it ruins my focus.

"The Squirrels' travel schedule for the game season. Gosh, if I owned the team, then I would change that name stat."

I review the paper skeptically, and she divided the info into subheadings and even highlighted dollar amounts. "Hmm, you are useful, it seems." I keep my voice neutral.

"Exactly, which is why it would be a shame if I were to abandon you like your other assistants."

I flip the page and briefly glance at her as though I'm not bothered. "Sure, you can go back to Yellow Hill or wherever it is where they have jam at farmers' markets."

"It's Everhope. And lucky for you, I'm not a quitter."

"Joy," I mundanely reply and toss the notes on the desk. "You are dismissed. When Clark arrives, you can see him right through."

She rolls her eyes. "Dismissed. Really? That is your choice of words. Sounds like something you would say to a submissive in her maid outfit." Immediately, her mouth gapes open because her rambling landed her in hot water.

A giant smirk forms on my face as my brows rise, and I lean back in my chair. "Wildly inappropriate to say to your boss. But, *of course*, it could be innocent provided the submissive maid's skirt is knee-length, *obviously*."

She bites her cheek and remains mute. The way she avoids making eye contact is a tease, because if she did, I'm positive our eyes would lock and force us to admit a mutual idea we shouldn't have. Savannah pivots and begins walking out of my office, and I return to stern mode.

"Savannah, please get rid of the fruit snacks. I think I saw a wrapper on your desk."

She lets out a disapproving noise and storms out.

Truthfully, I stole one of those things yesterday, and they're not half bad, but she doesn't need to know that. It's better to keep up the pretense that I enjoy making her life hell at times.

―――

CLARK SITS down on the leather sofa across from my chair in the sitting area of my office.

"It's been a while." I smile.

"Yeah, I think last year's Easter party at the country club up in Winnetka." That sounds about right.

I decide that today I'm in the mood to cut to the chase, so small talk isn't on my agenda. "Well, it's good to see you, and I'm happy that you had a chance to come in. That's great about your new team."

He waves me off. "Nah, it's a hobby. But we lack new staff to handle logistics, so here I am while we're in the hiring process."

He glances to the side when Savannah returns with his smoothie and a water for me. She sets his drink down on the coffee table with a polite smile before she walks away. His eyes wander, and the subtle, sly movement of his facial expression irks me a little.

"Would you be a doll and bring lunch early? I'm starving." He gives her his attention when she's halfway to the door, and the way he said that last word has an air of inappropriateness that only I get to have in my office. I'm familiar enough with Savannah to realize that she is silently cringing and pissed off that he called her "doll."

"Of course."

"Tell me, Savannah. Do you enjoy hockey?"

She seems surprised that he's asking her a question. For the most part, except for the friendly greetings and arranging the notes during or coordinating contracts after the meetings, the PAs don't tend to engage in much conversation during new client meetings.

"Oh, uh, I mean, I've been to a few games. How could I not? Haven handles all of the logistics for the Spinners and major teams out in the east that play across North America." She winds it back to dropping that reminder.

"Very true. That's why I'm here."

I really want to get this moving. "Savannah makes a good point. Thank you." She seizes the opportunity to leave. "We normally take on larger clients." That should be enough to dig into his pride, but also make him feel that we are making an exception. "The Squirrels would be smooth logistics; however, no cross-US border trips. Unlike our major teams, most of The Squirrels' games are via bus across the Midwest. We can easily ensure all gear arrives on time with the team."

"I assumed as much. I'm sure we're peanuts compared to your other teams, but I'm going to make The Squirrels big, attract an audience, and find the best players. Might be the minors, but even the teams at the top of the minors get noticed by the mainstream."

"I could perhaps agree. Ambitious plans if it's only a hobby to you."

He shrugs. "I mean, I might as well make a profit from it, right?"

"I assume we would start in the fall, as the hockey season is almost over for the year."

"Yes—" His attention swings to Savannah when she enters with a basket of sandwiches wrapped in paper. "Will you be joining us?" he asks her.

She avoids looking at him and instead focuses on placing the lunch on the circular table in my office. "No, you're in good hands with Julian."

"A shame. You know, you both should come to one of our games. It would be great if the company would make an appearance."

"Of course, branding is everything." I try to divert his attention, but the guy is fixated on *my* assistant. Maybe she notices or maybe not.

He lifts his head and tilts to the side as Savannah busies herself with unpacking the lunch.

I clear my throat and hope to regain his focus. "Shall we get into the finer details of what a contract would entail?"

"Yeah, sure." He refocuses when Savannah leaves my office and closes the door behind her. "I'm hoping we can reduce the fee, considering we go way back."

That isn't happening, and we don't go way back. "I'm sorry, but we stick to fixed rates, otherwise the compliance auditors have a field day," I lie. Our loyal and longstanding customers get a discount; new clients like him have no chance.

"That's a shame. However, I would like to wrap the contract up as soon as possible to prepare for next season."

I stand and grin tightly. "Of course. Now, if I understand

correctly, our assistants have talked, and this is one of your favorite spots for sandwiches."

He follows me to the table. "It is. I met a yoga instructor, and she insisted on breakfast there once after a night together. I ended up ditching her a few dates later, but I was hooked on the menu. I send my assistant there on my behalf."

One thing I hate during meetings is when clients decide that we're in a locker room to discuss things I reserve for drinks with the guys. "Interesting. Well, it looks delicious."

"My assistant looks like a librarian." He hitches his thumb over his shoulder toward the closed door. "Not like her. You're lucky. She's young, and I didn't notice a wedding ring. Is she seeing anybody?"

One of my hands grips the armrest of my chair, while my entire body begins to boil with a fury that I shouldn't be feeling. I grit my teeth and take a second to remind myself that I'm the bigger man and I have class.

"I don't believe that is either of our concern."

He bites into a kale chip and settles into his chair. "You're right. If my assistant looked like that, I wouldn't care if she didn't even know how to type." He grins sleazily.

Now protectiveness is coming over me; there's no denying it. "Actually, she's astute and capable of many things. She's worked here for a while and is loyal. So yes, I am lucky."

I unfold the paper of my sandwich, and it isn't the glimpse of sprouts that has me untucking the paper with aggression.

"You're extra lucky. She's the whole package."

Nothing inside of me is simmering down. "That's what my company provides, the whole package. What it doesn't provide is my assistant in any shape or form."

His eyes enlarge, and he crosses his arms with a cunning smirk. "Ah, I see. She really is *your* assistant."

As much as I don't want to give him the satisfaction of goading me, he has successfully tipped me over the edge.

Because there is a possessive side of me that is reserved only for Savannah, and it is blatantly apparent.

"You know what?" My tone is curt. "You clearly can't focus on the business side of your little hobby, and I only take on clients who are serious about running a tight ship when it comes to their teams or company."

Clark's mood changes really quickly. "Excuse me? I'm not sure you should be talking to your potential client that way."

I stand, causing my chair to scrape against the floor. "That's fine because you are no longer a potential client."

"I can't believe you would want to lose my business so easily."

"Our views don't align, and I own the company, which means I can decide how we run the business." I point at the door. "You know where the door is."

He scoffs and stands, with complete disapproval written all over his face. "People will hear about this."

"And? Do I seem like somebody who cares?" I remain resigned and confident with my choice.

Clark shakes his head in disgust and walks out, causing the door to swing open with so much force that it hits the wall with a bang. His pace is fast, and he doesn't even glance at Savannah sitting at her desk, completely lost about what's happening. I stride slowly, satisfied, and pause at my doorway to watch him go. When he reaches the elevator, he pokes the button several times because he's scurrying away from a man who holds the upper hand.

He grows frustrated that the elevator doesn't move faster, but when it arrives with a ding, he huffs and barges straight in.

The moment the door closes, I drive my eyes to Savannah, who is standing behind her desk, trying to grasp what's going on.

"What the he—"

"You." My voice is harsh, and she stares at me with her forehead wrinkled. I raise a finger and beckon her to follow me. "In my office. *Now*," I bite out.

I'm furious.

At her.

It's illogical.

But she is in trouble.

8
JULIAN

Savannah doesn't question my demand and, to my surprise, grasps the urgency and follows me, hot on my heels. I begin pacing in front of my desk once we're in my office.

"You are unbelievable," I tell her.

"Me?" She points to herself as she stands still in the middle of my office, completely bewildered. "What have I done now?"

I shake my head, pinching the bridge of my nose in the process as my headache forms. "Because of you, I lost that deal."

"W-What?" she stammers. "How? What did I do?"

I stop mid-pace, and I point my index finger at her. "It's you and your bewitching ways. That's what happened."

Her arms fall to her sides, and her jaw slides to the side because this is Savannah, and she is preparing herself for a debate. "Enlighten me," she volleys back dryly at me.

Taking a few steps her way, I'm well aware that I must look like a man crazed. "It's you and that dress or some mystical perfume or something."

Her mouth gapes open. "Really?" She snickers. "I am to blame for this?"

"Yes. It's because of you I told him to take a hike."

She crosses her arms over her chest, which only brings my attention to her respectable cleavage; even covered it can still send a man into a meltdown, especially since I've seen her down to her bare skin.

I continue, "I ruined the deal all because of you."

I'm staring at her back as she quickly goes to the open door and shuts it before she faces me again. "I will not accept blame for whatever happened, because I wasn't in the room."

"You don't need to be in the room," I nearly shout.

Her hand sweeps through her hair, which is down and framing her face, and she lets out a frustrated grumble. "You make zero sense right now."

"Clark couldn't care less about business, as he was more concerned with you and your lack of a wedding ring." I puff out my chest, and it only highlights that my heart rate is uneven.

Something about my sentence causes her to change her mood, and I swear that cursed sexy smirk of hers appears because she is the devil in my head. Her slow strides have me very concerned.

"Why would you care what he thinks of me?"

I look to the side and pretend to be unaffected. "I don't. But it was a waste of my time."

"Huh, not jealous?"

I scoff at the absurdness. "Of him? Never."

Our eyes meet and are instantly locked in a standoff. This woman has me thinking illogically, yet I'm very aware of the tether that is about to snap between us.

"He's a jerk anyway, so I doubt I'm the one to blame," she reminds me calmly in a rasp.

Now isn't the moment to highlight to her that she's right, or that I couldn't care less about a minor account.

We both step closer, closing the distance.

"You're a problem, Savannah." She shakes her head gingerly, disagreeing. "Yes, you are. You make people think irrationally."

"I'm not apologizing for that."

"I'm not saying you should. I'm merely commenting on how you are a horrible assistant."

Her hands drop to rest on the hourglass of her hips, and she is pissed. "I'm the best at what I do, so your feedback is not accepted."

I drag my hand across my face and jut my jaw out because I'm frustrated. "Fine. You're not a normal assistant."

"Feedback still not accepted."

"You take no accountability for your actions." Now I'm listing ridiculous accusations to buy me time.

She throws her hands in the air and growls. "What horrible boss are you? What action accountability should I take?"

We're bickering and going in circles, and I've got to stop this because maybe I'm redeemable in the next few seconds. I shouldn't have dragged her in here because of my own self-anger.

"Well, what is it, Mr. Haven? What is it that makes me the worst assistant ever?" she snipes at me.

That's it.

Time now struck, and I'm not at all a redeemable man.

In a quick movement, I take an easy step forward to close the space between us and tangle my hand in her hair to yank her away slightly, my eyes dropping to her lips before shooting back to her eyes, which show no sign of fear, only excitement. I bring her mouth closer to me, feeling her warmth. "You're a distraction. A complete fucking distraction that makes it impossible to work around you," I whisper before crashing my mouth onto hers.

The world goes quiet. I'm not used to that.

Our lips meet, and it's a long, firm kiss. She doesn't whimper, nor does she seem surprised by my quest to devour her lips. I feel her hands fisting the top of my blazer, and it isn't to push me away. She holds on tight and even brings me closer.

She's irritating, but we're buzzing with electricity. We're not starting with a gentle kiss; instead, it's hungry. The moment that our tongues touch, she becomes more intoxicating. Her murmur only encourages me not to break our kiss. That would be the wise choice. But a horrible one because I'm greedy for her.

The brief break we take to catch our breath doesn't deter us, because she answers me by bringing our contact deep and with intent. My hands cradle her face, and our noses brush before we find a better angle to continue our string of kisses, now hurried but still burning with fuel.

In a natural movement, my feet begin to walk her toward my desk, but my brain catches up, and I'm aware that putting her on my desk isn't a smart idea. I've already complicated our fragile working relationship, and that's purely with a kiss that is my guilty pleasure of the day.

I frame her face with my hands, and our lips brush slowly and softly because I'm reluctant to pull away. I can drag it out a little longer. When our lips seal together, it's different—it's tender, without the chaos. I would say this prolonged kiss is all my fault, except... she isn't pulling away.

We both want this.

That's *very* bad.

I have no idea how we are going to play this because logic hits me far too hard. My own recklessness is what she enjoys.

Which is why I begin to pull away, and my thumb traces her jaw to her swollen lips. Our breaths are ragged, and her eyes arrow straight into my chest, while my own focus is on her mouth.

"I... I'm going to go," she states calmly.

I step back and swipe my hands through my hair. "Yeah. It's a busy workday." My voice is soft, and I'm aware the air has shifted to an unknown.

Savannah steps to the side, and our arms graze as she walks away to the door. "Sure. I'll see you tomorrow."

Wait, what?

Was this such a colossal mistake that she has to run away, and I don't actually want her to?

I can't even reply because she's gone so fast… and the door closes behind her again and again.

My intuition tells me that I shouldn't chase her.

So I don't.

Great.

Just great.

I arrived at work this morning, and Savannah was nowhere to be found. Did I lose another assistant all because I had to kiss her to calm myself the fuck down?

It's 8:15, where is she? This isn't like her.

Making my own coffee at my machine in my office, I decide to proceed with my day. I've done this before, lacking an assistant.

It's just that I've never kissed one.

The knock on my open door causes excitement that she has arrived, but it's short-lived because Charles enters, smiling.

"Morning. Thought I would stop by for a quick catch-up."

I check that the level of my coffee in my cup is in ratio. "Sure. Why are you even in the building? You should be having a leisurely breakfast somewhere."

"We said I would be in two days a week until I'm officially retired."

"Help yourself to coffee."

"Nah, I'll get one when I go downstairs."

We both walk to my sitting area, and when we sit, he evaluates me.

"Everything okay? I heard the Gabes deal didn't go through."

I shrug as I sip on the coffee from the machine that my temptress of an assistant changed one day without my approval. "It's fine. He wasn't the right fit for us. Besides, let's not deal with minor teams."

"Fair enough. Only thought I would see if I missed anything. But if you say it's all okay, it is. I also wanted to remind you that in a few weeks, there is that speaking engagement that you agreed to out in Boston."

"I know. How to grow an empire or something of that sort." I'm not too excited for it, but if someone needs to hear how to be the best, I'm the guy for that.

He crosses his leg over his knee and spreads his arm along the back of the couch. "How is the assistant situation going?"

My body peaks because I'm wondering if this is the part where he tells me that Savannah resigned all because I was reckless.

"Fine. Why? Have you heard something else?" I cough into my fist before evening my voice.

He shakes his head. "No. I figured there wouldn't be any issues. She's great at her role."

"I don't remember her being so sassy, but I guess I get that privilege."

He lets out a hearty chuckle. "You do have the privilege, because we had a great working relationship, and her humor hit the mark, never sassy, though. Maybe it's the whole respect-your-elders thing. I guess you only saw her before as my assistant, sitting in on meetings. It takes a while for the new dynamic to gel together."

"Sure. Let's call it that," I agree dryly before bringing the cup to my lips.

"A laugh will do you good. You're lucky to have her. She comes from a family-oriented background and is positive-minded. I'm sure you're not used to any of that." We can thank my family for my hardened persona—survival of the fittest.

My jaw ticks, and I struggle to smile wryly. "Maybe."

Silence falls upon us, and it becomes disconcerting, and that's when I notice that Charles is holding his stare toward me.

"Yes?" I lift my shoulders.

He pretends to fix the band of his watch. "It's nothing."

"Obviously, it's something." And I'm curious.

"Julian, well, how do I say this?"

"Spit it out." I'm growing impatient.

He notices. "It isn't crazy if you might... it's Savannah, she's... All I'm saying is you two can work really well together... there are policies to ensure that."

I begin to laugh because he just advised that Savannah and I could be sleeping together, for all we want... but do it discreetly because of company policies. The guy may have hit retirement, but he is still bold. "Right," I play along. "Not an issue, but duly noted," I lie because I absolutely did everything I shouldn't have yesterday.

"Okay." His smile returns.

It's a very long beat, and something else crosses my mind. "The clause about her student debt. It only happens if she works for us for a set amount of time, right?"

"Yes. Two more years."

My lips quirk out, and I shake my head once. "You can get rid of the time limit. It will be paid either way."

Charles's eyes bug out. "Oh?"

"Yes. She can quit, and it won't matter."

He stands, unsure of what to say. "Has something happened?" he pries.

"No. Just get rid of the clause." My face must appear as stone, unreadable.

"I guess I could talk to HR. There are policies—"

I cut him right off. "And I own this company. Just get rid of the clause, and there is one more thing." He appears to be all ears. "Don't tell Savannah."

He appears completely gobsmacked. "What? Why?"

A sly smirk creeps up on the corner of my mouth. "Leverage," I simply explain.

He rolls his eyes, not impressed with my antics, but he obliges anyway. "Christ, I can't even begin to break this one down. Fine." He gives up, and when I don't respond, he decides it's his time to leave. "Well, that's me. The temp, my assistant, promised to have anything I needed to sign off on all ready for one go."

"Makes sense."

He walks to the open door and peeks out. "I thought Savannah would be back by now. I wanted to say hi."

"Back from where?"

His brows furrow. "She had to finish a paper last night and submit it first thing this morning. Remember? It's her big final paper deadline. She's finishing her master's."

Ah, shit. I need to remember these details. She's been working on this for a long time. It isn't a small feat. We even talked about it.

"Right. It slipped my mind." Or I should read my damn calendar, where she probably made a note that she would be in late.

He gives me a little salute goodbye.

I'm relieved that she is actually coming to work today. It's a mystery how we will face one another. Deciding to busy myself, I go back to my desk and make a few calls, and around 10 AM, I hear movement which captures my attention. Through the open door, I see that Savannah has arrived at her desk.

My pulse begins to quicken, and I push myself away from my desk and rise. I'll make the first move. I'm the older one, in a position of authority, and the man who decided her mouth was worth my lips.

I slowly saunter to the entrance of my office, and she doesn't even glance up as she tucks her purse into her drawer.

"Morning," I greet her while I lean against the doorframe.

"Oh, hi, thought you would be on a call. You have one now." She still doesn't make eye contact and continues setting up her desk for the day.

"They phoned earlier to reschedule. I guess you'll get an email about that."

She looks up real quick with a bright smile. "Okay. Anyhow, I need to catch up on your inbox. Let me know if you need anything." She plops herself onto her chair.

"Savannah..." I begin.

She looks at me as if all is normal. "Yeah? I think your four o'clock will most likely drag on. A heads up on that."

Brushing everything under the rug is how she wants to play this. Fine. I'll let her take the lead.

I turn, only to pause. "Savannah." But I'll try this again. "About—"

"Yes?"

Her beauty today hits differently when I see that her doe eyes search mine. "I wanted to say..." I don't have the words for it, which means I don't even want to approach the subject and will follow her policy. "I just wanted to say hope the paper went well."

"Thanks."

I leave her and close the door behind me.

It was a passionate angry kiss.

That's all.

Let it be in the past.

9

SAVANNAH

Streetlights highlight my wide smile. I'm on a video call with my Aunt Bea, catching up. How lucky I have been to have her in my life, I'll never take for granted.

"Fancy," she says.

I look around my surroundings from the back seat of an expensive car with dark leather seats, which picked me up from the office as darkness spread across the sky.

"Well, my not-so-stellar boss forgot a document that he needs to sign before 8 AM tomorrow, so he sent a car for me. Having billions means he doesn't need to put in the effort to return to the office to make up for *his* mistake. Instead, he decided that I needed to ruin my night by working extra."

It's not that I had plans. It's the principle of it all. He kissed me, and for whatever reason, my body didn't fight back. One second, he was angry, and the next, his decadent lips were on mine with such possession. They say sometimes arguments lead to passion. I'm not sure that's what it was, but I'm not complaining. I mean, I got to experience what it's like kissing Julian Haven, and I never thought I would think it, but lucky me. *Except...* it did little to cool us. I chose to ignore the need to address it, and his answer has been to return to being unbearable during work hours over the last week.

That's actually a good thing. We should be professional because I won't let attraction derail my career. Even if I have to battle the pull, it's a must.

"I hope he isn't working you too hard." Her forehead scrunches as she rests against the kitchen counter while holding her phone.

"Nah, I can handle it."

"Because you are excellent at your job. He's lucky to have you."

I chortle a laugh and bobble my head. "I'm not sure he sees it that way. Let's just say that I miss working with Charles. He is a soft soul. Julian is, well... not."

"Maybe he's missing something in his life. Is he close with his family?"

"No. Not at all." I've wondered a time or two if I would solve the mystery of his family. Maybe it would give insight into a reason why he's rough around the edges.

She gives me a knowing look. "Family can fill the heart. It must be lonely if he doesn't have that."

"I mean, he has friends. I'm sure he isn't alone on holidays or anything." Or at least, I hope not.

My aunt shakes her head at me. "It isn't the same. Think of the joy you have when we have chaotic family gatherings with your cousins."

She's right. I look forward to seeing everyone, and the way we all plan what to bring to holidays, picnics, BBQs, and any time we can find a reason to get together. Most of all, everyone comes with kindness and open arms. Every time I speak with my aunt, I'm thankful that she raised me. I couldn't have been more fortunate if I tried.

I press my lips together. "Maybe. Anyhow, enough about him. How are things in Everhope?"

"Same old. The only scandal is that we're getting a new donut shop on Main Street, and Foxy Rox coffeehouse isn't too happy."

That sounds about right. Our small town is quaint and lifts your soul because, considering the world and the way that it is, we're in a bubble away from it all.

"I hope they have donut holes." Because who can pass up donut holes? It causes her to grin. "But I actually meant how is Everhope and things with you?"

The developer seeking the docking permit renewal is an implication I don't want to think about. They have the power to make it happen and a promise to the county to bring in money and more tourism. The only problem is that it would ruin the feel of the town, probably destroy the river, and my aunt's business would be gone.

Her eyes dip low. "Don't concern yourself with it."

Her reply worries me, and I wiggle in the seat and straighten my spine to attention. "Aunt Bea, what's going on?"

She droops a shoulder when she sighs. "It's almost as good as done."

"What!" I wasn't expecting this. I thought there was more time to figure out a solution. Persuade the city council, find a loophole in a law, or even try to find some obscure plant in the river that can't be destroyed by construction. "You can't give up so easily."

"Sweetie, let's not talk about this now." That usually equates to her thinking about it more than she would like to admit.

The driver turns his head slightly, and he takes the moment of pause to speak. "Miss, we're here."

"You have got to be kidding me," I mutter to myself. I can't even finish my conversation because I've arrived at a place that won't in any way, shape, or form calm me down right now.

"Go. We'll talk later." She smiles weakly as the car comes to a stop.

I shake my head, aggravated at how today is going, and I quickly glance out the window to see that trickles of rain are beginning to fall.

"Fine. But this conversation isn't over," I warn her from a place of pure affection. "I love you."

"Love you too. Don't worry. Enjoy your evening."

When we end the call, I toss my phone into my bag, and my chest feels tight. As the driver opens the door for me, I grumble out some slivers of my mood and refocus on why I ended up here. Stepping out, I assess the building in front of me, and I'm in no way surprised—a high-rise with an expensive lobby and a man already holding the gold-handled door open for me. I never complain about my living situation because I got lucky with my rental, but this is a whole new level. It's elevated luxury.

I thank the driver as I link my arm through the strap of my bag. Smiling at the doorman, his bright welcoming smile is practiced yet honest.

"Good evening, Ms. May. Mr. Haven is expecting you." I'm sure he is.

The man walks with me to the elevator, quickly dips his arm in to punch a button, then steps back to ensure the door stays open as I enter. "His door is on the right."

Before I can say anything, the door is closing, and I'm all alone in an elevator. I contemplate changing into my flats from my bag because my feet are killing me, but heels scream, "I am not in the mood for bullshit."

As the light climbs the numbers above the door, I realize something horribly true. I'm curious about the way he lives. I shouldn't care nor be intrigued, but I am. I hate to admit it, but I have butterflies in my stomach because I doubt any of his previous assistants have been here. They didn't last that long. It runs deeper, though. He is letting me have a peek into his personal space. I feel somewhat special about that.

When the elevator stops and the doors slide open, I take a

deep breath because I remember why I'm here. Julian didn't even ask if it was okay for me to do him a favor. He ordered me. I'm well aware that when you sign up to be a PA at a major corporation, you're always on standby for the higher-ups. With Charles, he would always ask very nimbly and profusely apologize, then leave my favorite box of snacks on my desk the next day. Julian? He might grunt a good-morning before chastising me for some ridiculous matter, and I'm positive he does it to piss me off because that's what brings him joy in life.

I don't even need to knock when I arrive at his door because it quickly opens, as the front desk must have called up. I'm greeted by... casual Julian. Holy fuck, what world did I walk into? I'm devastated that I actually find him attractive right now. Dark jeans, white tee, and he must have had a shower because his hair is still damp and his body smells strongly of soap.

"Miss May," he greets me roguishly.

That sinful look could weaken me, but a millisecond in, I remember why I'm here. I tuck my hand into my bag and pull out the small binder with laminated pockets. I'm quick to almost throw it at him; instead, I opt for the shove-it-into-his-chest move. Also a mistake, because it makes his hands shoot up quickly and grab my wrists to hold the documents against his chest so they don't fall.

"Here." I'm quick to retrieve my hands back to my sides.

"Savannah, it's the Connors contract, a little more finesse would be appreciated. These are important documents here," he chastises me with cockiness in his voice.

I dagger my eyes at him. "Really? Someone here shouldn't have forgotten to sign them at the office instead of summoning his assistant because of his lack of competence."

My boldness doesn't surprise him, and he raises his brows. "Last time I checked, it is my personal assistant's job to ensure I don't forget things and to be on top of the ball."

I snicker from my fuming mood. "I believe I did so... three

times." I raise my voice. "Now, can you please go sign them and bring them back?" I instruct, with the full intention of speeding this along. "And why are you signing a contract? I thought they went with another company for their exporting of medical equipment."

An unapologetic smirk appears on his mouth. "It's simple. I had our guys reach out to a few clients who left the opposite party, dug up all their little mistakes, managed to figure out some numbers, then went back to Connors, exploiting the worst-case scenario and the damage control they would need should the other party take them on as a client. To sweeten the deal, I gave them a three percent decrease in pricing to be more attractive than the other party. Undermining confidence and having leverage is a powerful tool."

"You mean subtle manipulation?" He warned me he does what it takes. Briefly, I wonder whether it spills over into his personal life, but he can't be this way if there's no significant other.

He steps to the side and points to the front hall. "Don't you want to come in, or will you be staying in the hallway throwing a temper tantrum?"

"Hallway sounds good. I'm sure you have a pen somewhere on you, like a good CEO should, so we can move this along." I smile tightly with my lips pressed.

"I'm not that competent, remember? As a CEO only, of course." He throws my words back at me. "I have to get one from my office. Shouldn't you be carrying one around?"

Rolling my eyes, he has a point, and I fish in my bag for a pen, only to come up empty.

He notices, and it pleases him. "My oh my, what's your favorite word again?" He clicks his fingers in the air, pretending to search for a word. "Oh yeah, competence. So, would you be obliged to come in?"

My lips press tightly as I accept that I've been a hypocrite for the last minute. This is a headache of wanting to escape and wanting to stay because my body is a traitor, and my mind is captivated. "Fine."

Stepping over the threshold, I vaguely hear him pushing the door shut lazily, but I immediately forget that he's behind me because I'm too engrossed in the view of a very large open-plan living space with glass stairs. It's modern yet surprisingly welcoming.

"Huh. Kind of had you down as a Dracula dark-cave kind of vibe, and this is not that," I observe and slowly walk as the windows magnetize me. There's a lightning strike over the Chicago skyline that highlights the outline of the buildings and the height of being on a top floor.

"Imagine that. Savannah is wrong. Oh, the shock and horror," he flatly rebuffs. I feel him behind me, but he isn't close, a few strides. However, his presence is more domineering than it is in the office. It's him out of a suit that seems to heighten my body's awareness of his proximity. As though being casual stripped him down and thinned his walls to leave me unprotected.

I don't gift him a glance over my shoulder as I saunter around the room, letting my fingertips glide along the top of the sofa. "I believe time is ticking. Would you be a gentleman and sign those papers so I can ensure they are where they should be by 8 AM tomorrow?"

I hear a sound buried in his throat, and it resembles a hidden laugh. "Wait here. I'm sure you can follow instructions like a good girl."

My entire body locks up because the way he said that sends a wave straight to my center. It unleashes thoughts in my mind of how he would be in specific settings, and it's only ever been implied that he is anything but sweet and tender. Rolling my lips in, I decide to brave it by snapping my gaze when I turn to face him.

Julian's face is stone. It wasn't a slip of his tongue. I've felt his tongue on mine, and I'm now well-versed to know when he taunts, because it sharpens my awareness of him and it's a safe threat that doesn't scare me.

The only way to fix this possible detour is to lighten the mood. "Whatever you say, dear master." I'm frivolous, or so I thought, because maybe it still sounded sultry. He half-smirks to himself, mollified and posed, before he walks away.

My pulse is pounding, and I repeat in my head over and over that he has been a horrible boss. Even if I think he wanted to talk about the kiss, I wanted to hear nothing. Safety first.

Except, it's hard to bury.

I mosey around, studying the various paintings on the wall and the lack of framed family photos. Instead, I notice a tray of whiskey and crystal glasses. Next to it is a small shelf with more hard alcohol options and half a shelf of different playing card boxes. None of them look new. They're worn boxes with fonts and designs from long ago.

"Want a drink?" He startles me, and my body reacts.

I turn to see him strolling my way ever so slowly, hunting.

"No. It's fine. I should go." Where did my attitude go? My voice lacked it.

He holds up the folder, and I reach out to grab it, but he moves and holds the folder out of reach. "Tsk, tsk. Not so eager. Let me call you a car." His eyes catch mine, and it's clear that it's his way or no way. "It's the least I can do for causing you inconvenience." The politeness, however, is by no means serious.

I step back and sigh in exhaustion. "You can be quite insufferable, but fine."

He sets the file on the table in victory. "Time for a drink." Before I can object, he's already setting two glass tumblers in the middle of the tray.

"Aren't you going to arrange a car like a gentleman?"

His lips purse out as he opens the bottle of whiskey, and his eyes remain set on pouring drinks. "Nope." The P pops, and a sound of liquid pouring accompanies it. "Not yet. Might as well enjoy your glass of whiskey, since it cost a couple grand. Otherwise, it would be a crime to waste it."

He hands me a glass with his eyes arrowing straight into me. "Here."

Our fingers briefly touch when I wrap my hand around the tumbler, and they linger for a second longer than they should. Bringing the drink to my nose, I smell a sharp odor. I decide to go for it and take a sip, instantly feeling the sting on my throat.

"You are quite a rule-breaker. Not even toasting."

I give him an "oh, really" look. "What are we toasting? Indifference?" I suggest.

He looks away and fails terribly at hiding his tiny smile because he found it funny. "Fine." He swings his gaze back and taps my glass with his, indicating with his head to follow him. I do, but only because it's clear that it's straight to his couch.

The quiet in the room is unnerving. It has everything to do with our dynamic; professional yet crossing borders of professionalism in terms of jabs thrown and his commanding lips. I decide to break the tension.

"I noticed the card collection."

He smoothly drinks his own whiskey. "Mmm." He finishes his sip. "I collect playing cards. Some are from the 1920s, and others are special editions."

"Really?"

"You sound surprised."

I smile genuinely. "I am. Are you a poker player then?"

He licks his lips, and his cheeks tighten. It's sexy and strikes curiosity, especially when his smile is sincere. "You'll like this. No. I only play Go Fish."

"Funny." He shakes his head gingerly side to side. "You're serious?" He nods, and my entire face stretches in surprise with a wide grin. "No way! That is… hysterical and total blackmail material."

"I thought you would enjoy that."

We both continue to nurse our drinks. "Why Go Fish?"

He lifts a shoulder. "I don't know. It's easy. Doesn't require much brain power. It isn't poker, which I fucking hate. My da—" Julian stops himself from finishing the sentence, clearly poking a sensitive thought. I want to press him on why, but I sense that it isn't a good idea.

Instead, I ask, "Go Fish involves at least two people. Do you play a lot?" That was not subtle, and I could facepalm myself if I weren't holding a drink.

Julian shifts and positions his body to face me as we both lean against the back of the couch with one arm, as though we've been talking for hours. It's crazy, but a man holding a glass of whiskey with a watch like his yet wearing jeans is a turn-on for me. It's sophistication.

"Not here. No." His voice is unyielding, and his eyes pin me in place.

Part of me wants to say to hell with it, toss the expensive glass to the floor, and move to straddle him. The other part is much wiser.

"Right." I swallow.

"Don't have any antique stores near Purplehope, do you?"

The corner of my mouth snags. "You mean Everhope, and actually, there are a few in the county. I'm sure you can send someone to check them out. I'm not sure they'll take your gold card, though. They're simple people and enjoy staying behind in the times."

"Charming. Going all in on the theme of antiques, it seems."

I laugh. "Wow, you made a cheesy joke."

Julian takes a final swig of his drink. "I am capable. Plus, I have a pain-in-the-ass assistant whom I could send to look for me. Are you heading to Purpletop soon?" He mistakes the name purely for enjoyment.

"Hopefully. It's an easy drive for the weekend, but I want to go when I have a few extra days. I really want to see my aunt."

"You've mentioned her a few times now."

I smile with fondness. "A great woman. If she met you, she would offer you a drink and a cookie, no matter what mood you're in. I've come to realize that some parents let their kids down, but it's okay. Because you could be lucky and get something even better."

His face stills, and I realize I hit a nerve with my philosophy. No, that's not it. There is a hint of longing. Or complete numbness to whatever family baggage he carries. He stands and picks up his glass before he heads straight back to his whiskey table, clearly agitated because he pops the cork of the bottle with extra vigor.

Standing, I don't follow. Instead, I stare at the chiseled muscles of his back that the shirt covers tightly.

"I mean, I guess a lot of things are luck of the draw." I try to take down the insistence of my view.

He holds the bottle in the air. "Another?"

"No. I should head out."

Julian turns and perches against the table with a fresh drink in hand. "Do I scare you?"

"No." I'm amused.

"But I annoy you."

"Confirmed."

He tilts his head to the side and seems to be examining me. "And you didn't tell me to go fuck myself, either."

"I do. I simply don't say it aloud," I bounce back.

He smirks, even with the glass between his lips. "I'm sure, but I meant last week."

Oh.

It dawns on me a possibility. "Did you leave the file on purpose and demand I come here?"

He pushes himself off the edge of the table. "Now, why would I do that? Only someone very clever would think of that. I don't possess that competence, according to my assistant."

My entire body begins to melt, and my pussy starts to ache for his touch.

He did set this up.

"Subtle manipulation," I repeat faintly to myself the earlier thought from when he explained his dealings. It's a red flag. Yet, I place my glass on the coffee table. "He is capable of other things, though." Am I testing the waters of where this evening could go? That goes against everything I tell myself, remain professional, as in don't cross the darkest line of them all, because it can't be erased. A kiss is a kiss, but one touch more and it leads you down a road of no return.

"Is that so?" He stalks toward his prey, and my nipples harden because his prey is me.

But I stay even in my stance. "Maybe. He does irrational things, so it isn't always so clear."

Another step closer and another. His mouth dips down to my cheek, and his breath cascades against my skin to that delicate spot near my ear. "No. I'm direct when I want to be," he rasps before retreating.

I shiver slightly. I'm not sure he notices, but I want to have the upper hand, and when I open my mouth, he beats me to the punch.

"The papers."

I flutter my eyes to adjust to the swift change of direction, and I make a sound in acknowledgment.

"You should take them. I'll ensure a car is waiting for you by the time you're downstairs."

Is this happening?

Is he doing another 180 and flipping back to an arrogant man who calculates his every whisper and touch?

"Really?" I'm not impressed, mostly because I'm beginning to believe this is an addictive infatuation.

The twist of the corners of his mouth confirms he doesn't care. "I'm sure you have things to do, and I want to get ahead on some stock research."

I'm getting whiplash. Or is this payback because when he kissed me, it was me who left? Same in the sauna. Great maturity on his part.

"I do," I lie. "A friend's brother is in town for work. We're meeting up for drinks."

He didn't seem to be expecting that, and his body tenses and his jaw strains.

This is my upper card. I walk past him and pat his chest. "Where's that file?" I turn on my saccharine-toned voice. "Don't worry, I'll be sure to meet my deadlines. Not like drinks with a friend's older brother is going to get crazy." I sashay further on.

"Have fun. Don't forget the file is on your way out."

My eyes grow with annoyance, and I choose not to respond to him. Still, it's hard to ignore the sense of his eyes targeting my back.

Continuing, I follow my quest to get the hell out of here. I slide the folder off the side table, and my heels click against the floor as I walk toward the door.

"Oh, Savannah," he says, grabbing my attention, causing me to turn and look at him once more. "Thanks for stopping by. Huh…" He pretends to rub his head for a thought. "Did I mention that they actually only needed a digital signature?"

My face falls because the asshole set all this up. Disrupting my evening on a false ruse. My jaw grits with fury, even though logic begins to point out the obvious.

The man wants to have the last winning move of the night. That's frustrating and embroiling. However, he also made this move with only one possible outcome in mind. I would show up, and apparently, he wanted my presence.

I could throw his expensive piece-of-art bowl on the side table at him, or I can give him a smile, sweet as can be.

Choosing the latter, I play defiance. "That's okay, a simple thing to forget," I lie.

Turning, I swing the door open with gusto and roll my eyes with complete distaste written on my face.

Why do I do this to myself?

I should quit and get myself out of this web of confusion.

But I refuse to let him win.

10

SAVANNAH

I'm lucky to have Elodie as a good friend. Not many people would be willing to tag along on their friend's ridiculous tasks that her boss sets for her. Yet here I am standing in line at the dry cleaner's with Elodie by my side.

"Remind me again why we're here?" she asks as I stand on the balls of my feet to see what is taking the customer in front of me so long.

"Because Julian decided to go back to making my life hell during the lunchtime rush. Apparently, he *needs* this suit today despite having a whole closetful of options." I didn't see him yesterday, as he was away from the office, and this morning's greeting was throwing a receipt on my desk.

She nudges my arm with hers and has the audacity to give a knowing smirk. "But he kissed you." She sing-songs the reminder.

Not that I need one. The memory is part of the broader slew of issues. I can add the other night's visit to the list, too. He makes my heart race, but I don't want to be that woman who succumbs to his broody charms at the sign of interest. I held strong, but I didn't sleep a wink.

"Well, he can take that victory, but the other night I walked away because he doesn't get to snap his fingers to have the world go the way he wants." We step up when the customer in front of us leaves, and my hand darts out with a receipt to the man behind the counter.

He has a quick read of the numbers on the paper. "Thanks. I'll be right back."

"Yet, he has the power to send you on his ridiculous errands, probably because you denied him the Savannah goods." Elodie laughs.

I cringe at her sentence. "Can we not say goods? It sounds like my body is a bakery." She shrugs. "And secondly, being here shows the lengths of his pettiness, all because his feelings got hurt." I'm a little fired up on this. Not only his warped brain, but also, I was working on a project that held my interest, and I felt I could have added more input had I been given another hour or two. Instead, I sent it to Julian with what a normal assistant would provide because I've been dispatched to do his errands.

"Let it go. Maybe he really does need the suit. He's always at some event outside of work." My eyes grow wide at her, and she bubbles a laugh. "What? One of the cat ladies on my floor always gives us the latest gossip on him. Cute, kind of. I always took her for a knitting-and-painting-by-numbers kind of lady. Anyhow, at company events, he sticks around with the board, and I guess you need to dress well for that."

"Who cares? I'm starving on my lunchbreak and here to pick up my boss's dry cleaning."

"I think you do care and love playing the part of a disgruntled employee," she accuses me.

I'm about to defend myself, but I choke on my words because I know she's right. "It's safer that way."

"Miss, here you are," the man says as he passes me the bagged suit over the counter.

"Thanks. It's on his account, right?"

He nods. "Of course, no need to ask for Mr. Haven. By the way, though, when I checked his pockets before the cleaning, I found something." He hands me a small plastic bag that I usually receive when something is left in a pocket.

Disgruntled, I open the bag, already enraged that a woman gave him a number this time. I pull out the paper, unfold it, and instantly freeze.

Bad assistant. You lied.

It takes a few ticks for me to digest what I'm reading, only for my face to tighten due to my blood boiling. "I'm going to throttle him," I grind out.

Elodie has the nerve to chuckle cheekily. "Throttle. So many ways for interpretation."

I glance sidelong with an unimpressed look.

SITTING on the edge of Julian's desk with my legs crossed and one heeled shoe half off, I twitch my foot in the air and pop a fruit snack into my mouth. One thing about knowing his schedule is that I'm aware that at any moment, he will walk into his office.

His action with the piece of paper is so blatantly ridiculous, and I don't appreciate being called a liar when I have no clue what he is referencing.

I hear Julian walking toward his office, and he seems to be on his cell phone. The moment he opens his door and receives his welcoming view, his face stalls.

"I'll have to call you back, Hayes," he says and ends the call. His eyes narrow as he attempts to figure out my mood, but he doesn't need long, and that goddamn arrogant smirk makes an appearance as he closes the door lazily behind him.

I lift the empty gummy package and crumple it before ceremonially dropping it onto his desk.

"Ooh, someone has her claws out today."

"What the hell?" I'm so tempted to throw the paperweight next to me at him. "I should have torn that suit of yours into shreds, but I'm a professional at my job, and collecting your suit was my task of the day. *However,* I will not tolerate any extra remarks."

Julian strides closer, and his smirk inches bigger. "Ah, you found the note, did you? I thought it was a nice touch." He's proud.

"Care to explain how I'm a fucking liar?"

He loosens his tie as he slows his steps. "The other night. You didn't see a brother of a friend, now did you?"

I'm puzzled. "What? I don't understand."

"You see, a wonderful thing about arranging a car for you is that these days, safety comes first, so imagine that… an app told me that you went straight home." He tosses his tie to the side with not a care in the world where it lands.

"You followed me?" I'm flabbergasted. "First off…" I hold a finger up. "I could have gone home, changed, and then left." I add another finger in the air. "Secondly, this is borderline stalking, which is a little fucked up."

He arrives right in front of me. "It's called being concerned over your safety on a night in Chicago. Logical. So yes, you told a little white lie."

I shake my head. "Don't ever call me a liar again."

He shrugs, and his hand reaches out. My eyes fixate on his loose collar, and the way having him close causes a bolt of electricity in my body, I'm losing my mission.

"Fine. But calling you a *bad assistant* is up for debate?"

Pretending to be disgusted, I struggle as his finger delicately swipes a loose hair off my forehead. "We are not having this conversation."

He quirks his lips out and gingerly bobbles his head side to side. "You might want to get off my desk. Arriving at my office with a woman on my desk isn't exactly fair."

That's it. I hop off and break away from the bubble of tension. "I'm not sure what you did with your other assistants, but I have a little more class than that." *Today*, because being splayed out on his desk doesn't exactly cross my mind.

"Sure. Easy to do. No other assistants have had the privilege, so consider yourself an anomaly," he mentions casually before his demeanor turns formal. "Now, should we focus on work?" Julian doesn't let me answer and instead circles his desk to sit down in his throne.

Blowing out a sigh, I decide that it is a workday and I have a job to do. I drop onto the chair in front of his desk and inhale deeply.

"I need to talk to you about something," he begins, and my eyes grow wide because I fear that we have circled back to inappropriate again, and he senses it and grins. "Work. I'm talking about work," he reaffirms.

"Right, of course."

"Narrowing down candidates to replace Charles for the COO position is a lot of work. As much as I would promote internally, I'm not sensing anyone suitable. I'm left no choice but to search externally. I've thrown out some feelers in my network. When it comes time for interviews, I'm going to need your help. You see the tiny details, you've worked with Charles and know his day-to-day running better than anyone. Therefore, I'm relying on you to give input on candidates. The board will have to be involved at some point for decision-making, and that is a headache I need organized as well."

"Oh." I'm pleasantly surprised; I assumed I would have no part in this responsibility. Hiring a significant role within a corporation involves directors, not me. However, what he says makes sense. "It never crossed my mind, however, I would love to give input."

"Great. Not many personal assistants add value to the process."

Another 180. My face must show how I feel about his brazen comment. "Oh? We are not *just* assistants."

He holds his hand up. "That's not…" His face contorts when he probably replays his comment in his head. "What I meant is that you have a lot going for you with your experience and degree and all."

"Are you actually giving me a compliment?" Today is a full moon, it has to be.

His mouth stretches into a grin. "I guess I am."

I can't hide the smile because I appreciate the praise. "Thank you. Anything else?"

He shakes his head, and his grin stays put. "Not now."

I nod and stand, walking away with a little more pep in my step and my earlier fury now buried.

"Oh, wait," he calls out.

I turn halfway. "Yes?"

"I need you for Saturday's gala."

"Uh… why?" It's a personal event on his calendar.

Julian doesn't look up from his laptop. "In case someone comes along with an interest in clawing their way into a conversation about the vacant company role, and you have a sixth sense about it. Or I simply forget someone's name, and you can remind me."

I'm severely doubting his spiel. "Again, why?"

He glances up, and his eyes, which have a different glint today, bullet straight into me. "I assume you have a dress, as you have been to company events before."

"Okay, you're avoiding my question. This isn't exactly a company event. And yes, I do have a dress. Shall I meet you there, or would you like to track me by my phone as a good stalker does?" I list, and it causes the corner of his mouth to lift in humor.

"It doesn't matter what kind of event it is. Great about the dress, ensure it keeps straying eyes off you if we can. My PA is kindly requested to join. And no tracker, I'm not that crazy, and it really was a coincidence with the app. I'll pick you up," he answers in order.

"I'll meet you there. It means I can avoid travel time with you on my weekend."

"So be it."

I bite the inside of my cheek, rolling my lips as I debate in my head how to evaluate this situation. Something is underlying, and I have a feeling it's due to our sexual tension. We have unusual banter that borders on flirtation. Our breathing around one another is different, too.

My curiosity about him runs deep, and it's threatening.

A dress for straying eyes? Well, that might kill him. "Of course, I'll go to the gala."

I smile widely with satisfaction at the possibilities for driving him crazy.

11

JULIAN

Savannah obviously didn't understand the assignment because she's already gone off track.

The ballroom is buzzing with people, and the background jazz music is soft enough that it doesn't drown out conversation. Expensive drinks flow, and the amount of money in this room gives no excuse not to contribute to the cause—a good one too, the food bank. My whiskey is on point, and the man from my corporate circles next to me is talking about a new restaurant, but it's merely white noise. In this very second, all of those details are drowned out, because I'm trapped in a moment that I feared.

Savannah scans the room, and I'm lucky that it's me that she's searching for. Her dress? Well, that's the part where she didn't listen. While elegant, I don't appreciate how the dark blue satin fabric drapes down her back, revealing the length of her spine, or the way it curves around her breasts, taunting the imagination. Her hair is half curled and falls softly around the shape of her face, with her dark red lips. I already notice a trust fund kid to my right giving her a second glance. The way she presents herself in this very moment should be reserved for only me. She broke the rule that she isn't quite aware exists.

The moment she spots me, the corner of her mouth lifts faintly into a smile, and she walks my way. I knew I should have picked her up.

"Excuse me," I tell the man next to me. I'm quick to grab a flute of champagne off the tray of a passing waiter before I meet Savannah halfway.

"Good evening." She greets me brightly, as though she is oblivious to the fucking chaos she's causing in my head.

"Evening." I hand her the drink, and she seems appreciative. I clear my throat. "You look lovely."

She raises her brows at me, amused. "Yikes. You had to force that out. Is something wrong?" She begins to assess herself.

I touch her bare arm to calm her. "No, it's fine. It's…" She waits patiently for me to finish the sentence as I formulate my words. "I can create a map of half of your body."

She fights her smirk. "Well, be sure the compass direction is right," she quips.

Lifting my nose in acknowledgment, I snap out of being the Julian that loses the plot around this woman. "Really, you look beautiful," I calmy and genuinely compliment, and her response is an almost bashful smile.

"Thank you."

"It's refreshing to see a woman here not covered in jewelry that is ugly as hell but sends the message of their status."

She giggles once. "Well, I'm not a huge jewelry person. I did have a charm necklace that came in a little blue box when I turned 18, but I unfortunately lost it. A mystery where."

"That's a shame. A particular charm?"

"A simple one. A key. Classic, I guess."

She takes a sip of her champagne, and I give her an unimpressed look. "Uh-uh. How rude of you not to toast," I tease her.

The way she rolls her eyes playfully is what I've become

accustomed to. "What is it that we're toasting? That you successfully persuaded me to come to this thing?"

I touch her glass with my own. "That will work."

There is an odd moment of silence until she opens her mouth. "Julian, I'm here because you and I do this hot-and-cold thing. You've been a little frosty lately, so I'm hoping this will bring us back to a toned-down torment of each other phase."

That is a spot-on explanation of us. "Playing psychologist today?" Her feigned glare causes me to press my lips and smile. "Agreed. Moving away from cold to hot in your words. So, are we doing warm 'you need a sweater to cover your shoulders in that dress' or sauna hot on the scale? I need to adjust my behavior tonight accordingly."

Her eyes blaze at my comment, and she quickly takes another drink from her flute. My smile turns to a smirk as she searches the room, not uneasy, nor on a mission. When her eyes land back on me, she seems to ponder. "Nice tux. Not the one that I wasted my lunch hour on, but still, it's nice."

"Thank you. I have to be up to your standards."

"Yeah, yeah, yeah. Now, do we work the room, or have dinner, or hit the silent auction where you can pretend you want to buy lunch on a private yacht on Lake Michigan? What's my assignment?"

I do appreciate her breezy attitude and humor. "Let's stay away from the silent auction. Dinner is in a bit, and I guess this is the part where I need to be more social."

She looks at me peculiarly. "You're excellent at schmoozing, but I'm not sure why I haven't noticed before that you absolutely don't want to be at these types of events."

I tip my head to the side. "Solid observation." These things are stuffy, often pretentious, and remind me of everything I hated growing up. However, these events are part of my life and keep my business network strong.

Savannah looks around my shoulder. "Over there. Oswalt Jones is here."

A man who often visits the office due to his account with us. Saying hello is a must, and Savannah's already on it. I turn slightly to check, and sure enough, the portly older man catches my eye, and we smile.

"Well spotted, Ms. May."

She gladly accepts the praise as Oswalt arrives.

I rev my engine up for the overly polite conversations that will occupy the rest of the evening. "Oswalt, great to see you."

"You, too." He looks at Savannah and smiles. "You remember Ms. May," I preamble, and Savannah gives him a smile and small bow of her head as hello.

"Lovely to see you again. Is Charles here?"

She shakes her head in response. "No. He has a grandchild's birthday party."

Oswalt looks between us like a pendulum of a clock. "Ah, so you're here with Julian. Great to see two people enjoying life outside the office together."

Savannah almost chokes on her champagne but remains composed.

I have to let out a short laugh. "Well, Savannah is my personal assistant now. I think you might have heard the rumors that Charles is retiring soon."

"Yes. That's right."

"As luck would have it, I landed his talented and beautiful assistant," I cooly add on before taking a sip of my drink. My attention slips only once to Savannah who doesn't seem surprised by my choice of words.

It's a minute more of pleasantries before Oswalt is summoned by his wife to another conversation, and turning to face Savannah with a fixed wry smile is priceless.

I lift a shoulder. "Nothing wrong with giving someone a gray area of interpretation."

She shakes her head ruefully. "I don't know what to do with you, to be honest. You're either cranky most of the time, infuriating the other times, and for a few seconds, actually intriguing in a good way."

I can't help but grin. "You should tell me more about those few seconds." I indicate with my head in the direction of our assigned table for dinner, and we walk together. I set my fingertips on her lower back to guide her, and neither one of us think about it because it's far too natural.

"I mean, don't get me wrong… *if* I wasn't working for you and was watching from the sidelines, then you *might* get points for your ridiculousness because it is a *smidgen* funny some of the things you have done recently." She is quick to point a finger at me. "But I do work for you," she reminds me. "Therefore, you are a despicable boss, instead."

"I could say you're a horrible assistant, and would your heart be as wounded as mine every time you say I'm a horrible boss?" I'm sarcastic.

She shakes her head gently as we reach our seats and greet the others at the table. When we sit down, she sighs and leans back in her chair to angle herself toward me.

"It isn't a trap, you know. You can knock yourself off of your award pedestal," she remarks.

My brows rise. "A trap?"

"I doubt I'm here because of your need for an assistant. I'm surprised you didn't pull out your contact list for other options."

I lick my lips because she's stating the obvious of what we both already know. "I burn numbers, I do not keep them. You being here solves a problem. I needed someone here, and you keep it simple." Or so I believed. My plan is already backfiring because I'm loosening more than I would at these events. Apparently, she holds a string that I didn't know existed. Which is why I lean in closer to her, keeping my mouth a respectable distance from her ear, but being this close to her is enough to drive me wild. Especially when my nose feathers her hair and I inhale her berry scent. "As for a trap? You willingly showed up, well aware that there isn't even a trap."

She turns her gaze sharply to me, and her look is so angelic and confident that I could kiss her right now. A sensitive ripple floats between us along our skin.

"Touche, Mr. Haven," she says, her voice low.

Finally, we may actually agree on something.

DINNER WAS TYPICAL. Small talk, laughs with a few people whose company I actually enjoy, and speeches that are not always genuine. I don't need the noise, and I follow the silent-donor route. Savannah was by my side, and although we didn't get much chance to speak to one another, our eyes met enough times that we could probably create a whole new language. I also have no illusions, the way my hand would casually touch her elbow or back gave away the message to others that she's mine, and that's what I intended. Touching her is also an addiction. One that she might be experiencing too, as her body brushed past mine on several occasions, causing me to tell my dick to calm down.

Finally, dinner is over, the remnants of chocolate mousse in a glass pot in front of me, and people navigate to the dance floor for the band playing classic jazz while I sink into the seat. We get a chance to breathe, and Savannah half-turns her body to talk to me.

"I'm not even going to ask if you were the silent donor whose donation had that many zeros attached, as I already know the answer. But it is very kind of you."

I shrug it off. "You didn't ask, so I don't have to answer." She nods gently at my logic. "Can I ask you something?"

"Sure."

"They really don't interest you, people with money, do they?"

She grins at my directness. "No. Why should they? I would be working at the wrong place if they did. Plus, I would much rather have a good coffee or be at a festival in town. I'm not sure you would understand. We had different upbringings."

Her answer has zero bullshit in it, and I'm not used to that when women are around me. "I guess I wouldn't," I reply softly with honesty I wish I didn't need. The idea of growing up with a family that actually spent time with one another is a foreign concept to me.

She grabs her glass of water and takes a sip before setting it down. She's about to say something, but an older woman in her black dress and a thick ruby necklace stops by beside me and smiles.

"I thought that was you," her scratchy voice greets me.

Being polite, I stand. "It's been a long time, Penelope." She's an old neighbor from when I was younger.

"It's good to see you." She glances down at Savannah who smiles, before Penelope returns her attention to me. "Lovely to see you in good spirits."

I drag my thumb above my lip. "Yeah, well… I guess it's been quite a few years. Everything good with Matt?" Her son was a few years older than me when I was at school.

She nods gleefully. "Very much. He's down in Denver, and his wife is about to have baby number two." It doesn't surprise me that he has a young family, many men my age do. Me? It doesn't cross my mind, probably because I haven't had a situation where I need to think about it.

"Tell him I say hello." It's only to be polite, I don't particularly care.

"Sure thing. How is the rest of the family? I ran into your sister about a year ago, and I haven't seen your father in years."

My entire body constricts, and that feeling of distaste quickly ignites. "Excuse me. I believe I promised Savannah a dance." I'm quick to offer her my hand, and she seems to understand the urgency and accepts it as she stands. "Good to see you," I tell Penelope and head straight to the dance floor as a slower tune begins.

I wind Savannah into me tightly until her middle meets mine, and she drapes her arms over my shoulders. Instantly, the last minute disperses, and my body relaxes. It's all because of *her*. The woman in my arms whose rapid pulse I feel is due to me. That's not me being cocky, it's the truth, because it mirrors mine.

My eyes meet hers, and she isn't curious nor sympathetic, instead only peaceful.

"You're not going to ask me about all of that?"

She presses her lips out and continues to sway as my hand slides down to her hip. "No. If there was something you wanted to share, you would. I'm not going to ask." She answers so simply, and it blows my mind. People tend to want to dig into the issue.

"Well, I would rather not get into it on a dance floor with eyes all around."

"Okay." We continue to move, and our bodies so easily mold together. Yet again, another problem about her, and my body doesn't accept the warning. In view over her shoulder, I notice Clark Gabes by the bar, and he catches my location. It didn't cross my mind that he would be here, though I'm not surprised.

"Savannah, you need to be a little closer." I yank her slightly, nearly causing her to lose her step and crash into my chest, with a little yelp released from her lips. I ensure that my hand is splayed perfectly on her back, the part that shows her bare shoulder blades, making a point to invite his irritation at the view he's witnessing.

Her brows furrow at me for the sudden bolt of insistence that our embrace changes. "A little lighter on the moves, please, I'm in heels," she complains.

"Sorry, I saw an opening to show you off, and I took it," I admit.

"An opening to what?"

Laughing once, it's sinister. "Clark Gabes is by the bar and holding his glass a little too hard with envy."

Savannah instantly fumes, and her fingers dig into my chest as she begins to push me away, but I place my palms on top of them to stop her. "You're using me? Is this why I'm here? So you can add me to your methods of having the upper hand with people?"

I squeeze her hands tightly against my chest to ease her. "Absolutely not. It's by chance he's here. I didn't anticipate that."

Her eyes remain wide. "I'm not a pawn."

My gaze snaps and pierces straight into her eyes. "You're not, but a smart man takes opportunities to ensure victory." It earns me her eyes sliding to the side with utter dismay. "Can you blame me for wanting to show you off?" I mean it sincerely.

"I'm not something to be shown off." She isn't thrilled, and I've clearly offended her, which is fair enough. I could have explained it with a bit more tact.

Rubbing circles with my thumb on top of her hands, I try to calm her. "Trust me, this is all by chance. Despite what you may think, you are a stunning woman, and every man in here is envious. I'm the one lucky that you're here with me… and not about to knee me."

She doesn't respond, deliberating with herself whether now is the time to flee.

"Really." I ensure I capture her sight to reassure her, and hopefully she can see my authenticity. "I want to dance with you, so please stay with me. I won't pull any more bullshit."

Her jaw juts out, and she considers for another beat. "Don't make me regret this."

"Promise." I lead us right back into a swaying rhythm, and we stay that way for a little while.

"You're a good dancer," she admits.

I smirk to myself because I know she's about to smile. "I took ballroom dancing lessons when I was younger, my grandmother insisted."

She bursts out with a beaming look. "I didn't see that coming, but the lessons paid off."

"Thanks. Plus, it helps that I have a partner who knows how to move."

Her entire appearance turns sultry, and I'm completely in trouble. "I do know how to move."

"This is a classy event," I chide.

"It's okay. The dynamic with my boss has thawed." Her voice is neutral.

"I would say so." I tip her to the side without warning and pull her back to me tightly. A new spark forms between us, only proven by the way she wraps her arms loosely around my shoulders and begins to play with the hair on the back of my neck. "Can I ask you something?"

"That seems to be the theme of the night, so yes."

"Why haven't you brought up the kiss?"

She looks away, nearly bashful, before her gaze shifts back to me. "Well… no need to, right? We were angry, and it seemed to diffuse the situation."

I repeat my earlier move and tip her to the side, this time even farther back, before bringing her up flush with my body, leaving her no choice but to tie our gazes together and hang on to me to keep her balance. "Very true. I was unreasonable pissed."

She chuffs a laugh. "Unreasonable is an understatement."

"Maybe it's good you haven't brought it up. We've been able to maintain a professional relationship."

"Right," she clearly lies. "We might want to improve on that.

Everyone can see us right now and might get the wrong impression."

"It doesn't matter what people think when it is perfectly harmless for a successful man to dance with his assistant if they have nothing to hide. We have company policies, after all. I've always followed them." We continue to move. "Except…" Her eyes grow as she waits. "I've never been in a position to break them." I'm surprised I didn't keep that thought locked away. Her eyes change light, and I can't make out what she's thinking. "Maybe our method of communicating is borderline unprofessional, or the fact you're here in my arms after I've seen you naked and kissed you is questionable, too."

"Very," she replies.

"Okay, we agree on that." I want to be unprofessional, which makes me a horrible person because she deserves respect that comes with work experience, as she'll be going places. She's smart. But I'm entirely selfish. I'm addicted to her, with every jab striking me even further into an abyss I can't escape.

"Julian…" She doesn't say my name often, but when she does, it clings to me. "I don't want to be one of those people who fall into an office judgment from people. I want to be respected for my work. Also, well, your company is clearing me of any financial debt. Adding this… hmmm, not sure what to call it—"

I interrupt with honesty that we need to admit out loud. "Chemistry."

"Exactly. Adding it to the mix has made it harder. Yet, I can't seem to gravitate away from things. Hence, why I'm here."

"Interesting." I continue to lead her in a dance that's disappeared into standing in place with a gentle sway. "And I'm not someone who appreciates the cliché rendezvous with their assistant. Yet, my compass won't change direction."

It's a long few beats of stalemate at our joint realization. It's a beast inside trying to rip open our barriers. She blows out a breath and averts her gaze. "Anyhow, I should probably go soon."

"Makes sense. I'll take you home."

"Okay."

The worst idea ever.

S<small>AVANNAH DIDN'T BLINK TWICE</small> when a driver picked us up from valet. Being down to earth makes her even more attractive. The drive through the city is pure luck, with no traffic, and our conversation was like Lake Michigan on a still summer night, calm and quiet except for the occasional wave.

Truthfully, the most calming aspect of the night is sitting in the back and allowing my eyes to drift every so often to my side to see Savannah with my suit coat draped over her shoulders and her face eased, with a tiny, closed smile etched on her lips as she watches the city outside the window.

We don't need to say much because we're both soaking in the calm air between us.

The driver finds a free spot outside her place in the East Lincoln Park neighborhood. "Nice place." We pay well, but this well for an assistant role? It surprises me.

She skates her gaze between me and the house with what appears to be two apartments, one on top of the other. "I got lucky. A friend from college was sent on a company assignment to Brazil, so her company pays half the lease, and I pay the other while I stay there."

"In this city, yeah, that's fortunate."

She seems humored by me. "I doubt you can understand with your bank account."

"I'm not ignorant, you should know that by now." I unbuckle my seatbelt.

"Whoa there, mister. Where are you going?"

Immediately, I'm not impressed. "It's night in Chicago. I don't care if you have to walk three feet, I'm walking you to your door because I'm a fucking gentleman."

She scoffs. "Really? Going into the broody demanding mode, right now?" She opens her door and gets out, only to turn back. "Fine… you might have a point."

I'm quick to hop out, close the door, and circle the car to her. We leisurely walk up the steps, probably to stretch time. "Thanks for coming tonight."

"No problem." She shakes off my tux jacket that was around her shoulders to keep her warm. "This is yours. I assume I'll be picking it up from the dry cleaner sometime soon."

I titter a laugh at her reference and accept the jacket. "Tempting. But I might actually change your job profile and take that item off the list."

"Oh gee, how thankful I shall be," she deadpans.

We reach the final step and her door. "I'm still a little pissed, though."

"Oh God, what now?" Her aggravation is beginning, and it's that turn-on that I hate.

"The dress. Really unfair to me." I'm dead serious.

She throws her arms up in exasperation. "You have to be fucking kidding me. You don't get to decide how I dress, and if you can't keep it together, that's your problem." She's offended, as she should be.

"Hey, tone down your snark for a second."

She swats my shoulder. "I'm not snarky, I'm standing up for my dress collection and all the hard work I've done on my legs in Pilates class," she justifies.

"And nothing in that sentence helps the situation." My voice rises.

"I don't care. Nothing about you in a suit and your cocky attitude is fair, yet the world keeps turning."

Everything inside of me that was building in that second

bursts. "What about me *without* a suit? Does your world keep turning then?" I counter, and she pauses with her lips parted slightly open.

I step closer to her, and the way her chest moves up and down only heightens the tension around us because it's clearly visible even under the dim streetlight that she's worked up. I'm well aware that subconsciously, I'm leading us down a dangerous path, and that is my full intention.

She glances up to the sky and drops her gaze back to me. "Are we bickering about clothes? You, *grrr*, gosh, you are…" She lets out a slew of words that make zero sense, and she shakes her hands as her face contorts in different positions.

The moment stops, and she gives in by stepping forward and moving to frame my face with her hands, but I'm quick, and I grab her wrists to meet her halfway when our mouths meet in a fervent kiss. I make an indication behind my back to the waiting driver to leave before I snatch the keys from her hand and walk her back to her door.

It's impossible to say how I managed to get the door open because neither one of us was focusing on the logistics, instead stuck in our determination for more.

When the door opens, she fists my shirt and yanks me in.

And I kick the door closed behind me.

12

SAVANNAH

Lately, it's been impossible to ignore the tide drawing us closer. We didn't need to say anything because everything pulsed between us.

We are so tightly wound that I didn't even hear the door close. I only know it did because Julian pulls me close and spins me around, pinning me to the closed door.

His lips kissing me so fervently causes my body to tighten with an overpowering need to take whatever he'll give me.

He wraps his hand at the base of my neck. It should scare me, but it doesn't. It's light enough, but it leaves little doubt that he is the one in power.

"This is the part where you kick me out and tell me I'm the man you can't stand." His voice is rough, filled with a need for something that I don't want to stop.

"Oh, shut up," I snipe. It's all I manage to say as desire takes over my body. My lips feel heavily touched.

"Only after you wrap your legs around me like a good girl." His grin is sinful before he kisses me harder, and he hauls me up, my legs wrapping instinctively around him and my dress bunching at my waist.

He doesn't ask for directions and walks us as our mouths remain fused. There is no space between us, we are sewn together, and I dig my fingers into his shoulders as our tongues meet, rough and greedy.

We have no control over what we're doing, letting desire lead us.

Somehow, without separating, we shamble down my short hallway, ricocheting off the walls, until we reach my living room and the end of the sofa. He sets me down, quick to twirl me until my back is against his front. I feel his hard length against my back, and my panties are already ruined.

The moment gives us a brief pause while he grazes the back of his hand down the curve of my body. Slowly, purposefully. His movement causes my skin to tingle and my nipples to pebble. His breath against my neck is heavy and hot. The moment his fingers pinch the zipper of my dress, I feel a change.

Clothes are about to come off, and this is my chance to second-guess what's transpiring. But I don't.

Agonizingly slowly, he pulls the zipper down. "So beautiful," he whispers.

I close my eyes as the fabric slips down my body to a pool at my feet. Stepping out of the pile, I turn to face him. There is a flicker of marvel in his eyes as he reviews me.

One step is all it takes from him, before he dips his mouth down to latch onto a nipple. My head falls back, and I moan under my breath. At first, he's gentle, flicking his tongue, but he adds more pressure, with his fingers twisting my other nipple. I seem to encourage him further when my hands rake through his hair. I swallow, feeling exposed, yet completely confident that this is where I should be.

The moment he parts from my breasts, I seize the opportunity and slide my hands up his back, feeling his muscles beneath his shirt. I trace them on the path that leads me to his front, and I begin to undo another one of his shirt buttons, nearly ripping them in the process.

Our eyes connect, and it's a reminder that we don't need touch to burst into flames because we're capable of driving one another wild purely through eye contact.

His shirt falls to the floor, and I yank on his belt. I want to see more of him. I want to touch him in places that could cure my aching.

"Everything off, even the heels," he commands.

I give him a strange look because most men want the heels to stay on. The corner of his mouth curves because he knows how to read my mind.

"I want to try you in a few different ways, and they might create an obstacle we don't need."

"Really? It isn't your ego that's the problem?" I tease him in this moment.

I yelp when I feel the palm of his hand slap the side of my ass. "Watch it. Otherwise, I'll make you red and begging."

There is no further discussion because he drops to his knees, and his mouth traces the waistband of my lace panties, purposefully almost brushing over my sensitive spot, ensuring our eyes remain locked. He isn't seeking my approval; he has a point to prove.

One that sends me straight into a moan when he hooks his fingers under the fabric and yanks them down. He hovers his lips over my pussy for a mere second. Taunting me, giving me a glimpse of his intentions.

The moment his tongue darts out and hits my clit, I don't get the relief I hoped for. Instead, my body only gets wound more tightly. Julian circles my clit before sucking. I'm about to lose balance, and his answer is to fill my pussy with two fingers. He does nothing with them; instead, he uses his mouth to drive me wild.

"Fuck," I moan, and he laps up my juices.

"You taste sweet. And you're soaking for me, desperate for my cock." His voice swelters.

My own hands begin to caress my breasts because my entire body is floating, and every touch is heightened.

"I think you're desperate for my pussy, you're the one on your knees."

It seems to trigger him, as he instantly stops. He stands, then pushes my shoulders down, indicating that I get on my knees, and I do. He unzips his pants and pulls out his thick, long cock that meets my eye level.

"Now you're the one on your knees." He traces the tip of his cock across the line of my mouth. "Open."

I obey and bring my hands to his shaft as I take his cock into my mouth. He sounds approving as I begin to suck, and I'm eager to take more. There is comfort with my mouth full of him. Oral has never been a thing for me, but this? It's a whole new addiction.

My mouth salivates, and I feel a dribble of drool escaping the corner of my mouth.

"So fucking good, Savannah," he praises, and he grips my hair around his fist to guide the speed. I look up to see him in pure relaxation. "Taking it all in your mouth. Look at you. So beautiful as you do this."

I murmur sounds I didn't know I could make, but I'm eager to please him, and the praise only blazes inside of me to want more. I'm so overloaded with a desire for an orgasm that I bring my fingers to my pussy to rub.

"Tsk, tsk, only I get to do that." He takes hold of my arm with force, causing me to stand.

He guides me back onto the sofa, and I crawl back until my back is against a throw pillow in the corner. He follows me as though I'm his prey, right before he parts my legs and jolts me forward to spread me wide.

His tongue is back on me, and he licks. Instantly, I try to stay in this world, but it's a struggle, especially when his determination pays off and my pussy begins to vibrate around his mouth, and I softly scream my orgasm. His mouth doesn't abandon me until I calm.

But I only get a few seconds' reprieve, and during that time, he grabs a condom. The moment he slides into me, we sync. First, slowly an inch, then deeper and deeper.

Our murmurs blend, my walls tighten around his cock, and my body molds to him as he moves in and out, inching more inside of me with every thrust. We speed up together, and our mouths wander. I'm on fire, especially when he hits me deep.

I bring my legs around his waist, with my toes digging into his ass cheeks. I'm holding on as our movements become more intense. He slams his cock into me, and the sound fills my ears of our skin smacking.

"You have two options. I either come right now, or you get on top of me to fuck and milk me dry."

Gosh, his dirty mouth. I love it.

I push him away, and we quickly switch positions to enable me to straddle him. I sink down on top of him, and a new angle sends me keening.

The one problem, however, is that now we're in an embrace where we stare directly into one another's eyes. In a moment, the pace is uneven as we adapt to the position, and I choose to ignore the extra beat my heartbeat dragged.

His smug look lacks humor. Only understanding that this evening is unexpected, but maybe we were waiting.

I don't let the thoughts linger as I bounce, and his hands hold my hips steady. We move, and my arms snake around his neck as I begin to come, my walls tremoring all around his cock.

"That's it. Come all over my cock. Be good for me."

But he chases me, and soon, he groans as his own orgasm hits.

We're left a tangled mess of two souls completely spent on

giving in to attraction and chemistry that is far too natural when it comes to sex.

Once isn't enough, but again would be dangerous.

Yet a few minutes later, when he returns from the bathroom, neither one of us makes an effort to find clothes.

Instead, he holds his hand out to me as he stands over the couch. I accept it and join him, leading him straight to my bedroom for more.

13
JULIAN

It's the curve of Savannah's shoulder blade. Why can't I look away? Maybe because it's a piece of her body that is perfection. It's also the safest option because her magnetic eyes and angelic face are doing something to me. Unwrapping me. Making me a man who has been coming unhinged lately.

Lying on my side with my head propped against my bent arm, she lifts one eyelid from where she's on her belly with a pillow bunched under her head and a sheet hanging low on her back. A bemused smile ghosts her lips.

"Something you care to share with the class?"

I crack a grin. "Nah. I'm just impressed with your stamina."

She flips like a pancake to her back. "Uhm, that should be my line. I'm the one who's younger with more energy."

My fingers feather up her arm. "Let's not judge based on a number."

"Fine."

I've taken this woman on her couch and in her bed, and I've come to the conclusion that I'm drowning in her. I learned how to swim long ago, but for some reason now, I can no longer swim to safety.

The way she smiles when she's riding the wave of endorphins is new to me. It's a good look on her.

"I should send my dress to the dry cleaner and make you pick it up," she quips.

"Nah, that's what I have money for. I'll just buy you a new one."

She pinches me, and I yelp to play along. "Are you saying I could have just used the company credit card and bought you new suits?"

"What fun would that be?" I let my eyes drift away from her and really explore her bedroom. It's simple, except for a wall with a bunch of photos in various frames.

"Family?" I tip my head in their direction.

She doesn't even need to follow my sight. "Yep. A few friends as well."

Sure, I see people with family photos on their phones or when I go to somebody's house. In this situation? It hits a little differently. Maybe because Savannah's always distinct in a way that is only reserved for talking about her family. She has a unique aura. It's a foreign concept for me.

I notice a framed piece of paper with lines from a crayon. "What in the world is that?"

It causes her to glance over her shoulder, and she smiles. "From my goddaughter."

"It's literally two lines that make zero sense. How does that end up in a frame?"

She swats me and laughs. "She's just turned two. It was her first time holding crayons, and she drew a picture for me. I shall cherish it forever."

"Yeah, no, not happening. I don't think my parents even kept my prize-winning sea drawing I did when I was in first grade, let alone crayon lines. If I ever have a kid, I'm setting some rules."

I'm not sure why any of that left my mouth. Both topics I do not wish to discuss.

"You want kids one day?" To be fair, I walked into that question.

I shrug. "Probably not. I would assume you want ten or something. Have to help on the farm in Purplehope."

She snickers playfully. "First off, no way I'd have ten. I don't live on a farm, and it's Everhope, as you very well know. But no kids in my future anytime soon. I'm young still."

"You are."

"Anyhow, I'm going to enjoy my family not meddling right now. In ten years, if I live alone with a cat, then they'll be sending men my way, I'm sure. Nobody loves meddling family," she says lightheartedly, but my ears didn't hear the tone.

Instead, the words strike me. "Absolutely fucking not," I agree, but out loud and with grit in my tone. When I realize I let it slip, I sigh as I move and rest my head on the pillow next to her.

She looks at me, and her lips roll in, but she doesn't say anything. Her face is pained, but it's for me because she senses that there has been a shift in my mind. But it's Savannah and she won't pry. We may constantly snark and bicker with one another, yet she holds respect for topics that I wish to be untouched.

Maybe that's the reason I find her more compelling. "I don't talk to my dad at all. Not a single word. It's been that way for years." And it seems I'm letting her in.

She nods gingerly. "I've heard."

"I was close with my grandmother, and when she passed when I was in college, it was in her will that I would become head of her company, but only once I graduated. My dad was interim CEO and made some moves to ensure I never got the company."

"I'm sorry."

"It gets better." I grin bitterly to myself.

She cringes. "I don't feel like it does."

"Ding, ding. Points for Savannah. My dad was having an

affair… with my sister's sorority roommate. To add a cherry on top of that, my mother is the one who discovered the photos of them together. She got a nice divorce settlement and travels the world sending an email to check in only twice a year at best."

"Ouch."

"In the end, it's a win for me. I have more interest in what I'm doing now, with zero strings to my family in terms of my company."

She seems slightly disheartened to hear that. "I'm going to be honest whether you want me to be or not, but you're probably holding on to a lot of anger."

"Maybe."

Savannah hums a sound. "I'm giving you a free pass and we can move on from a topic that I don't think you would even pay a therapist for. But thank you for sharing. It connects a few dots."

This woman. She's pure. That's quite possibly why I've been hard on her in the office. I'm not that blind. She's everything that scares me. Savannah is everything in one package. Looks, smarts, humor, and now proven to drive me wild in bed.

It spells disaster because she deserves a man who sends her roses. Yet, she doesn't give a hint that she's dwelling on what this is. It's simply sex. It has to be.

But right now, the world only exists outside, and I'm going to steal every second of this moment.

Her long finger taps my biceps. "I never actually got to the root of why you named your company Haven Crossroads. Haven, okay, makes sense. But why Crossroads?"

The corners of my mouth twist, and I consider whether to share or keep her guessing. "Maybe one day you'll find out."

She mocks a pout, and my response is to sneak my hand under the sheet and quickly find my destination; her soft thigh, with skin that feels warmer the higher I go.

She touches my face, her thumb swiping across my lips. I

capture her thumb for a quick nip. "Julian," she purrs. "What are you doing?"

I place kisses along her jawline, leading me to dive into her neck with an urge to bite her skin, mark her, and she gets a small nibble. She murmurs as she tilts her head back, which causes her neck to be on further display.

"I'm taking you because you're naked and next to me," I whisper against her skin.

"And how do you plan on doing that this time?" Her hand snakes around her body to touch my hard cock.

My nails claw into her skin on her hip. "Take you from behind with your ass up and your face against the mattress. There's less chance of your mouth getting feisty on me."

She lets out a derisive laugh. "You bring out the worst in me."

I give a low chuckle. "I beg to differ. I've very much seen the best of you. Not a scrap of clothing and my cock deep inside your pussy."

"I really wish that didn't turn me on, you seem to have victory in bed."

I swirl my finger around her soaking clit. "Glad we acknowledge that," I say hoarsely.

"Such an arrogant ass." There's too much truth in her tone.

My devilish laugh should warn her, and I don't respond to her comment. Instead, I lead us straight into position so I can slip inside her.

I should have left her after what transpired on the couch. But I'm a self-seeking winner, so every warning I give her, it's not merely words, it's the truth.

Her hips buck, when I thrust into her with blunt force, and it causes her to gasp. It's my full intention to take over her body. I want control. And watching her claw the sheets feels like success.

But falling asleep after? That's my failure.

THE SUN IS RISING. I can tell by the tint of light that appears in the crack in the curtains. I slowly sit up and rub my eyes before driving my sight to Savannah next to me, lying peacefully.

Did I get what I wanted last night? Now that I've had my fix, can I return to friction in the office? Maybe we've ruined that. She's unpredictable at work, I'm not chasing, but my actions always seem to continue the game we play.

She begins to stir, and I debate whether I should sneak out now, or at least give her a good-morning. A small part of me contemplates ordering us breakfast, but that would entail staying longer. It could get messy that way.

I make my decision and search for my boxer briefs on the floor. Sliding out of bed, I swoop them up and dress in a hurry. The rest of my clothes are scattered across her living room. I'm about to quietly tread to the bedroom door with what I have on, but I indulge myself with another glance at Savannah, naked in bed with a sheet draped slightly above the curve of her full breasts, and her hair is splayed across her pillow.

The corner of my mouth snags up because it's impossible not to smile at her gentle beauty.

I lean down and rest my hands on the mattress to reach her forehead where I plant the faintest of kisses.

I'm not a coward. I'm ensuring our dynamic remains attainable.

Which is why I walk away, leaving her be.

14

SAVANNAH

A smile begins to etch on the corner of my mouth, but I can't commit to it because there's a dose of nerves behind it. All due to sleeping with my boss because our level of sexual tension broke, but then he was gone. I don't know what I expected. I mean, I knew the score. It was purely physical, and we had to get it out of our systems. That's why I shouldn't let any part of me think otherwise.

I snap my attention back to Elodie when she passes me a lid for my coffee. We're standing next to the table against the wall, with little packs of sugar, stir sticks, and options of spices or cocoa to add to our coffee. She managed to drop her daughter off early, and we decided to grab a quick to-go beverage from a little place around the corner that has far better coffee than our building.

"Right? Such a scandal," she says, and it causes my stomach to tighten.

"Scandal?" That word is a little harsh. Is that what it is when the CEO's assistant sleeps with him? Wait, how does she know about my exceptional evening in bed? Nobody is aware, because my career is due to my own hard work, not the result of sleeping with the boss, and I don't want anyone to get the wrong idea.

She looks at me strangely and uses her back to open the café door. "Yeah. The Everhope Summer Festival. The battle for the winning pie. According to my parents, it's coming down to the lemon meringue and the blueberry. Both bakers hate one another, so it could be interesting."

Pie. Really? This is the conversation that is starting my day? I guess it's better than the alternative. I'm not sure how this morning in the office with Julian will go.

"Oh yeah, the festival."

"Are you heading home for it?"

I take a quick sip of my coffee, and the ratio of milk and coffee hits just right. "It's still a while away, but yeah, probably."

"Obviously, I'm there, as my parents will lose it if I deprive them of their granddaughter for the annual festival."

A warm smile finds me because everything about that sentence is calming. Zero room for interpretation or negativity. Unlike the possibility of what I'm about to face.

I'm not sure yet how to play it. Disappointment or indifference. I'll decide the moment Julian's piercing gaze meets mine.

We continue down the sidewalk, and the coffee is kicking in. Still, I'm not very engaged in our conversation, and it has nothing to do with Elodie's part.

She nudges my arm. "Did you get the news yet?" she coaxes me with a grimace.

She doesn't need to explain further. "I actually looked this morning, as they released all the grades and confirmations at 6 AM."

"Aaaand?"

In all my recent entanglements, I almost forgot about my master's until this morning when my calendar reminded me that I had a degree to conquer.

We enter our busy building and follow the crowd to the elevators. "All passed with exceptional grades, thank you very much." I smile proudly.

"Eeek, I'm so happy! When will you have your graduation ceremony?"

I take another drink, probably to prolong having to answer, but I have to. "I won't. I asked them to mail me my diploma."

"What?" she shrieks.

"I don't want to make a big deal about it," I answer as we wait for the elevator. "I don't like that attention on me. It feels as though I'm... bragging. Is that the right word? I'm not sure, but I'm aware it's crazy, and my aunt will not be pleased, but she has enough going on. It's better that I casually slip it into conversation next time we speak."

I glance to my side and see that my friend seems completely bewildered. "Wow, that's a lot of nonsense for an intelligent woman. You should celebrate your big accomplishment. Nobody thinks that you're being showy. It's even tradition to celebrate."

All I do is shrug as we enter the elevator.

"Well, at least let me take you for a drink?"

"Sure. I might need one later." Or three. My body is going haywire because the pops of unrealistic secret thrill and possibility are playing a game inside me.

She pauses for a second and studies me. "Is everything else okay? You seem a little out if it."

I don't like lying to her, but I'm not ready to talk about my situation with Julian. I need to process it all myself.

"Yeah, it's fine. I'm a little tired." That's an understatement. I'm a little sore, too.

She touches my arm for comfort. "Okay. Well, hopefully the coffee will kick in soon. Don't forget to eat breakfast, too." The elevator dings, and it's her floor to get off.

"Yes, Mom." I give her a little salute.

She leaves me, and the moment the doors close, I'm wide

awake, my entire body spiking with adrenaline, and it only gets worse when I reach two floors up and I leave the elevator.

I'm met with quiet, except for the sound of someone printing something down the hall. One deep breath and straightening my shoulders, I walk to my desk with confidence, even if it's all for show.

For a brief moment, my heart lifts when I spot a vase with flowers on my desk. Okay, I wasn't expecting these, and I smile because he sent me flowers, that isn't a bad sign. Suddenly, there's more pep to my step. When I arrive at my desk, I set down my cup of coffee, and I pick up the card only to completely deflate. It's only from a supplier, to get in Julian's good graces, I'm sure. I toss the card to the side, and my bag slides down my arm that I set on my chair. Good luck to them, he hates flowers.

With a mix of disappointment and even a tad of anger, I abruptly pick up the vase and carry it to the staff room to leave them for others to enjoy because I sure as hell won't. If they are placed anywhere near my desk, they will only goad me. It's the flowers that trigger me, because suddenly, it's clear to me how I will handle the day. I'm feeling things that I shouldn't, and I will take the leap so Julian doesn't have to. We can erase any memory of the weekend, even if I can't.

I snatch up a blueberry bagel from the basket on the counter and skip cream cheese. I bite into it like an animal as my entire mind and body prepare for the morning ahead, ready to defend my dignity.

Gobbling my bagel, I walk with a fast pace straight to my desk and flop the bagel down before wiping my hands and tousling my hair. Julian's door is closed, and by the waft of his cologne trailing to his office, it makes me aware he arrived while I was re-aligning my mood.

One deep breath and I decide to get this over with. I stride straight to his office and don't even bother knocking on the door, instead opening it with gusto.

His eyes instantly float up to see that it's me. Our eyes connecting causes the clock to temporarily stop. The current message between us is recognition for what happened and that we have now been intimate, and that binds us in a different way.

He leans back in his chair and tosses his pen onto his desk. He opted to leave his top three buttons undone, and his eyes are sea blue today. It's the sun reflecting through the window, I'm sure. He nearly has me in complete submission to the control that he exudes, because that's all he knows.

But I don't waver.

My eyes drop to the floor to ensure he doesn't entrap me in the spell that he gives off. "Look, it is what it is. We don't need to have a full-fledged conversation about the weekend. We're professionals and that's that." My tone is simple yet to the point. I blink a few times when I realize that I should have more dominance right now.

He sighs. "Savannah." My name is heavy when it leaves his lips, and I see the struggle on his face. "It's… you… it's—" He looks up at the ceiling as he formulates his thoughts and drops his attention straight to me as I stand in the middle of his office. "I don't do romance. I don't do relationships. I'm no good at either. We had fun, and it probably shouldn't happen again."

Hearing him say it, even if anticipated, still stings. Sure, some people can sleep with someone and leave it at that. But sleeping with someone when there is a stronger connection, an unimaginable magnetism that keeps drawing you to one another. The banter, the flirtation, the little facts that you begin to learn. It makes it all feel like a little more than sleeping together.

But he's right, and I can't have any other expectations.

"Exactly," I agree.

He stands, only to turn his back to me, pushing the sides of his blazer back to rest his hands on his hips and gaze out the window. "I don't sleep with employees, so you can get that out of your head."

"It wasn't in my head. You mentioned it already once," I reply bluntly. That is one factor that I quickly learned is true.

"And even if there is a spark..." He doesn't even glance over his shoulder. "You should stay away from me."

Now, he hit a nerve, and I'm quick to defend. "Are you seriously putting this on me? I haven't been chasing you, if that's what you're implying."

Julian turns and rests his hands on the back of his chair, and our bodies are both ready for a standoff. My entire middle tightens because I'm not sure if it's him or me that is about to snap.

"I didn't mean it to come out like that. I'm the problem. I'm highlighting that you should stay away from me... in that way." It feels like a warning that he doesn't want to give about himself but feels obligated to do so.

I take a step forward and place one hand on my hip, and with the other, I point a finger in the air. "You know, I came here with... not quite the acceptance of how this would go but for the most part the expectation of how this was going to go. And your warning is the biggest BS. Also, while we're at it, we are the total epitome of mixed messages."

"Agreed."

"Whatever game this is, you're the one who sets the rules, and I don't like that."

He uses his thumbs to rub his temples. "This is what it is... Let's move on." He sounds frustrated with himself.

I claw my hair. "Fine."

The silence in the room still roars because there's a storm of tension. I pivot to leave, only to pause. "Julian."

He flicks his gaze back to me. "Yes?"

"Do you regret what happened?" I shouldn't ask, I should leave it, but I'm not always logical.

He traps his tongue between his teeth, and it's a second or two before he audibly breathes. "Would saying yes makes it easier?"

Typical Julian. A blurred answer. It's an unfair strategy.

"I'm not answering that."

A sharp muffled sound leaves him. "Of course, you wouldn't. You don't make my life easy," he remarks affectionately.

"Ditto," I counter softly.

It's a long stretch of seconds that we get lost staring at each other. My chest thrums, and he appears conflicted yet able to remain reserved.

I pretend to wipe my hands and erase the tone. "Done and dusted. Back to work." It's my effort to move us along with the day.

Even if it's clear that no eraser will help us because neither one of us can forget.

SOME PEOPLE really need to read the instructions better. It would make my life easier. Someone from IT reset the system incorrectly, which set almost everyone back a few hours of work. I have zero regrets that I went out for lunch and did some shopping, including picking up a new box of fruit snack gummies. I'm mentally preparing myself for the hours of work ahead. It'll be a long day.

When I approach my desk with my shopping bag in hand, my eyes squint because I notice a small box on my desk. I set my things down and shimmy off my sweater as I examine the blue box with a white ribbon. Unlike the flowers, this has a little card with my name on it. I pick it up and open the envelope to pull out the card with beautifully typed wording.

Congratulations on completing your degree.
Haven Crossroads

Strange. Unless Elodie spread news like wildfire, I haven't informed anybody else. I untie the satin ribbon and lift the lid of the blue cardboard box, brush the tissue paper to the side, and I completely stall because my heart jumps.

A necklace with a key charm.

Why would this be the present? It dawns on me that I mentioned something to Julian. Barely a sentence, yet he must have remembered.

This man.

He's making my head spin again.

But right now, I can only smile softly and appreciate the gesture. Only to acknowledge with disappointment that it is another turn in the labyrinth of a game neither of us can decide whether we want to win or lose. The tide inside me turns again when I realize how this isn't a scenario that I should've found myself in. It only causes anger, and here I go from zero to a hundred again today.

Storming to Julian's office, I don't bother knocking on his open door, as he is busy typing on his laptop.

"Strange." I grab his attention purely with my voice, and he whips his attention to me. "I received a company gift because of a special occasion."

"Did you? HR arranges those things." He plays oblivious as he settles back in his chair.

I'm annoyed that he's deflecting.

I walk straight to his desk and drop the gift in front of him. His eyes pierce the box, but he doesn't move. "I'm not a whore."

He brings the knuckle of his long finger up to drag across his upper lip, and his sight remains drilled to the present. "You are not a whore," he echoes back.

"We can't fuck and you buy a necklace as if nothing happened." There is rage in my voice.

His jaw ticks, and he bites the inside of his cheek as he accepts my wrath. "That's not what I'm doing. Trust me, jewelry and women are a dangerous move that blurs expectations… It would be irresponsible of me to forget that rule." I sense the struggle as he realizes his actions, the awareness bleeds through him, and it's apparent. "As I said, HR—"

"Sends expensive pens as gifts for employee milestones. Not necklaces." Pointing a finger at him, he has now turned unreadable. I continue. "Cut the crap, and either way, I shouldn't accept such a thing, but somebody clearly picked it out with knowledge."

"Maybe." His look is resigned.

"That person should know it could be seen as thoughtful, even if they have a fucked-up way of communicating most of the time. They might even be a coward."

He stretches his neck, uncomfortable, clearly offended by my suggestion. "You should really take up your concerns with HR."

I shake my head, now irritated how he wants to hide behind a façade.

At least my suspicious are confirmed. He doesn't want to forget the weekend, and he does believe he could be destined for more than just sex with someone, I'm twisting everything inside of him. For now, a confirmation is all I need. Everything else will revolve the way it should, in either direction.

Sighing, I give up on this conversation. Pivoting, I walk away, maybe even with an intentional sway. "This talk is a waste of time, just as much as the mess that IT left us all."

I'm about to leave, but Julian saying my name stops me.

"Congratulations. You should be proud."

I glance over my shoulder. "How did you know?"

His cheeks tighten, and he fights an affectionate smile. "I overheard you talking with Elodie. And no, I wasn't stalking, you were literally in our office building, and I made a point for you not to notice me because it made the morning easier."

"And did it?"

He chuckles quietly to himself. "Not even a dent."

I almost grin but keep myself in check. "Sorry to hear that."

Julian rubs his face with his hands. "You should leave. *Now.*" There is a smile he wants to stop when he says it.

Because he isn't immune to succumbing to a woman, and he is only beginning to realize that.

And it happens to be me.

15

JULIAN

The clink of utensils and bouncing chatter fill my ears when I should be focusing on my sister across from me, having lunch at Jupiter. My mistake, since this place reminds me of Savannah and the night we had unexpected drinks and some obscure mushroom with cheese.

Vaguely, I hear my sister Caroline saying my name on repeat, and I bring my attention back to her. We only meet a few times a year, and that suits us. There's no bad blood, quite the contrary. We're just not, well, close-knit people who need to chat every day. I'm career-driven, and while she does have a career with her boutique art gallery, she would rather be spending money in France. Her pantsuit today is a little too dull for a woman her age, but to each their own.

"As I was saying, are you sure you don't want to attend a meeting?"

I grimace tightly. "And break tradition? Why would I do that?" I answer sarcastically.

"You're really never going to show an interest?"

I shake my head proudly before happily taking a bite of my BLT.

"I know you have no intention of seeing Dad again, and I don't enjoy that annual, distant nod in his direction. But grandmother left us those shares, and we shouldn't let them be taken from us."

"True. But I'm quite satisfied with you voting on my behalf for whatever is on the agenda."

Her eyes bug out. "You really don't even read the agenda?"

"Why would I do that? That's what I have you for. Unless voting harms the man who's no longer a father to us, abstain from every vote. Abstaining always disrupts the vote count for whatever agenda they're pushing. I see my shares as merely stock—the last tie to what grandmother wanted."

She cuts the chicken in her salad and wobbles her head. "That also works."

"Then why do you insist on going?"

Caroline shrugs, before popping the food into her mouth. "I don't know. Curiosity, perhaps." She speaks with her mouth full.

"Well, you enjoy that and don't let me know how it goes. I'll even let you vote on my behalf for once as your early birthday present. So go wild as long as it screws something up."

She holds her palm up to ease me. "Fine. I get the hint. No more discussion on this." She drops her hand. "What else is new? You know, I've decided that I'm putting in my will that if I die, you get my kids."

I look at her strangely. "You don't have kids."

"Yes. But maybe one day I will." She's playing hypotheticals again. Sometimes, out of nowhere, she plans her life. Last time, it was a vacation house in Aspen—she hates snow.

"Don't do something so stupid. I'm horrible with kids."

"Speaking of which, how's the hunt for a wife going?"

I scratch my chin. "I'll take that as, is there a woman in my life?"

She grins because she enjoys putting me on the spot. "Yep."

My chest tightens. Conflict hits hard—a surge of fear, resentment, and hope. "There's nobody." Except someone twisting everything inside me—everything I hate. Yet for the first time, someone is winning me over, and it terrifies me.

"Oh, that's a shame. Someone mentioned they saw you at the gala with someone."

I hum in acknowledgment. "That was my assistant, Savannah."

She butters her roll, and I'm beginning to lose my own appetite because thoughts of Savannah can't be escaped. To the point that I'm debating if I should bring her a piece of s'mores pie back to the office, as it's an award-winning dessert here, although she is probably the best dessert on the menu today. But my last gift of a necklace was not well received, probably because I shamefully didn't own up to it. It's complicated between us, but I wanted her to have something nice to celebrate her accomplishment. I failed to think through the coward angle.

"Ah, okay. I admittedly searched the internet for a photo from the night, and my eye caught one. She's pretty. Younger, but pretty. Beautiful, actually. Hopefully, you keep her around for a while."

She isn't going to make a suggestion that Savannah and I could be anything else because we both despise mixing work with pleasure. Yet, that's all I seem to be doing lately.

A glance at my watch reminds me of the meeting I have in half an hour, and an odd sensation of wanting to stay longer tugs at me. I mask it with a joke as I flag down the waiter. "It's been fun, we should do this more often. Let's say in six months?"

My sister smiles. "Totally."

When the waiter approaches, I debate ordering dessert. But for the first time lately, I'm smart.

———

SAVANNAH and I watch as another candidate for the COO position vanishes into the elevator. The moment the doors close, I tip my head in the direction of my office, and she follows me in tow, closing the door behind her. If it weren't for the fact that I need privacy during calls and meetings, I think I would rip the door off its hinges to ensure I can never be in a closed room with her. It's tempting, risky, and far too confronting of the memory of the curve of her spine.

"That was horrible," she begins.

"Very," I agree, reaching the coffee machine. We saw the last candidate only as a favor to my high-up in finance; he was stiff and would never think outside the box. I start my coffee, then give her a brief glance and raise a cup to see if she wants one. Inviting her to stay for coffee has been another dicey move lately.

She shakes her head. "No, thanks. It's after 12. You shouldn't drink so much coffee. It isn't good for sleep."

"I sleep fine, as you kn—" I stop myself from finishing the sentence, but the damage is done, and we both know what I meant.

"Fine. You shouldn't drink it because it spikes your blood sugar before making you crash. It wrecks your mood. We go from nearly tolerable Julian to devil incarnate. It's bad for humanity." Her knack for keeping us on track is a godsend.

The corner of my mouth tugs from her humor, but I don't let her see as I keep my back to her while finishing my coffee. "You've highlighted that many times."

"It wasn't in my job description, so I took the liberty of adding it. Anyhow, you need someone for the job who is an all-rounder, smiles, yet can relate to someone who thinks in numbers or IT."

"In other words, the socially awkward."

Turning, I'm faced with her unimpressed look. "They are not socially awkward."

"Tell me, if you had more experience, would you want the COO job?" I'm curious. On a completely professional level, actually. "I mean, we are paying off your degree in a field that suits." I'm still holding up the pretense.

She blinks a few times, clearly not having expected my question. "I mean, it crossed my mind a few times." She's unsure, but after a few seconds, everything in her posture grows comfortable. "Actually, no."

Huh. That's blunt. "You wouldn't want to be the COO for a billion-dollar company?" I'm doubtful.

"No. Don't let it hurt your ego, but your company isn't the end-all for some. I think I would stay here for the years promised, plus a few more to get more experience. But I think something smaller and closer to Everhope might be of interest. For now, I will help my aunt when I can with her business."

My lips quirk out, and I appreciate her honesty. "I wasn't expecting your answer. But you always catch me off guard."

A bright smile stretches on her gorgeous face. "I do." Her tone is soft, and our eyes catch while silence swims around us. We allow it to happen for a few more seconds until her eyes drift to the side. "Uhm, anyhow. We have the trip for your speaking engagement. You'll need to be at the airport on time. There will be a business lounge to sit in before we board."

"Business lounge? Why would I need that? I'm going straight to my jet."

She grimaces with a mix of fear and satisfaction. "We're flying commercial."

I drained the last sip of my caffeine and set it back on the table. "Why the fuck would we do that?"

"Because where you're going to speak is very environmentally friendly. Arriving by personal jet isn't exactly great for your optics."

I clench my fists. "Damn it." She's right. "Fine. But they better have scotch on hand."

"I'll bring a small bottle in case," she promises, but she isn't serious, which is a shame.

My phone vibrates in my pocket. I reach in and see Hayes's name on the screen.

"I need to take this," I say.

"Sure. Oh, and I got this for you for the flight." She stuffs her hand into her dress pocket as she walks toward the door, and she tosses me a small box in passing. "You might get bored, flying commercial and all." She glances over her shoulder and winks at me before she closes the door.

I swipe my phone and bring it to my ear as I head to my desk. "Hey." I could use the break from this office. So be it, a simple call from a buddy is what it has to be today.

"Hey. Thought I would check in with you. I wanted to send you a candidate for the job if you're interested. I can email you his details."

"Firstly, no business discussion. Secondly, if we were to discuss business, it would be about convincing you to join my company." I lean back, throw my feet onto the desk, and glance at the contents of the box in my hand.

A pack of playing cards.

And they're not the normal kind that you can pick up at the store for two dollars.

The colors are faded, and the case is gray. Their box looks aged by years, by no means new.

I smile to myself. She *is* full of surprises.

"Since we will not be discussing business, surprise me and tell me what else is new."

"Uh." I slide my jaw side to side and ponder, unable to look away from the box I continue to examine. "Shit." That isn't a lie.

He chuckles, and I hate that I just opened the door for him. "I have a feeling why, but you set the no-business-discussion rule. I'll assume your issues involve a certain employee."

I place the box on my desk and pinch the bridge of my nose. "No comment."

"That's a yes. You know if it were simply a physical thing, she wouldn't be wreaking havoc in your life. Therefore, I'm going to go with the idea that there is perhaps a *little* more."

"You can say that again." I let out a long exhale. "And now we're about to go on a business trip together."

He laughs for a solid few seconds. "Good luck with that. It's only risky because clearly she brings more to the table than her looks."

"That's the problem. She's funny, gives as good as she gets, and knows me better than most. And I've seen her naked."

"Ah, so yeah, you went full swing on this."

I'm getting a headache. "I don't want to be that guy who hooks up with his assistant. She deserves a hell of a lot more respect than that. Plus, it isn't that. It's something else that I can't pinpoint, but it's gnawing at me."

"I'm not the guy to be telling you to explore that. I have zero experience, but it would seem to be the obvious advice someone would give. It only takes one person to flip your world, right?"

I swivel my chair as I contemplate. "I'm not the relationship type of guy. I can't offer her much."

"Fine. Have fun watching her receive flowers from some guy named Steven, who she probably had a date with because her friends set her up."

The hint of jealousy for a fictitious what-if is deeply concerning.

"I have a no-flower policy," I deadpan.

"Don't be stubborn. You are about to be stuck with the woman on a business trip. At least be open-minded. Tell me, are your rooms next to one another? No, even better, let's hope they misbooked, and boom, you two need to share a room."

"Funny."

"Anyhow, I have to run. If you can hold an engaging conversation with her and there's attraction, you might as well stop being an ass. Don't let good things get away. I mean, fuck, I still think about that woman from a few years ago and my stupidity for not exchanging details."

I snort a laugh. "Really? Are you bringing that up again? I hope your therapist evaluates that more."

"This isn't about me." I can hear him smile. "All I'm saying is sometimes we have to look at things from a different angle, even if that means it involves a physical or non-physical connection with your PA."

Rolling my lips in, I'm struggling to accept his logic, even though I know he's right. "She makes it impossible to focus, invades my space, and messes with my rationality. What's worse is that I believe she is well aware."

"Easy. Break down a layer or two. Maybe you'll prove the world wrong and be a good catch. Hell, it'll be refreshing to hear that you decided to take the next step."

"I have been an ass lately. Still, she hasn't quit. But that's work. Who knows on the personal level?"

"Well, you should figure that out. Anyhow, I need to go."

We say our goodbyes, and I'm left to consider some of his views. It's a solid five minutes, then seven, then ten before I decide to take a plunge and tell Savannah that we should talk.

Getting up from my chair, I almost charge to my door, which I open with force, and Savannah quickly looks up. She must have put on a fresh coat of lip gloss, damn that move.

"For the trip. You and me, we should discuss…" It's on the tip of my tongue, but my throat clogs, and I'm unable to find the words except… "Be sure to bring your A-game on this trip," I instruct, and I sound condescending, to be honest.

No wonder her eyes turn to saucers. "And this is why I ensured I booked my seat on the plane, not next to you."

"Really?" Damn, that's hardcore avoidance.

"Yeah. I didn't want to take the risk that you're having a

moment when you're a complete jerk." The widespread attitude in her voice drives me wild.

I hate her for that. "Let's hope your seat has a life vest in case of emergency."

"Yeah. Thanks for that. Completely cursing our flight," she flatly replies.

"You're welcome. A-game, only that," I remind her with firmness in my voice before I pivot back into my office and slam the door shut.

Because Savannah is causing me to lose my grip, and I'm struggling to hang on. I'm the one who needs a damn life vest, even if there's no water.

16

SAVANNAH

I was saved by a row of seats on an airplane. Also spared by Julian being on his phone for the entire journey to the hotel and check-in. By luck, a talkative woman from the event, with a little too much makeup, met us in the lobby to lead us to Julian's speaking engagement.

What am I not saved from? Being mesmerized by the way he speaks in front of hundreds. I'm furious that I'm joining the crowd that listens intently in utter awe of a man whose success is easy to envy, but it's the charismatic way that he delivers his words that has everyone captivated.

And I'm no exception.

I really want to hate the guy. As soon as he takes a step forward, it's two steps back on the scale in winning our little game of attraction. Yet it only makes me more attracted to him. I try to keep reminding myself that he's a jerk on his good days, but a whisper in my brain reminds me that I've seen glimpses of a man who is softer and might actually be breaking a brick from his wall.

Watching from the side of the stage behind the curtain, I

double-check the time on my phone to see that Julian has already gone over by five minutes.

He stands behind the podium. "You are constantly making decisions that serve your business interests. Not everyone on that path will appreciate that, because people like soft communication. However, blunt directness brings clarity to all involved."

My jaw goes slack. Is he fucking kidding me? Clarity is not his forte, at least, not when it comes to me.

"With that comes the ability to lead. I don't need to make friends; I need solutions to ensure my company gets further success. Nobody wants to be the bad guy, but sometimes you need to be for the ending to be golden. For example, I've followed my policy, and Haven Crossroads is a place that treats its employees well and can reward hard work with great benefits. That wouldn't be possible without my way of driving on the road."

Gah, why are people so intrigued by this? And why must it all be true? Checkmark for a great place to work, company success, and to some extent, his ability to lead. A hard fail on his policy to drive on the road. I'm well aware that I'm projecting my feelings into analyzing this.

"So, ladies and gentlemen, the moral of the story is to consider the way you present yourself. Ensure you are a wall of steel that will only accept the answers you need to find success. Remember, once you reach the top, you can still go further; the roof has a lot of levels underneath it, but you still have the sky with more possibilities." He concludes with a suave grin that weakens the female population and warns the world that he will come out the winner.

As the audience claps, he exits the stage. I can't help but give him a death stare, and his lips form a contrite grin at me as he brushes past me, bumping my arm in the process.

Most people would say this is when they resign. But I'm not a quitter, and I think I've found a new craving I can't shake.

I quietly groan to myself and trail behind him, while the event organizer sings his praises. And yes, I notice how she insists on staying close by his side as others give him compliments. She even throws in a little arm touch. Luckily, he shows zero interest in her.

This is not going to be a fun car ride back to the hotel.

Only proven by the stiff silence in the car an hour later, where we both pretend to be buried in our phones as we sit in the back.

"Did you see that email from Compliance? An audit is coming up. The head of the import division also needs another meeting. I've sent you your reservation for your trip to Seattle, pay attention since I won't be there."

Julian's head whips in my direction. "What do you mean you won't be there?" He isn't impressed, but his tone also carries concern.

"I'm not really needed for that trip. It's quick, plus I want to try and get home," I easily explain.

"Some hoedown or something?"

I ignore his jab and grab my bag to pull out a fruit snack pouch.

"You have snacks, I see." He sounds slightly judgmental.

"You never know when you might get deserted somewhere." I rip the bag open and notice his eyes on it. A tiny grin forms, and I offer him the bag.

"Don't be ridiculous." I stare at him, sure of myself. "Fine. One." He takes a red strawberry shape.

I take the win and sink into the leather seat. "You're good at spewing out bullshit, to be honest," I remark.

"Enlighten me on which part you felt was incorrect." He's facing forward, but I can feel his eyes gravitate to me.

I lean my head against the headrest and turn to the side to greet his precarious eyes. "The part about how your personality brings clarity. Lie of the century."

"Savannah, do I not get results for my company?"

"You do," I agree. "But that is the only part."

He holds my eyes hostage with his own. "If you are referring to other matters, then that is open for interpretation."

I snicker. "Lack of accountability isn't your style."

I can see that I've ignited something inside him, as pure annoyance bubbles up. "That's probably because of you."

Now, I'm riled. "Me? Always my fault," I raise my voice.

"Yes!" He curls his fingers into a fist as though he were squeezing a stress ball. "You're different. Nobody is like you."

A pin pops the tension in the car and deflates the balloon between us.

"You bring out the fiery side of me. Not many people can do that. Actually, nobody," I admit, in delicate defense.

Even with a seatbelt on, a sharp right turn makes me slide to the middle slightly and into Julian, his arm instantly steadying me. We end up closer, his arms embracing me, his eyes dropping down, mine looking up. Feeling his body against mine sends my senses into overload.

"What am I going to do with you?" he whispers. It's not even sexual; there's vulnerability, a hint at his thought process.

I shake my head, feeling his chest beneath my cheek. "It's not my decision. I don't even know my options," I rasp.

We both feel the car slow down, and I peer out the window to see that we're back at the hotel and pulling up to the lobby. I escape his clutches and sit back, already unbuckling my seatbelt with full intention of fleeing the car.

Being near him is overwhelming. I need distance, space to clear my head.

"Savannah." I hear him say my name as I open the door.

I slide from my seat, dragging my bag. I ignore him but glance back to see him rubbing his temples in frustration.

We both need to cool off.

THANK GOODNESS FOR ROOM SERVICE. It gives me privacy and the ability to stay locked away from the world. Or at least I try to be. My room is next to the hotel's executive suite. There will be only a few walls between Julian and me when we sleep tonight. I'm already prepared that I might be restless. For now, I need to cool off. That's how Julian and I work. We hit our peak, then mellow out, before heading right back up the mountain.

The hotel robe covering my naked body is divine after a shower, and I'm about to pull back the covers on my bed to settle in for the night with food and watching a hockey game when I hear a knock on my door. Strange. I already received my food and declined the evening turndown service.

"Savannah," Julian says my name from the other side of the door, then knocks again with a light tap.

Oh.

My entire body hesitates. I'm reluctant to open the door because I don't know what to expect. My thoughts spin around him, trying to find direction.

"If it's work, you can send me an email," I say, stepping back from the door.

"It's not work."

Oh.

My fingers pause on the door handle. I brace myself, inhale, and open the door to find Julian. Damn it. He does it to me again: jeans and a t-shirt. Completely unfair. But I'm strong today.

As his feet remain fixed to the floor in front of me, he doesn't seem annoyed, nor angry, nor in the mood to squabble.

"The clause that you have to stay to have your degree paid for was taken out. It'll be paid either way… I changed it. A while ago, actually. I just never told you."

A sting jabs at my stomach. "I've been free to quit all this time without the risk of student debt hanging over my head?" He says nothing.

"Fuck you," I spit out. "Decided now is the time to pull that card out?" I'm furious.

His eyes latch onto mine. "You're right. But I can't lie to myself, and I did it because I always want you to have security." My body softens, more willing to calm and listen. "I'm telling you because you're right. I am a coward. It's useless for me to ignore what is transpiring between us. I don't have any fuel left inside me to fight it. I'm not the best at clarity and getting rid of gray areas when it comes to… well, it's because you drive me fucking insane. You are invading my life, and I can't control that I'm letting you."

My eyes enlarge because I wasn't expecting this. He's laying it on the table in his own form of validating that I'm right. I use the remote to mute the game and choose to listen.

Everything in this moment feels raw. My anger, sharp and unexpected, floats into the past even as the man in front of me opens up, vulnerable because of me. The shift is jarring—my own frustration echoes as I witness his honesty. That's not an easy feat.

"Well, it seems we finally meet on the same page." It feels like eternity as I wait for him to spell it out for me what he's expecting.

"I can only offer you risk." He's implying us. "But I'm laying that on the table for you to choose."

My lids flutter as I consider his offer. I can either stay in unbearable friction or take a chance and have him for as long as I can, with no clear path. My body strains for a logical choice, but one side clearly wins.

He senses my answer. "It's not simple. Nor public. I can't pretend it's more than this, but I wouldn't touch you if I didn't care." It's his way of highlighting the boundaries of who we would be and ensuring I'm confident in my choice.

With one step forward, I make a decision that could ruin me, but it would haunt me if I didn't take the chance.

"Okay." It floats from my lips, and he seems relieved. His lips press together, and he smiles wryly, aware that I made the choice he wanted.

The moment his arm extends and his hand meets my skin, I nuzzle my face into his palm, inhaling his scent and soaking in his touch. "Logistics might be a pain," I joke.

"My desk is ready for you," he teases.

"We may be private, but I refuse to feel like a dirty little secret."

He kisses my forehead. The man with an iron heart just gave a chaste little kiss. "No. You're not. I mean, I haven't tested your Go Fish skills yet, but I'm confident that you'll pass." I kiss his wrist softly. "Congratulations… you are the one to break me," he whispers, and his other hand rises to cup my face.

A smile that hurts my cheeks forms on my face. "I would say you can send me flowers for that accomplishment, but my boss is a dick and has a no-flowers policy."

"He is an ass. An absolute one. I'm everything you should run from."

I shrug and keep my smile intact. "Yet, here I am."

He steps forward, causing me to step back, and everything in my body pulses faster.

"I need to be inside you."

We are about to cross the threshold of my room, but he guides our direction in a circle and away from the door.

"My beautiful assistant booked the penthouse. We should probably use that. There are many surfaces to try, maybe a snack to replenish our energy, and we can talk while you lie naked in my bed."

"That all sounds promising."

He encourages me to hop up and straddle him. My body

buzzes for him. I want him to hurry us to a destination of his choosing.

"Only you do this. Only you get this from me," he pledges.

Now we can both breathe, because everything seems to fall into place for now.

I'M snug in Julian's arms, after being sharply tugged into him with a kiss that is a collision, a clash of teeth. His hand tangles in my hair while I claw his shirt as though I'm starved to touch his skin. He lifts and shoves me against the door to his room with force. I gasp and laugh as I nibble on his earlobe. His grin is boyish and vicious, pleased that I'm on board for haste and rough.

I drop my head back when he mouths my throat, his stubble scraping, and my clit is on fire. He doesn't bite my collarbone; instead, he sucks for a long beat while I pull at his shirt. He sets me down to peel it off, and his hands return quickly to me by locking his hands around my hips and turning me to face the wall, until I need to brace myself with my palms. His chest is pressed against my back, and my breath is already ragged. He rips open my bathrobe and yanks it off my body. The apex of my thighs already feels wet, and he inspects me when his now naked body holds me tightly from behind. He kisses the back of my shoulder, hot and heavy.

"Julian," I plead, because I can feel his hard cock against my lower back.

His finger circles around my clit, and his other palm kneads the flesh of my waist. "I'm going to fuck you, baby. Hard, though." He speaks low with swelter, and using an endearing name revs me up to a thousand. My response is to moan as I ache for more. "Can I take you like this? I want to feel you wet around my cock."

Oh. I didn't think about that. I'm on birth control, but I've never actually been without a condom. It makes it extra special in a way. A part of me is envious that he has maybe been this way with others. "Have you ever…"

He must sense my hesitation. "I don't do this, and I'm safe. It will feel better for both of us if you want."

Lust overtakes me, and my mind eases. "Yes."

I brace my hands against the wall as the tip of his cock caresses me between my legs. We both make a sound because it already feels too good. I feel him working his way in as he locks his hands on my hips.

His chest is pressed against my back. His breath is ragged, which syncs with my own shuddering moans. I arch, shoving myself back onto him, and he slams further into me. There is no slow, not even when my legs weaken. Instead, he links his arm around my middle to hold me upright, and his finger explores my clit.

I'm shamelessly loud with my body in overload.

My cheek is smooshed against the wall as he thrusts bluntly. "I'm so close," I call out.

He fists my hair and tugs enough to tilt my head, and everything about him inside me and touching me in this moment is raw. "Not yet." He speaks as though he rules my body, and that is a further turn-on.

We're starving for one another.

He pulls out, and I'm needy for more.

He turns me, and as though all of his rough insistence stops, he cradles my face to give me a slow, tender kiss. A reminder perhaps that this isn't just sex. Only a moment later, he returns us to our pace, and he guides me to the bed and pushes me onto the mattress.

He spreads my legs wide, and my entire body arches off the bed when he strokes me with his tongue, and he makes a noise as if he's sucking on a dessert spoon. My nails dig into the bed as my voice rises in response.

His lips move to kiss my inner thighs, and I'm throbbing. "I needed to taste you before I fill you with my cum."

My eyes roll to the back of my head because I could orgasm purely from his filthy mouth.

"Please," I beg, and my body writhes, trying to encourage him.

He grins slyly as he pins my arms above my head, instructing me to keep them there. Easing my legs open, he enters me and continues his promise to fuck me hard. He grunts, and I moan. I enjoy seeing him use me the way he wants while I benefit by feeling so incredibly wanted and pleasured.

My legs get thrown over both his shoulders, hitting another angle, and I can't handle it. I begin to palm my breasts, and I'm a few thrusts away from coming undone.

"Be a good girl and come while I'm inside you." His breath is now labored.

I let go and tremble and coo. It doesn't stop because he's speeding up his movements instead of slowing down to give me a break. He keeps going until I feel him pulse inside me, and he stills.

Julian collapses on top of me but holds his weight up as we both come down from a high.

"Fuck, Savannah." He remains inside me.

"I know. I know." It was a new level.

He kisses my mouth as he slips out, and I feel his cum spill onto my thighs.

Julian nuzzles into my neck as he attempts to even his breath, and we both sigh, completely satisfied.

―――

I JAB my toe into his thigh where we're sitting on the floor next to the floor-to-ceiling window. I'm balancing my hand of cards while I hold up the sheet that's draped around me. I watch Julian study his cards while in only boxer briefs and don't let my smile ease.

"Have any fives?" he asks.

"Go fish," I reply, and he takes a card from the deck.

He closes one eye and studies me before I burst out laughing.

"I'm sorry." I try to stop, but I can't. "This is…"

Julian begins to tickle up my leg. "You know my secret, don't judge."

"Okay." I attempt to give him a serious look, but it fails, and I can't stop. He rolls his eyes, amused, and I take a breath to try to calm down. "It's funny."

He tosses his cards onto the floor. "I'll spank you later for this judgment," he teases.

I wiggle my eyebrows and give up on my cards. "No complaints."

"I didn't ask. Where did you get these?"

Truthfully, I put a little effort into it. "A friend sent them to me. There's a secret place near Everhope."

"A secret place, eh?"

"Yep."

"I should have thrown them on your desk."

It doesn't take a genius to understand what he's hinting at. "Payback for me dropping expensive jewelry on your desk?"

"Something like that." He leans back against the glass and blows out a raspberry. "You were right… I'm a coward."

I lift a shoulder. "Tell me that you at least got it yourself and didn't actually make HR arrange the gift."

"I'm not a complete idiot."

I lift my nose and inspect him coyly. "If you say so."

He grabs hold of my ankles and slides me forward to him

until my bent legs are between his. "It's in my desk drawer if you ever want it."

I bring my finger to my chin and loudly hum. "Hmm, let me think. No. I'm good. Maybe one day."

He drags the back of his finger along my knee, drawing circles. "Fair enough. However, you shouldn't ignore your accomplishment."

"My decision."

"Stubborn."

"Yep."

Now, his finger taps against my skin, and my pussy is aching again.

"So, tell me more about your aunt. Why is it you're going back?"

My face creases. "Uh, because you don't need a reason to visit family."

"Right." His T extends. "Normal family life."

I take hold of his other hand and interlace our fingers, as I can see the sting, whether he wants to admit it or not. He lacks the experience of family life. "It must suck."

"Nah, it's okay. It's all I know. I actually saw my sister the other day. Mostly business, though."

"No chitchat about life?"

"A little, and I'm okay with that."

"Liar," I accuse in a neutral tone, but he doesn't respond, and it's obvious that he wants to move on. "Anyhow, it's the festival. It's a big thing. I've never missed a year. Everything you probably hate. Pie competitions, awards for the best cow, live music, the market, and all the little things that you might consider sappy."

"I-I mean... probably."

I chuckle because he agrees. "Anyhow, there's that, but there's also my aunt's business. It's facing some challenges, and I want to see how I can help."

Concern finds his face. "Tell me."

"Long story, but even if you own a docked boat, you don't own the river. The town is being persuaded by some big corporation to let them buy the pier from the city and end the docking lease. Their goal would be to push her business out. They want to make Everhope a little more touristy, I guess. It's Lake Spark County, one of the best weekend spots in the States. Everhope doesn't have Lake Spark, itself, but they have a beautiful river."

"I didn't realize it's that big of an issue."

"Yeah, well, maybe if I think of a few ways to challenge or find a loophole, it might work out. Granted, the boat also needs some work."

He squeezes my leg to comfort me. "If you need any help, let me know."

"Thanks. I appreciate that, but there's nothing you can do."

Julian begins to guide my legs and yanks me closer, naturally spreading my thighs around him. He has a sly smirk, and I know I'm in trouble.

"Do you have plans?" I purr as I drown in his orbit.

"Depends. Were you a good assistant and change our flight so we could sleep in?"

I give him a pretend warning glare. "Yes. Because I'm damn good at my job, *but* can we find some way to separate this? It's not good to mix business with pleasure, and that's exactly what we're doing." I'm already going against my principles, but I can't control it.

"You're right. We won't discuss work when clothes are off."

"And also, when we have a leisurely dinner?" My sentence trails because maybe that isn't something he sees us doing.

"We could do that. Breakfast should be added to that list," he says as he pulls me tighter to him.

The feeling of his erect cock pressing against my thigh causes me to feel arousal between my legs.

"But I kind of enjoy calling you boss." I pinch my lips together.

His nails drag the sheet up until it bunches at my waist. "I enjoy hearing you say it, especially when an orgasm is involved, or when you beg."

Humming a sound, I wrap my arms around his neck while his hands plant on my waist to ensure that we remain tightly wound. "We'll be discreet. While we... you know... figure things out?" I'm unsure of how to broach the topic.

He blows a raspberry, yet the cute act sounds sinister. "We can try, but I don't really follow the rules. If some guy tries to make a move, I will stake my claim."

"Likewise, however, it's important that nobody in the office gets a drift about us. I don't want people to assume that I'm only in my role because I sleep with you."

"Who said anything about sleeping?" His face is completely full of mischief when he says that, and it throws me off. "I kind of plan on keeping you active during the night, so not much sleep is happening."

I shove his shoulder. "Get it together. Your cock might be dangerously close to my pussy right now, but let's think beyond that."

His face eases, and he brings his fingers to my ear to tuck hair tenderly behind my ear. "We're on the same page for the rules. Since I'm a bit more tolerable to you, will you be sitting next to me on the plane this time? Or am I stuck with some guy who insists on eating four bags of peanuts?"

I nuzzle his nose with mine, with full intention to lead us to a kiss. "I might have already been persuaded to change the reservation, so it might be your lucky day."

"Savannah." The way he says my name now sounds different; it's sweeter yet already practiced that my name on his lips is a firm possession. "You're mine. Let me lead the way." I listen contentedly. "I'm new to this." He means what we're doing. "But I never fail at things. I hope you understand what that means."

There's a knot between my breasts; it's in my chest next to an organ that beats. My man of gray communication suddenly changed, and it's in my favor. "Just don't hurt me." That is very much true.

"I won't," he barely whispers.

I see it in his eyes, even if he's unsure of himself, he believes in everything he says.

Our mouths seal together for a deep kiss. I need his touch on my clit, need relief from how much I want him.

"Look into the window. See your reflection," he whispers, his warm breath near my earlobe that he captures between his teeth. A wave of extra sensitivity flows through me as I glance to the side to toward the window. "Watch how you look as someone who is mine, with my cock filling you up."

The sheet tangled around me drops to reveal my breasts, and I bring my fingers to pinch a nipple as he takes the other nipple in his mouth for a quick suck.

"I see."

"You see how needy you are?"

"Yes." My breath is heavy. His mouth trails down my neck, and my head tips back as I enjoy his lips on my skin.

He traces my collarbone, then pauses. "It's only for me. Say it," he murmurs before returning on his quest.

"I'm wet only for you. Always." My eyes hood closed as I begin to get lost in ecstasy.

"Good girl. Now I'm going to take you slowly, and we are going to watch our reflection on the glass."

I look, and I see a man completely enamored by me, taking possession of my body. But the way he touches me is an element of more. This isn't merely physical between us.

It's a struggle as my senses have surrendered to him because

everything tonight has caused me to feel safe around him as it seems the game is over. We won each other.
    And that only makes me elated.

17
JULIAN

Dragging the back of my finger along my upper lip as I sit back behind my desk, I read over my screen. I'm not sure if I like the direction or wording of the document. It's a stiff minute before I drag my sight up to face Savannah standing in front of my desk, patiently waiting for my reaction.

To my surprise, well, utter amazement, really. When we're in the office, we are simply two people at work, and we leave our personal dynamic at the door. I should pat myself on the back that I haven't attempted to bend her over my desk even once, and it's been a week since our trip. Hell, even that flirtatious banter that we had before I knocked on her door has vanished. But it all comes down to one reason.

I have her.

I shouldn't have shown up at her bedroom door, not with the risk hanging between us. One that neither of us had prepared for. But I showed up because I couldn't stop myself. Inside me, there's been a thin layer of fragile ice. I've built up my walls for reasons, yet with Savannah, they're wearing thin. All the more reason to be guarded, but that policy sits in the back of my mind.

Every time our feet leave the office, she's in my life differently. An instant switch where professional us gets left behind and we do whatever the hell we please.

Right now, though? I'm going to be critical, and I won't have a shred of remorse.

"Rewrite the second paragraph, the schedule doesn't make sense, and if I have to repeat once more that I don't want Harold from accounts in on the meeting, my level of pissed-off will reach new heights."

We have a new client meeting tomorrow, and a simple agenda has turned into a headache because they're so demanding. Every single person in middle management feels they need to be present, and senior management wants to give them a chance.

She rolls her eyes and grumbles to herself, "Compromise. Give them a nibble of the big fish."

Creases form on my forehead, and I'm not sure if it's because of her odd reference or the fact that she used nibble and big in the same sentence. "No," I affirm my wish tersely.

She throws her arms up into the air. "Fine. I'll be the bad guy and email Harold and his boss. Because that's not going to make him go home and complain to his wife at dinner about how he isn't understood." Savannah is a little annoyed and satirical.

I straighten my back and shut my laptop screen. "You know, delivering my thoughts to others in a tactful way is part of your job, right?"

"Of course it is. If we had you doing that, half the company would be in tears."

I've often heard that having a woman in one's life could soften a man. Unfortunately for the world, ruthlessness is too imprinted inside me. I don't even glance at her; instead, I sweep my eyes to my phone to check the time. Tonight can't be a late office day, as I have places to be.

Noticing that Savannah hasn't left aggravates me, as I don't need any delays. My eyes peer up at her unimpressed look. "Chop, chop, Savannah. The clock says you should let them know now before the end of the business day." I lean back and rest my elbows on the armrest while I steeple my fingers. "Again, I expect everyone at Haven Crossroads to be a 9-to-5 kind of employee."

Her brows rise. "Wow. You really are a piece of work this afternoon."

"And?" I merely reply.

She sighs, and her cheeks puff out. "Fine. I'll go be the messenger of doom."

I plaster on a fake smile for her. "Much obliged."

The next hour, I managed to work my way through three calls. One of which lasted only a minute when I cut them off because I wasn't going to listen to another word. I quickly type a message to my driver so he knows to wait for me downstairs. I grab my suit blazer from the coat rack next to my door. When I open the door, Savannah takes no notice of me, as she is focused on writing something on her pink Post-It note. Walking to her desk, I grab some fruit snacks from her jar, and she still ignores me.

"Ms. May, I believe it is time to leave the office."

She glances up, but her pen continues to write on the paper. "Sure. Give me a sec. Need to remind myself that when I arrange coffee for tomorrow's meeting, I should be careful not to use the jar of poison that I sometimes contemplate using for your drinks." Her little quip makes her grimace to herself, and I fight my smile.

"Now, you wouldn't do that. You have many reasons not to," I remind her lightheartedly. Maybe that's enough of a cue that it's time to leave the day behind.

Savannah drops her pen and neatly moves a few things on her desk. "Fine."

"See you in five," I tell her, and then routinely leave.

And five minutes later, she is sliding into the back seat of the car waiting at the service entrance.

She's quick to put her seatbelt on, but I stop her even though the car begins to move. My hand stays put on her wrist.

"Uh, safety first," she chastises me.

"You'll only need to take it off," I inform her.

That warm smile of hers begins to spread. "We are *not* having sex in the car." She felt awkward about it the first time, considering my driver is in the front, behind the dark partition. But it was a must-do, a rite of passage, as crazy as that sounds.

"Get your mind out of the gutter, baby. We have places to be."

"Really?" She's confused. "I thought we were leaving work to order in and take it easy because you have a call with Hong Kong at nine."

That's what my nights have become. Dinners at my place or a hidden corner in a restaurant. Either way, we end up having sex. Getting to know which positions we enjoy has been an excellent use of time.

My fingers crawl up her arm, and I watch their movement. "I changed our plans, and we won't be staying in because I have a surprise for you."

Our eyes meet, and she's curious. "Oh?"

I'm well aware that I've hit a snag in our dynamic. This evening's idea came on a whim—or not a whim. It's not clear why I'm about to make her smile, only that I want to. Show her that I've paid attention to the finer details from the start, and it matters.

"Yeah. I forgot that I had donated once to the ballet here in the city, and they have a special performance with the Paris ballet visiting. You mentioned you used to go with your aunt."

She titters a laugh. "The ballet? You?"

I go along with her teasing. "Yes, me."

She almost seems skeptical, yet that smile I love crawls on her face. "We're going to the ballet?"

"Yes. We even have discreet box seats. Nobody will notice us."

"Wow, okay." She gives herself the once-over. "But can we swing by my place? I'm in my work clothes and would rather be in something that doesn't scream office."

I boop her nose with my finger. "No time, babe. Now look on the floor."

Her eyes search the car's interior, and she spots the white box with a dark green ribbon. "What's this?"

"A dress."

She sputters a laugh as she eyes the box. "You bought me a dress?"

I shift in my seat and angle myself toward her because she's a tad more astonished than I was going for. "It's not so crazy."

"*Uh*, it kind of is. First, I have now seen you as a decent human, but it's… Well, I don't think it crossed my mind that you could be a hopeless romantic."

That word, as a compliment, scares the hell out of me, but hearing it feels like praise, which I'm enjoying.

"Neither did I. Now open the box," I instruct.

She unties the satin bow. "How did you even get this? I mean, to guess my size and pick something out." The ribbon falls onto the seat between us, but I quickly sweep it up because I might need it later.

I look at her like she's crazy. "Your size? I believe my eyes and tongue have measured every inch of you. And as for the dress? I paid money and had someone from the store choose based on a photo of you."

"Geez, you really thought it out." She lifts the lid and pulls away the tissue paper, and I realize my bank account really did pay off because the brightness on her face from a gushing smile is worth it as she lifts the dress out of the box. It's black, classic, off-the-shoulder, and if my request is fulfilled, it means she'll be showing a little of her back that my hand will cover. She might be cold, but there is something that kind of inflames inside me when she wears my blazer around her shoulders to stay warm.

"Put it on."

Savannah moves to the edge of her seat and finds the zipper of her work dress, quickly pulling it down and off.

"Fuck me," I curse myself and bite my curled fist to hold myself back as I drink up the scene of Savannah left in a black lace thong. I miscalculated how a simple outfit change would take us off course. "How am I not supposed to lick you right now?" I move to drag my lips along the smooth curve of her shoulder. Even with her mesh lace bra, I see the tips of her breasts are pointy.

"Julian," her voice vibrates.

The palm of my hand is flat against her belly and slides down, causing her to lean back. "I need to check something." My voice is thick with desire, nor does she shoo me away as my fingers dip into her panties. She croons for me as the tips of my fingers feel her wet heat. Her body goes slack as she moans. "Nice and wet for me. Spread your legs." My request is direct.

I love it when she obeys. "Julian." Her whisper has a hint of warning right before she moves, pushing her hand against my chest, causing me to abandon her pussy and sit normally in my seat. Well, somewhat, because she's quick to straddle me.

"We don't have time, remember?" she taunts me as she circles her pussy around my cock that's hard underneath my pants. "Now help me get dressed."

She lifts the dress from the box and finds the bottom. Raising her arms, she lifts them over her head. I assist in sheathing the material down the curves of her body until the smoothness of the satin bunches around her waist due to its length. Her naughty smile, as she stares into my eyes, fades into something else. It's new, yet promising. It mirrors my mood. We don't break contact even while I slowly drag the zipper on the side up. Savannah lifts her hair over her shoulder, and she musses the strands with her fingers. It gives me a prime opportunity to kiss slowly up from her cleavage along the line of her neck, only to stop when I reach her chin.

Savannah loops her arms around my neck, and the quiet around us is calming. "I don't want to use the word sweet that you arranged this all. We know how you hate the word sweet."

I swipe her loose hair behind her ear. "As I said, I remember you mentioned once coming to the city with your aunt and watching the ballet."

She half-smirks. "Now I'm 100% using the word sweet."

"I'll allow it. I'll spank you for it later, though," I say, right before I steal a deep kiss from her.

The idea to do all of this came out of left field for me, yet as soon as I thought it out, I had to get the wheels in motion. Excitement was too intense. I want her to be happy, and due to me would be a bonus.

She jabs my chest with her finger. "So, Mr. Romantic, what are we seeing?"

"*Giselle*," I announce casually, and continue to watch my fingers feather down her arm.

She sputters a laugh, and I look up at her, confused about what I did. "You do realize the story of that ballet, right?"

I shake my head. "No. Do I look like someone who would?" Savannah's laugh should concern me, but it's good to hear and see—it swings our work life even further away.

"It's about a rich man who seduces a peasant," she deadpans. "A little familiar, no?" I'm amused, and my grin must show it. "He betrays her, and she heads to the forest and joins women scorned. She's heartbroken."

My face turns sour. "Yikes."

"Is this some foreshadowing of my destiny? Should I be worried?"

I scoff at the thought. "Absolutely not."

She pretends to wipe away sweat from her forehead. "Phew. Please don't leave me scorned and cause me to disappear into a forest."

My hands move to her back, and I lift my hips, causing her thighs to tighten around me. "Don't you worry," I promise.

And I'm scared how desperately I want to mean it.

18

JULIAN

Walking into my bedroom, I shadow behind Savannah as she crouches down to slip out of one heeled shoe, followed by the other. Tossing my suit jacket onto the chaise lounge, I don't have any intention of prolonging the inevitable.

"The talent on that stage really put me in a trance and into a whole different world. Didn't it relax you a bit?" She's been jabbering about the show since we left.

"Mmmhmm," I reply, choosing not to explain that I was lost in observing *her* all two hours, plus the twenty-minute intermission where my hand remained on any part of her that seemed appropriate in public.

"It was a great night, thank you." She finally turns to face me. "Really, it was the perfect surprise."

My fingers undo the buttons of my shirt as our eyes remain locked. "I'm happy to do anything for you, but if you really want to thank me then answer me truthfully."

Her brows pinch together, and her smile turns nervous. "Okay. What might that be?"

I scoop the ribbon out of my pocket, the one that's been

burning a hole in my pocket since I saved it from the dress box earlier. I aim to use it if she'll let me. Dangling the fabric in the air, I ensure our eyes latch in a stronghold because I'm serious. "Can I use this on you?" She seems intrigued as her facial expression eases slightly. "To tie you to the bed or blindfold you? You'll have no use of your hands or be unable to see. It's complete trust in me... Only if you want, of course."

Her smile turns to a mischievous smirk. "I trust you, and I'm kind of addicted to your control," she voices, simple, direct, and with a hint of eagerness.

Good. She's on the same wavelength as me. I would want her even if she said no. I can do slow for her.

"So what will it be? Eyes or hands?"

She doesn't even take a second. "Hands."

"I was hoping you would say that." I hear the swelter of sin in my voice. "We need a safe word."

"Hmm... White. We've both thrown a white flag to end our hostilities toward each other." There is slight cheekiness when she says it, but it suits us perfectly.

"White it is." Stepping forward, I bring my hand to her cheek to allow my thumb to circle affectionately on her cheek. "You are something, you know that?" I tell her tenderly.

She answers by simply placing a soft kiss on my inner wrist.

"Clothes off. Panties stay on."

We take a few moments to get out of our clothes. I leave my boxer briefs on, as well as my shirt, but keep it unbuttoned. Without my cue, she crawls onto the mattress to the headboard and lies down on her back with her long hair all across the pillow. She's a complete display of a goddess, the temptation that I get to devour.

"Preparing already. Such a good girl." I walk on my knees to her, leaning down for a kiss on her lips. "Hands above your head on the pillow." She obeys, and I pin them against each other before I move the ribbon, the silk feathering her skin in the process. I loop the fabric around her wrists, forcing them tight together. As I tie a knot, I notice her small flinch but a ghost of a smile on her lips. The back of my knuckles glide down the warm skin of her arms. "Pull. I need to know you can't escape."

She yanks once, and I'm satisfied. Anticipation must be burning in both our eyes.

Savannah already appears wanton and needy. Not so gently, I cup her jaw to tilt her gaze up.

"You look innocent, but I know better, which is why I have every intention of touching you so we'll both enjoy." My rasp is deep. Her eyes widen, but I'm quick to focus on the way her throat is bared for me in this position, noticing her swallow. Dipping my mouth down, I dart my tongue out to touch below her chin, then trail down to the base of her throat, where I nip at her skin with my teeth, and she makes a little sound.

"Want to guess what one of my favorite things to do with you is?" I whisper.

"Tell me," she pleads softly.

"Mark you as much as I can because you're mine."

Her sigh is heavy yet pleased.

Continuing, I latch onto the tip of her breast, circling the pebbled softness. Her body arches up, giving the signal for my hands to get greedy. I fill my palm with her other breast and squeeze while I adjust to sitting on my knees. Popping my lips off of one nipple, I use my fingers to pinch them both, and she lets out a moan. I refuse to offer her more, and my hands trace down the outline of her ribs, going down to her lower belly. I quickly glance at her thighs, which she presses together.

Savannah's breath changes, and she's doing her signature move of biting her lower lip when she wants more. Hovering down her body, I let two of my fingers drag up her silky inner thigh, and her legs naturally part open. Her skin is hot, and she appears needy.

"Your pussy is on full display for me. That's the way it should always be."

My mouth grazes below her belly button to her lace panties, my nose nuzzles against the wet fabric, and I can smell her sweetness. She hums a little sound, and her body bucks.

She's probably as impatient as I am.

Pressing my mouth onto the fabric, I taste her. My tongue laps up and down her slit, pausing at her clit to flick. "Fucking good," I mumble as my pointed tongue remains busy on her clit.

"Fuuuck," she breaths out.

"I'm not taking these off until I fuck your pussy, so get used to having lace between my tongue and your needy clit." I continue to work her, and she ripples with a shake. My eyes peer up to see her wrists straining against the fabric as she tries to break through to use her hands for stability.

I take her to the edge, but stop, my mouth traveling to her upper thigh, and I bite once. Not hard, but not gentle either. Sneaking two fingers under the fabric, I slide them into her wet pussy and feel how much she wants me. Retrieving them, I stuff them straight into her mouth.

"Suck." Her mouth does just that. Retrieving my fingers, I stand and remove my boxer briefs, walking to the side of the bed, then my knee dips back onto the mattress near her head to bring my tip to her mouth. She needs no instruction, and she begins to lick and then wraps her mouth around my cock.

"Deeper, Savannah. All the way to the back of your throat." I bring my hand to guide her head. Her wet mouth continues to move, and her eyes search mine for approval, and I only move faster, slightly harder. "Taking it like a good girl."

With my balls heavy and her wet panties still on display, I abandon her mouth. My hand follows the curve of her body, moving her slightly onto her side as I appraise the best position to take her in.

I spank her ass once with my palm. Quickly, I check her facial expression to see if I have taken it too far.

But all I see is her wicked little mouth. "Have I been a bad girl?"

"Very." I chuckle under my breath. "I'm going to fuck you until I wreck you."

"Please. Now," she begs.

I get between her parted legs. Quickly, I yank down her panties and throw them on the floor. I see her glistening pussy, and I'm not going to prolong this. Running my cock along her thigh, I land between her folds. I hook my arms under her knees and part her even wider.

"It's going to be hard," I say as my tip plays with her clit.

"I don't expect anything else." She smirks, her breath a near gasp.

Inching into her, I remind myself to remain in control. She's tight, wet, and my cock is thick, and my balls are swollen. My first push drags a whimper from her, and I stall for a moment. I'm about to ask if she's okay, but she mouths to go on. Pushing deeper, I begin to grind into her, her walls clenching around me.

"Your pussy was created for me, I swear," I groan, thankful I have restraint. This woman's body will make me lose my mind; hell, *she* makes me lose my mind. Grabbing a pillow, I lift her hips and place it under her body, giving me an even better angle. Rolling my hips, I fill her to the brim. I don't second-guess as my thrusts are blunt, and her body jiggles on every move. I have to hold her hips down to keep her in place.

"Julian," she nearly yells.

No hesitation, I continue to fuck her. I admire the way her jaw is slack due to the moans that escape her.

With her hands tied above her, I lean forward as I ease my thrusts. My force comes from fisting her hair to dart my gaze directly into her.

"Feel that, Savannah?" My voice is gravelly and panting. A

sheen of sweat breaks out on my body. "Feel how deep I am?" She nods. "All of you is mine." I let her head go and continue my pursuit.

"I'm yours."

Her toes dig into the mattress, my thumb finds her clit, and I drive into her like a crazed man. Because she makes me one, in the best possible way.

My pursuit is rougher, taking pleasure in the fact that her hands are helpless in this moment. Our sounds mingle, and our breathing is rapid. "I'm going to come inside of you, fill you up all night any fucking way I want, Savannah. Is that what you want?"

"Please come inside me, you can have me any way you please," she says as a moan hits her in full force. Her eyes begin to close as she feels me relentlessly, and her body begins to tremble.

I smirk, with my pride roaring inside. She is submitting to everything I want, from her own choice.

"Yours," she whispers as her hips meet my thrusts.

I lean down to kiss her lips, ensuring that our tongues meet. "And I'm yours," I whisper back. As much as I enjoy this style of fucking, I want to be tender with her, too.

I'm confused if it's my admission or my thrusts that cause her to begin to vibrate around my cock, but it feels good.

"Julian," she coos as her orgasm takes over.

My nails dig into her hips. "Did I say you can come?"

"I don't care right now. You can spank me for that." She already sounds drowsy, even though I continue my quest inside of her. "Just come inside me like I want."

I feel my orgasm on the cusp. "It isn't just want. You *need* it."

My grunt is fiercer than normal as I release inside her, my pulse on fire, and my body heading straight into bliss.

When I collapse onto the bed next to her, I blow out a long breath, my vision going near white.

I untie the ribbon, and her arms become free, and I'm quick to bring her wrists to my mouth so I can kiss both pulse points before I begin to massage her arms gently, all while her spent body hangs onto me like a rag doll.

Savannah's hand disappears between us and returns with my cum on her fingers that she swiped from between her legs. She pops her fingers into her mouth and sucks.

I'm dead.

This woman just killed me purely with her dirty mind.

"I'll draw us a bath in a second, just let the old man recover," I quip, and it causes her to giggle under her breath. "Need anything? What can I get you?" I ask seriously.

Her lips stamp a little kiss on my shoulder. "Nothing. It's perfect right here. You know, your dirty mouth isn't unexpected, neither is your need for control, but you pulling the cover over us right now for a cuddle session still surprises me every time."

I ensure the blanket covers her body. "It's what I have in my arms that causes me to do it without even asking. You little temptress... Plus, you deserve it."

I hook her leg over my hip to ensure she can't escape and rub soothing circles on her back. My mind begins to drift, wondering how this woman can connect with me on so many levels, not just in the bedroom.

It should scare me.

Yet it doesn't.

PLAYING a simple tune on the piano, I'm not sure what I'm aimlessly thinking about. Maybe it's actually nothing. I haven't had a clear mind in a long time, and I have an idea why suddenly a moment of my life isn't occupied by work; instead, I'm eased by relaxation.

Savannah.

She's flipped my life upside down.

A throat clearing causes me to swing my gaze to the bottom of my penthouse stairs, where I see Savannah in one of my shirts that reaches her knees. It's not even sunrise yet.

"Ah, so you do play piano beyond do-re-mi."

Opening my arms, I indicate for her to join me on the bench. "Maybe."

She strides my way with that angelic, closed-mouth half-smile that shows she's in bliss. "You didn't know what the ballet was about, but you can play a song from it."

Clicking my tongue, I use one arm to pull her closer when she sits next to me, and my other hand's fingers press a few keys. "I pick up notes by sound. I can't read music. My grandmother was insistent that I learn to play the piano. I had a Swiss teacher I was petrified of. I had to stop when I turned twelve, but it still kind of stuck with me."

She rests the side of her head against my shoulder. "Ooh, I learned another fact about you."

"Is it surprising?"

"Yeah. Deep down, you're a family man who does things for the ones you love, like your grandmother. It only takes one person. It was piano lessons for her that you remember thirty years later."

Perhaps, but I push it under a rock in my head. I'd rather explain it as honoring my grandmother's memory, and that's it.

I'll focus on the other part, and I give her a sideways glare. "Twenty-five years, thank you very much. No need to remind us of the age thing."

She giggles softly. "It's fun."

Kissing the top of her head, I hate that the morning will be here soon when the switch returns of who we are to one another.

"You should be sleeping," I whisper against her hair.

"Hard to do in an empty bed. Why aren't you there?" she notes.

I think about it, but my mind draws a blank. "Not sure. I couldn't sleep, but my head isn't occupied, either. My body might not be physically used to this. The calm, I mean."

She hugs my arm close. "Trust me, I never thought I would see you in a... normal and relaxed state? Nor did I think I would have ended up here."

Simpering a deep chuckle, I have to disagree. "Nah, we both knew we would end up fucking the moment you walked into my office as my new assistant."

Her grip on me loosens. "Right. Fucking."

She begins to move, but I reel her back close to me. "*Then*," I assure her. "Then. Now is different. You wouldn't be here in my home at who knows what hour in the morning if we were just fucking. We're a little more than that." There is no way to deny it being anything else.

"A little." She still sounds deflated.

My intended explanation needs to be clearer. My finger guides her chin in my direction, forcing her eyes to accept my intense gaze. "Unless it's related to money in business, I've never been able to envision the future. But right now, it's misty, though it's clearing. Tell me where your head is at."

Her mouth parts open, but only a dry, cracked sound escapes. She's afraid.

"Tell me," I say, more adamant.

"This doesn't feel like infatuation. I'm guarded, though, maybe."

That's a fair answer.

"We're on the same road."

She nods gingerly before I kiss her.

This time, it's tender, slow, hopeful, no need to escalate to any scrap of fabric on her coming off. It's simply a feeling of being clasped to someone.

Wanting to be with them so much that you hope that the clasp never breaks.

19
SAVANNAH

The sun streams through the large windows of Julian's kitchen. Twirling my yogurt in my bowl, I lean against the counter in my tank and pajama shorts. I hear Julian down the hall, deep in a business conversation. I've gotten used to this over the last few weeks. A few nights a week, my evenings and mornings are here, unless he's away on a business trip or at a business dinner. He has thought of a million excuses why I should join him on every trip, but I laugh off every justification he gives. Sometimes space is needed.

I'm overwhelmed with us, to be honest.

Smart me would take a moment to assess and breathe, remind myself that I shouldn't get attached. The other part of me is riding this wave because I sense things changing between us, in Julian. I'm in an intuitive state to hold on. Everything inside of me screams to do so. I'm reminded too often that I'm now almost elated, when a month ago, he had me fuming in misery some days.

Routine has found us, and it's the little things that make me nibble on my bottom lip, because I love the view, and it reminds me of everything that is right in life.

Exhibit A would be him approaching the kitchen with the phone to his ear, his eyes landing on me with an intensity that displays possession. Something about seeing Julian casual at home, his white shirt still untucked, yet his face already shaded to a man who takes no prisoners.

Sucking the remaining yogurt off my spoon, I watch him. He's wrapping up his conversation and grabs a coffee cup for his machine, which I still haven't figured out how to work, so, to his dismay, I brought over a classic filter-drip coffee machine that I picked up on sale. He hates it. And I love that.

He gives a firm deadline to whoever is on the phone before hanging up, without even a goodbye.

"Making someone's day miserable, and it isn't even 7?"

"No. It's not 7… they're in Belgium. Their day is almost over." He smirks to himself because he's being a smart-ass and continues to make his cup of coffee. He glances to the side at my coffee machine. "Get rid of it," he demands without even looking at me.

Spinning on my feet, I place the bowl in the sink. "Nope."

"Subpar coffee doesn't belong in my home," he reminds me.

I walk behind him and rub his back. "Get a machine that doesn't require reading an entire novel to understand."

He presses a button. "You have a master's degree. You figured out the machine at the office. You're a smart cookie."

Turning around, he faces me and yanks me close. "We're going together to the office?"

I shake my head. "Nope. My boss has a breakfast meeting at 8:30 sharp at that place on Michigan Avenue. I shall be grabbing the L."

"Over your boss's dead body. Your boss will have a driver take you."

Truthfully, as independent as I am, there is something about someone taking care of me with an air of security. "Fine.

Anyhow, I need to go shower. It's safe since you're already dressed."

"I mean, I could probably stretch the schedule to take them off and join you." I ensure that my face is unreadable while I bat my lashes, and he stunts a laugh. "Message received."

"I want to be dressed in a normal amount of time."

"Fair enough." He lets me escape his hold. "There is one thing that I've kind of been wanting to run by you."

I'm curious enough to ignore the time on the clock. "Make it quick."

"We can't be a secret forever, you know that, right?"

"Yes."

This conversation was bound to happen, but I always assumed that I would be the one to bring it up. Him bringing this up causes a shallow feeling in my stomach from fear. Is this the end?

Julian tilts his head slightly to the side. He's trying to sense my thoughts. "Don't you think that time is coming sooner rather than later?"

"Yes."

He rolls his eyes humorously. "Going to keep saying yes in this convo?"

Julian's buoyancy is a good sign, and my body eases.

"Now I might only say yes if it annoys you."

He begins to undo one button of his shirt. "Do that, and there will be consequences."

Taking a few steps, I return to him and replace his fingers with my own, except I button him right back up. "Not everything is solved with sex, you know."

"Exactly." His hands hold mine in place. "I'm trying to have a normal conversation with you."

"Miracle of all miracles," I convey with a straight face. It's easy to rile him. His controlled expression says he doesn't appreciate my tactic, and I turn serious. "You're right, and yes, it has crossed my mind."

"A timeline?"

"Oh." I search for an opinion in my head, but the question of why he's invested in having this conversation now takes over. "That's specific."

He holds my gaze. "I think somewhere during the night, it filled my mind. I can't hide you forever, and I'm well aware that if we were ever to be in the open, well... there will be a little scrutiny."

"You mean that I'm your assistant or that people will assume that I'm a gold-digger? There are so many options."

That comment makes his jaw tick and his eyes turn stormy. "I'm not talking about that. Well, I mean, I know the assistant thing will come up. It's more, the media is interested in my dating life."

"Could have fooled me," I mutter, one-toned.

"You're being a bit sassy today."

I exhale an audible breath. "What am I supposed to say? It feels like the external pressure is causing you to confront a choice. Plus, it's not you who will be under the magnifying glass. It's me. Who knows what awkward photo they'll dig up?"

His smirk is cocky. "Hopefully, one of you as Miss Everhope."

Now I'm the one who doesn't appreciate his antics. "I'm saying it's different for you than me, and quite frankly, this conversation is coming out of left field."

He scratches the back of his head. "Right."

Shaking my head lightly, I rub my face with my hands because he's being the way I know him best, stubborn and closed off. "Julian, just say it," I encourage.

He combs his hand through the hair on my right side, and I turn his hand into a pillow. "It's poking me inside. Hiding us, I mean. It doesn't make sense to do that anymore."

My head leaves his hold, and he slides his hands down the curve of my sides as though he can persuade me to agree to anything with his mere touch. I sigh. "Out in the open isn't a small deal. It means something." It feels like I just slapped him in the face because he seems to be offended. Although true, I shouldn't be scared right now, and I grin because I said it all wrong. "I didn't mean it to sound like that. It's not casual. It's another step. And if you're comfortable with it, then…" I want to be honest with myself. "I'm only human. I can't ignore how I feel. It threatens to unravel my career that I'm still figuring out."

"Let me fix it. I will find a way. I want to consider all aspects. Explore options."

"I'm not a stock option for your portfolio," I rebuff. Sighing, I'm a little exhausted with his insistence that he can solve everything. Life isn't always solved through money and human chess pieces. "It's pointless for me to say anything. You already have your mind set."

"You know me so well." He flashes his eyes at me.

"Julian, I have nothing to hide about the way I'm beginning to feel about you. It can't be one-sided, though. I'm hoping you're suggesting this means it's not."

It's an almost whimsical smile and poise that causes me to believe that he doesn't doubt his suggestion. "I can't predict the future a year or two from now. I'm still a risk. Right now, however, there is a step that I think I want to explore."

My lips press, and I search inside myself for any hesitation, but it can't be found. "Obviously, if there was a way for us" —I point between him and me— "to not be so secretive and for my career not to sink completely, I want to hear it. Plus, gotta make the women in finance jealous." I try to bury my truth in humor because what I want is so strong that it scares me.

Him. I want him. And he wants me, he's chosen me.

"For someone who usually doesn't hold back, today you are," he muses.

I've been called out because he now sees me inside and out. Maybe not every nook, but most.

I hoist myself up to sit on the counter behind me. "Trust me, even I'm surprised how you have me in a chokehold that causes me to malfunction."

Now his finger glides along my bare thigh. "Baby, this isn't a chokehold. I can show you what one really is." His one-track mind, of course. I cast my eyes to the ceiling, unamused, but I can't help my smile. "But I'm very proud that I get the honor of turning your world upside down."

"Gotta feed your arrogance, obviously," I say, sarcastic.

"Alright. Back to the original question."

We both turn serious because we've reached a point between us. One that is moving, and I'm beginning to wonder if slow is in his vocabulary. My ability to think with caution left me the moment I stepped through his door and faced his smug face.

"Secrets only tear things apart. Us being hidden from the world is one of them. I don't want that to happen." I accidentally release my thought aloud, and my mouth parts open from the realization.

It doesn't deter Julian. "Which means?" He's coaxing me into my answer.

My body relaxes, and a ridiculous smile forms. "You're right."

20
JULIAN

Stepping off the elevator, my jaw ticks due to a smirk that wants to form. All because I notice Savannah smelling a single pink rose as she twirls side to side in her desk chair. Her subtle smile is angelic. I slow my pace toward her desk, and she's oblivious to my arrival, and I kind of enjoy that. I get to see her lost in her own world.

I give my throat a quick clear to grab her attention. "Ms. May. What could you possibly be thinking right now?"

Her cheeks rise and her smile brightens to the brim. "That I arrived to find a single rose lying on my desk, but it's a shame that I'll have to get rid of it because my boss is a real pain. He hates flowers anywhere near my workspace."

"Sounds like he's a real ass."

She sets the flower down near her keyboard. Her eyes do a quick glance in both directions of the hall. "He has a nice one, at least. But yeah, what's a girl to do when he has rules?"

"Maybe your boss will make an exception. He wasn't alone when he woke up on the right said of the bed this morning." I give her a wicked grin.

"Hmm, okay. But I didn't even get a note to know who gave such a kind gesture."

"Probably some guy who was a coward once and used HR as an excuse to give you a necklace," I own up.

It causes her to chuckle. "Well, he's making up for it by being romantic."

Our eyes pin to one another, and I'm hit with the thought of how lucky I am and that today she's happy and it's because of me. "He's trying," I whisper.

"He's succeeding," she softly voices back.

The corner of my mouth snags to a half-closed smile. "Good to know." I check my watch and see the time. "It's lunchtime, if you care to head out for lunch."

My reminder causes her to gather her purse. "Can't. I already promised Elodie. But I ordered your usual, and it will be delivered shortly."

I make a mental note that I really should get to know her friend better. I have to share Savannah with her, after all.

"Okay." I accept my defeat.

She gives me a wink before she leaves.

Five minutes later, my chicken wrap arrives, and I bite into it as I read over proposals. I lose time until a knock on my door causes my eyes to shoot up.

"Thanks for stopping by," I greet Charles as he enters my office. Staying put in my chair, I close my laptop to give him my attention. Savannah is out to lunch, which is best for this conversation.

"No problem. Any closer to solving the 'get me out of here so I can retire' problem?" He takes a seat in front of me with a grin.

A muted chuckle finds me at his choice of phrasing. "Hopefully. I'm still pressuring Hayes, and if I know him well enough, then I'm on the tipping point of making him realize that this" —

my hands display my office— "is the place for his success. You're free to go and spread your wings."

"He would be a great fit. Let me know what I can do to sweeten the deal."

Nodding in understanding, I lean back, and my finger glides above my lip while I stall. I look over his shoulder while I prepare to utter the words. The unimaginable thought has haunted me all week, and I no longer believe I can battle it.

"There is something else I wanted to talk to you about." Charles looks at me peculiarly. "Run something by you."

"Which would be?"

"Savannah."

His chin rises, and his good mood changes. "Ah, I see."

Strange. Standing, I turn to half look out the window, buttoning my blazer in the process. "What does that mean?"

"There isn't a single bone in my body that thinks you are about to say you want to fire her, so have it out. Let me hear it." He has a closed, repressed smile.

Of course, he's waiting. The man is smart.

Opting to settle against the glass window, I take a moment for a deep breath. "What would one do if they were in a certain, very powerful position, and that said person might be in a relationship with someone that could be questionable?"

"I would tell him that it wouldn't look good to many people. Some competitors might even feel they struck gold with a reason to swoop in and steal a certain someone away, knowing they have the insights into your day-to-day operations."

"She would never take a job from a competitor, and she has the non-compete clause and an NDA. It isn't an issue," I remind him.

He takes time to analyze me. "Said person would have to consider the optics, a cliché, might turn heads on the board."

Crossing my arms, I'm hearing everything I already realized.

"*However,*" he continues, "not everyone would be surprised. Hell, they might even figure out that someone had a hidden agenda to send her your way." He ends the ruse. "Why don't you spell out the obvious?"

A smile tickles the corners of my mouth because he pushed her at me. "Savannah and I seem to have found ourselves in a predicament, well, more than. I want to get a sense of what to do because being hidden away no longer feels right."

The respect that I have for her is too high, and the pride that she's mine roars inside. None of this was part of the plan. Hell, I still have no outlook for the long game. One little step forward is what I can give.

"I was confident she would bring out a side in you that you've kept closed off." He bounces his shoulders up. "It crossed my mind that having her report to you could lead to something else. It seems I was right."

"Looking out for me as always." My voice is thin, soft, appreciative. "But what do I do now?"

His fingers tap the arm of the chair once before he points at me. "Find a way to keep work out of it. How? I'm not sure, because you actually do need her as your PA. But it's not realistic to have both. Look into a solution that ensures she stays with Haven Crossroads and shows the value of her work, but doesn't show favoritism."

I tread to the side of my office as I contemplate the whiskey bottle near the coffee machine. Problem-solving sometimes needs it. I pop open the cork to pour a drink. "Give me some time. You have another meeting?"

"Yeah… want me to come back after?"

Nodding, I bring the glass to my lips.

Charles stands and walks by me, patting my back for luck, and leaves. "I'll do that then." When he reaches the doorway, I sense his pause. "Savannah must really mean something to you if you're willing to puzzle piece your empire." That's his parting thought.

It makes the air feel heavy. My drink comes with me to the couch, where I lie down and breathe long and controlled.

Opening up has never been a step forward for me—it's always been a weakness. But for the first time, I'm not convinced that it would be a mistake.

21
SAVANNAH

A fussy toddler wiggles in my arms. Lola, Elodie's daughter, was sent home sick from the company daycare. It was on my lunch break, and Elodie needed to get more children's medicine, so here I am at the pharmacy near work with a cranky kid as Elodie searches the shelf.

"Bubblegum flavor," I recommend when I spot the bottle.

She shakes her head in disagreement. "Lola hates that. Strawberry is the only way."

Frowning at my goddaughter, I grab hold of her hand. "What's wrong with you not liking bubblegum flavor? Is your mom not raising you right?" I coo at her.

"Being sick is horrible. She's extra cranky yet extra cuddly. It'll be a long night."

"Give me a call if you need help." Elodie is strong, but she's done everything alone. Lola's dad isn't in the picture because he doesn't even know, for many reasons. I'll always come running to help my friend.

She shakes her head as she grabs a box. "Don't be silly. You'll risk getting sick, and I have a feeling you have other plans."

"Maybe." I have a sheepish grin. "I'm sorry I've been a little MIA. I'm lost in a world I didn't know existed."

"Really? Shocking," she replies dryly, and it causes me to smile more. "How is it going since your work trip situation?" When I told her a week ago that I ended up in bed with Julian and had been together for the last few weeks, she squealed for a solid minute before a wave of concern washed over her at the way my time with Julian is unfolding.

I bounce Lola on my hip as we begin to walk down the aisle. "It's not a situation."

"Many couples tend to keep it to themselves at the start. It's... This is different. Sneaking around, and he may never change his mind. Don't get too attached."

"We... upgraded our relationship."

Her eyes widen, caught off guard. "Really?"

"I mean, I think so. He indicated that he doesn't want to keep us a secret anymore."

"Wow. That's a step. I can't really imagine him in a relationship, but I trust your judgment, so if you're happy, I'm happy. I would say if he hurts you, then I'll kill him, but I kind of need my job because it has free daycare," she proclaims in jest.

"I think he's trying. He even abolished the 'no fruit snacks on my desk' rule. That shows he cares."

Elodie snorts a laugh and notices the vitamin water on the end shelf of the aisle and evaluates the options. "It's kind of weird you're telling me these little things he does that make him seem human."

"I'm beginning to think he's only this way with me." And inside, I gush with happiness every time.

"He is. Everybody in my department thinks he has been extra grouchy lately."

"I'm trying to change that," I reflect lightheartedly.

"Actually, he was at the daycare real quick earlier today. Marketing needed a photo to show how great it is to work there, with top benefits, and clearly, the bossman stops by daily to say hello to the kids," she mocks.

I chuckle at the whole setup. "Yeah, when marketing asked for me to book some time, I had to laugh and warn them of their mistake."

She grabs a bottle and adds it to her basket as Lola whines. "I truly hope everything becomes the fairytale you deserve. He's lucky," she voices with such warmth and care, yet a waft of jealousy ghosts her words.

"Thanks." I need to say it out loud because I've been overanalyzing in my head. "It's like I'm addicted to his control and possessiveness; it's his way of showing his feelings. But it's the power dynamic, it makes me want it, and I'm happy." She looks at me blankly. "You'll have something similar one day, too."

She is about to say something, but Lola begins to gag, and the next thing I know, my black dress is covered in orange vomit that has a rancid smell. I'm shocked, but not as shocked as Elodie, who quickly drops her basket and scoops up a crying Lola from my arms.

"Oh my God, I'm so sorry." She feels Lola's forehead and pulls her close.

People around us stare, and my jaw still hangs low, my body frozen from the quick turn of events.

"Uh… it happens," I squeak out. Elodie seems mortified, and I push my disgusting misfortune to the side. "Don't worry about it. Let's get you the medicine and get out of here."

"This is horrible. Your dress is completely ruined." Elodie is panicking.

I reach out and touch her shoulder to calm her. "I didn't like the dress much, anyway." A complete lie, but it doesn't matter.

A store clerk must have seen the scene, and she appears with a paper towel. I gratefully accept it and blot my dress, but it makes it worse.

"Oh no, do you have to go back to work?"

My face strains because I won't have time to find something else to wear. I need to be back to ensure Julian has his notes for his 4 o'clock meeting. "I always have extra clothes in the office in case of a cream cheese bagel incident." If only I were so smart.

She releases a deep breath. "Phew. You can still impress your new beau."

I laugh at her ability to find comedy in this situation. "Nah, he won't care. I've already impressed him enough."

I'm sure Julian from a few weeks ago would have had a snide remark. Today? Not so much.

As soon as the elevator doors open to the office, I hear shouting. Julian's harsh voice floats in the air, with apparent disapproval in his tone.

The door is cracked open, and I recognize the other voice as Charles. I've learned that when Julian is in full-steam heated discussion mode with others, I stay out of it. That's precisely why I walk to my desk and tuck my purse into my drawer, accepting the events of the day.

Vomit on my clothes, and Julian is in a foul mood. My cell vibrates, and I see it's my aunt, so I'm quick to pick up.

"Hi."

"Hi, sweetie. I'm sorry to bother you at work." Her voice causes concern.

"Is everything okay?"

"With you? Why do I hear commotion?"

I huff from the classic Julian office meeting. "That's my boss in a mood today. He's in a meeting with someone." She has no idea about Julian's role in my life now.

"Oh, must have woken up on the wrong side of the bed." Not exactly. We were stuck in the middle of the bed, we don't choose sides.

"Anyhow, I was wondering the chance that you would come home this weekend?"

I sense it isn't a question but more of a nudge. "I could manage." It's been a while since we really had an opportunity to catch up. "If I schedule right, perhaps I can get away early from work for the weekend."

"That would be great." She means it, but there is something underlying. More serious, perhaps. My gut tells me I need to go back to Everhope.

"I'll text you when I know what time I'll be back tomorrow, okay?"

"Love you, sweetie. Drive safe."

When I end the call, I open my laptop, but I don't get much opportunity to check my calendar because Charles storms out of Julian's office, with Julian not far behind.

"You're crazy!" Charles tells Julian. Charles never argues to this level, but I can see that this discussion isn't cause for concern, and at the core is twisted humor.

Julian crosses his arms and leans against the office doorframe. "You've mentioned. But you told me to think before you returned, and I did."

"Seriously, now you're *over*thinking this."

"I'm not. It's logical," Julian justifies.

My eyes swing between them as I sit here wishing for popcorn.

"I honestly can't deal with you when you're being stubborn."

"I'm allowed to be. It's *my* company."

Charles rubs the side of his head and takes Julian's claim with a grain of salt. "I'm out of here. I have a soccer game for the grandkids to go to." He begins to walk, looking my way. "Congratulations. I knew you could tame him. It was a risky move on my part, but clearly it paid off." He winks at me as he moves along.

My jaw drops from the revelation that he's now privy to the full extent of Julian and me. My mind screams that he might have set us up all along. Kill two birds with one stone. Fix Julian's disorganized office life *and* make it something more, as though he could see the match and we didn't.

I stand, wanting to say something, but Charles is already entering the elevator, and I direct my gaze to Julian, who is already on his way to his desk. I'm hot on his heels, though.

"What was all of that?" I point behind me.

"Nothing. Charles just delivered news that I did not appreciate." He sits down behind his desk cooly and searches for what seems to be a Post-It note, and he never uses those.

"He knows about us?" My voice pitches higher.

Julian nods as his eyes scan his desk. "I told him earlier today. Although he kind of already guessed it. Something about one of the reasons you had the perfect resume to be sent my way. But anyhow, he didn't succeed at what I needed."

"He never disappoints you, so what the hell could he have done?"

Julian massages the back of his neck and doesn't look at me. "My old assistant decided she won't be returning after her baby goes to daycare full-time, plus said she would never work for me again."

I plant my palms on his desk to enable me to loom over him. "What! Were you going to fire me? And by the way, she quit, in case you forgot."

"Charles did point that out." At last, Julian snaps his gaze up to me. "I wasn't going to fire you, merely *reassign* you."

Now I'm pissed. "And when were you going to tell me this? I don't deserve that."

He stands, his fingertips gliding along the glass as he circles his desk to land right in front of me, an intoxicatingly close distance.

"Baby, I'm doing this for us. Having the old assistant back would mean we don't need to worry about any confusing lines. It's a win for us."

I utter a sound of complete disagreement and turn away from him. "A win would be discussing this with me beforehand."

"You're right. I'm... wanting to explore, I guess. No obstacles. Is that crazy?"

Damn it. There are a few solid points there. But still, it's completely twisted.

I throw my arms in the air and breathe in exasperation before spinning to meet his gaze. "I can't deal with you."

"But you do."

"Yes. Because in some bizarre way, I like you like this." I raise a finger and give him a cutting look. "I'm only going to end this argument because I recognize a hint of effort, although a little fucked up. And if you ever make employment decisions without me, I will lose it. Full-on. Don't play that game with me," I reprimand with firmness.

He nods once. "Okay. I'm learning."

"Fine," I huff.

The silence causes Julian to notice my dress, and he begins to sniff. "What the hell is that awful smell?"

"Lola threw up on me."

He winces and covers his nose with his forearm. "What the hell is your friend feeding her kid?"

I drop my eyes to my dress. "I'm not 100% sure, but by the looks of it, I'm going to guess orange juice and oatmeal."

"Eeek."

"Getting vomited on by kids is what we do for friends and family."

He narrows his eyes on me. "Don't you have an extra set of clothes or something?"

"Being judgmental today? And no."

His arm falls, and his interest is piqued. "Really? So does that mean you need to take the dress off?"

Now I crack a grin. "Could be. I was going to ask if I can steal one of your spare shirts and sneak out, as I was going to ask to leave early, anyhow."

He folds his arms and sits on the edge of his desk. "I'll answer if you take off the dress." He's dead serious.

I give myself a second to decide if I should give in or play it tough. Another line crossed if we break our own rule of keeping things physically separate in the office.

But after being thrown up on, my boyfriend going a little batshit crazy, and the relief of knowing I will have a calm weekend, I decide to throw caution to the wind. I march to the door of his office and close it, only to sashay my way back to him slowly. Stopping right in front of him, I reach behind me to find the zipper and pull it down. All the while, our eyes tie, and I don't blink once, as I'm sure of my choice. I slide my shoulder out of one sleeve, then the other, and the dress drops down to the floor, leaving me there in a blue bra and panties. The stockings with suspenders happen to be his luck for the day.

His gaze sweeps over me, unhurried and thorough, satisfaction settling in his expression, enticement clear.

"Anything else?"

"Yes. Turn around," he directs.

I move slowly until my back is to him. Sensing him stand and approach me, he hisses a sound right before his knuckles touch my back. Instantly, I suck in a breath, and a tiny gasp escapes me.

"So fucking beautiful." The sound of a slap and the sting on my ass makes me yelp. "Fucking naughty, too. You shouldn't be wearing this to work. Too tempting, and it makes me want to cancel my next meeting so I can lick you on my desk." He stands behind me and brings our bodies flush. He draws his palm across my side to my front and lowers to my panties, and his fingers disappear under the fabric. The pressure he puts on my clit causes me to lean back into his body as he begins to stroke me. "Soaking for me, too. Why is that again?" His deep, low voice speaks against the back of my neck, his lips dragging.

His touch already has me desperately needing him to make me come. "Because I'm only yours."

"That's right, baby." His other hand grips some of my hair to pull back and tilting my head. He kisses the crook of my neck while his other hand drives me wild. He plunges two fingers inside me. "Tight for me, too. Why is that?"

I bite my bottom lip, and I recognize that my body is turning to liquid. "My pussy is only for you."

"Good girl." He kisses my mouth and dips his tongue inside. I'm possessed again, and it's all his doing.

But just as I think he'll give me more, he removes his hand, and I feel another spank on my ass. "You're going to have to hold your orgasms until later. I mean it, don't make yourself come or there will be consequences." He steps back, creating space, and I hate that.

Blinking a few times, I try to adjust to the lack of his touch. "How long is the wait?" My breath is still thick from his trance. "I'm heading home for the weekend, so I won't see you. It's a bit last-minute, but my workload and schedule will help support my case. I'm going to use some vacation time to take tomorrow off."

Suddenly, the air changes, and I smile as I turn to face him because I enjoy seeing the confusion on his face.

"Why?"

"Family stuff. You'll be fine. Your dick may not, but I trust it can handle it." I grin cheekily.

Julian combs his hands through his hair. "Funny. Fine. You'll be away for the weekend."

As I begin searching for my dirty dress, I have no choice but to put it back on. "Family," I remind him.

"Right."

I drag my dress up my body, trying to find the zipper, but it gets stuck.

"I'll come with you."

My gaze shoots to him, and I see that he is very sober in his expression, his array of thoughts and schemes today long vanished. Now, it's pure clarity.

"You're coming with me?"

"Yes. To Yellowtop." His lips twitch because he loves doing that.

I'm trying to figure him out right now. "You want to come with me? To Everhope?"

He steps toward me and helps with my zipper. "Everhope and your aunt come up a lot in conversation. I'm curious."

I snicker in surprise. "You want to meet my family?"

"I will casually check out the town and see your aunt."

He's too easy-breezy about this.

"You're really full swing, huh. Telling Charles, trying to find me a replacement, heading to my small town, meeting family. Where is this all coming from?" I'm torn between being guarded and letting loose the glee inside.

He places a kiss on my forehead and rubs my arms with his palms. "I'm not sure, in all honesty."

My eyes flutter as I'm trying to digest Julian being very committed to a relationship that he's sworn off for years.

"Okay. Double-checking that I'm hearing you right. You. Everhope. My family."

He hesitates, but a comfortable half-smile blooms. "This weekend."

I take a deep breath and come to terms with his persistence, which surprises me. It's not a tiny move. But it's welcome.

"You'll be staying at the bed-and-breakfast in town," I inform him and give him a pointed look.

"Alone?"

I love my aunt, and she's with the times, but staying at home with a man who thinks sleep involves multiple orgasms would feel strange. "I haven't decided. We're supposed to be flying under the radar."

His cheeks fill with air before he releases a breath. "Okay," he agrees.

Lines crease my forehead. "And you would still want to come to Everhope, either way?"

"Sure."

My heart stutters at the risk of this all, but there's no doubt in me when I see the sincerity in his eyes. "Well then, leave your suit at home. To Everhope we go."

22

JULIAN

My tires screech a tad when I pull into the parking lot on Everhope's Main Street. Savannah stares at me from the sidewalk next to a newspaper dispenser as she holds two cups of to-go coffee. She has that wry smile that shields her amusement. The moment that I park and get out of my car, I feel a flicker inside my chest.

This is all new to me—if I'm honest, it's slightly nerve-wracking because of that. Never in a million years did I imagine I'd end up in a small town because of a woman ten years younger than me, a woman who was supposed to be nothing more than my personal assistant. Except it's blatantly obvious she's more than that. And what unsettles me most isn't just her—it's me. I can feel a piece of my wall cracking, breaking away, and I'm fully aware of it as it happens.

"Really? Had to bring the expensive sports car?" she greets me and hands me a coffee. Savannah left first thing this morning, and I drove out after one meeting I had at the office.

I accept the coffee and step closer to lean in for a kiss, but she steps back and tuts at me. "Strategy. Nobody knows we're together. Let's keep it low-key for the next hour until my aunt knows."

Feigning a scowl, I accept her plan. "I shall obey. This time only, though," I say and take a sip of my coffee. "Damn, good coffee." We begin to walk side by side.

"Mmm." She takes a sip from her own drink. "It's from Foxy Rox." She indicates with her head farther up to a coffeehouse on the left. "A must for visiting Everhope."

Main Street is pristine, classic, and brings calm. Time already feels different here. No bustle, only people walking leisurely and the sound of the occasional bell over a door. I'm already overwhelmed with the friendly smiles and the sound of people greeting strangers.

"Quaint."

Savannah gives me side-eye. "Is that good or bad?"

"Good."

"Well, I'm happy you found your way here."

I chuckle lightly. "The GPS didn't need to do much. Pure cornfields once I left the suburbs. I only nearly made a wrong turn when there was a detour once I crossed the Lake Spark county line."

"It's duck season. We stop traffic in all directions when a family of ducks decides to sit in the middle of the road." It should scare me that she isn't joking, but the fact is simple and light.

We continue our stroll, and I notice a man walking out of a store, carrying a box, with a little girl holding his hand, and people almost swarm him.

"Poor guy. That's our mayor. He used to be the sheriff. Everyone bothers him for something. Never fear, it isn't the city, no crazy under-the-table deals. Mostly, it's about town support for farming initiatives or cultural activities. Well, that was until now…" Savannah pauses, and her lips pinch for a second. "Anyway, he actually ended up remarrying his ex-wife, Rosie, when she got pregnant. That's their little girl. If you're into yoga, Rosie teaches a Saturday class at the gazebo in the park if the weather permits."

"I think you know my answer on that one."

She laughs. "I do." She tips her nose up. "I guess that's the new donut shop. Apparently, they have bagels at lunch. Foxy Rox is not happy about that. Loyalty is being tested in this town. Maybe tomorrow we can try them."

"If you feel like we won't have a target on our backs," I joke.

"Nah. They need me for the summer festival."

I continue drinking my coffee as I take in my surroundings. "Why is that?"

She touches my arm, and we stop our stroll, forcing me to look at her. There's a humorous smile fighting to break out in full force on her face. "Promise you won't tease me about something?"

"By the sounds of this? No can do." She shoots me a warning scowl. "Fine," I agree.

She looks away bashfully and swings her gaze back. "I kind of have to be at the festival. Remember how I said I was Miss Everhope once?"

"Yeah. I enjoy picturing you with a crown. Never knew it could lead to certain scenarios in my head." I lift my shoulder. That comment earns me a playful shove from Savannah.

"Well, this year I've been chosen to help choose the pie competition winner. I found out today."

I don't say anything, nor blink. First, I'm trying to figure out what exactly that entails. Secondly, I'm not sure if I should laugh. I stand there complexed, and she can see it, which causes her to grin.

"It's been ten years since I was crowned Miss Everhope, and it's tradition that one returns to help taste pie, wear the crown, and give the trophy to the winner."

"Math right now is reminding me that ten years ago you were in high school, and that makes me feel slightly old. I forget about our age difference."

She lifts her shoulders, then drops them. "Because your heart is young and cold."

"Hasn't bothered us. Anyways, I didn't really have the whole queen with tiara as the plot twist of our conversation. But it's cute."

She brings her hand to her hip. "Cute?"

Maybe I didn't use the right word.

"Yeah. What am I supposed to say? I already feel like I'm in a different world here."

We begin to move again. "Because it is. I mean, have you even been on your phone in the last ten minutes?"

"No."

"Exactly. I've heard your phone vibrate three times, and you didn't even notice. You've escaped and got quiet in your head."

Huh, I guess she's right. I didn't notice. Nor have I even thought of anything work-related. "So it seems."

"Listen, about my Aunt Bea. She is graceful and sweet and accepts that times are what they are today. But as I've mentioned, I booked you a room at the inn in town. Her house is lovely, and she redid the basement to make it a guest area. I… haven't exactly… told her." Her voice drawls out.

I stop us instantly because I wasn't expecting this. "Why not?" For some reason, I'm slightly offended, and I can't pinpoint exactly the reason.

"Because you're my boss. The one I might not have had many nice things to say about over the course of time since I started working at your company."

"Thanks for that reminder." I toss my empty cup into the garbage bin behind me.

She smirks softly. "We're new. I'm not sure how to present the change to her. I mean, she has met guys before you—"

I gawk at her. "No need to finish that sentence."

She can't stop smiling. "Okay, well, let me work it into the conversation."

"Am I *really* sleeping alone tonight?"

The palm of her hand covers my hand on her shoulder. A connection that is calming. "Nah, she'll be fine and also understands that space is a good idea. I don't think I could even get in the mood while in the house. Besides, I've never actually stayed at the Schoolhouse Inn. It's the old schoolhouse that was completely refurbished and is now an award-winning bed-and-breakfast. It brings in tourists."

"Brings in charming men, too." I flash my eyes at her.

She makes a sound as her head tips to one side. "Charming is a stretch," she teases. She steps back and offers me her hand after she throws her coffee cup away. "Come on, let's walk by the Riverbell."

"Sounds good."

Our journey to the river is easy. Occasional hellos, little facts, tidbits of gossip, and that feeling nagging me that everything here grabs you to leave the city behind and turn off for a while.

Main Street turns from flat to slightly downhill toward the river and park. We end our walk when we reach the small pier that is big enough only for two small speedboats and the big two-deck steamboat that appears classic. The kind that reminds you of the Mississippi River. I see people sitting at tables on the upper deck while waiters, dressed casually, hurry inside the boat, carrying trays of food.

Savannah splays her hands out. "This is the Riverbell."

"Wow. I'm not sure what I was expecting, but it's impressive." I take a few steps to the right to get a better view. "You don't want to head onboard?"

"Not now. They're busy, and I really want to go see my aunt. But this is the place that hopefully will always remain. A landmark, really. I've been to so many parties and weddings on this thing. Everyone loves it. The menu is a staple at lunch, simple comfort food. The chicken salad sandwich is to die for. I would hate to see it all disappear. But corporations have influence, especially if it brings in money that could lower property taxes out here. It's a great town with excellent schools. That comes at a price, though: high property taxes, and people get influenced easily, those who vote on the city council."

"All because someone sees tourist potential."

She nods somberly. "I mean, we get tourists here. But it's the kind who appreciate quaint towns and want to feel like a local. Not tourists who want souvenirs and casinos. It's not only tourism, though; the disruption from new construction can really mess with the river's natural currents and dams."

The way she sighs heavily makes me want to scoop her up in my arms, and I do. I pull her to me, kiss the top of her head, and let her nuzzle her head into my chest. Wrapping my arms tightly around her, I wish they could protect her from powerless choices.

"It'll be okay."

She mumbles something, but I don't hear. When she creates space between her face and my body, I see it written all over her. She's disheartened. "Enough wallowing. I haven't even spoken to my aunt, and I still need to give you the grand tour." Her attempt to smile is weak, but I appreciate the effort.

"Yeah. I hear I have an exam at the schoolhouse later." I add a bit of swelter to it, hoping it raises her mood.

"Sounds kind of dirty."

I crack a grin. "I was going for that."

The rest of the hour is pure admiration for her honest intention to care for others, and gushing about where she grew up, which adds to it. She's pure, with zero tolerance for fake ways of life.

"What's next?"

"Meeting family."

Right. I'm doing this. I already know that our versions of family are different. We both struggle to conceptualize how the other may be.

Savannah looks at me peculiarly. "Still on board?"

"Yeah. I'm thinking. That's all."

Her brows rise, and she searches my eyes. "It's okay if you changed your mind. We are kind of... new."

"Want to get rid of me?" She shakes her head. "Great. I have a bottle of wine in the back of my car, and I look forward to seeing how you introduce me to your aunt."

She sputters a laugh, and that's a good start.

I CHECKED into the inn and was impressed by the antique furniture and smooth wooden floors. The four-bedroom inn was quiet, and no signs of children since they have a no-young-kids policy—a win for me. Also, I appreciate how private the place is.

We took my car, and I listened to Savannah's directions.

"This is Everhope Road," she announces as we turn. A woman pushing a stroller waves to Savannah. "That's Hailey, a neighbor. Her daughter must be walking by now. She secretly married her brother's best friend. The whole town found out on the Riverbell," she chirps happily.

I slow the car when she points to a house up on the left. The houses on the street are not cookie-cutter; each has its own charm, although they're all updated and kept in good standing: no overgrown yards, flowers on porches, and a lot of flags.

"What's the deal with the flags?"

"It's for the high school. One of the coaches lives down the street. It's baseball season now, but during football season, whoa. Everyone in town heads to a Friday-night game. They're quite good and made state three years ago."

My lips quirk out. "Impressive. We didn't have anything like that in high school."

"You mean when dinosaurs roamed the earth?"

I manage to let a hand loose from the wheel and pinch her side for that remark. "Easy there, you might regret that later."

She fakes her pain. "Fine. In all seriousness, though, I don't particularly see football being a thing at boarding school."

A dull ache in my stomach comes to fruition, as I sometimes forget about it. "I mean, there was. Crew, lacrosse, and hockey were more of a thing. Cold parents and pretentious parties were a bonus." I have zero good memories from that time, except for some great parties when somebody's parents were away on vacation.

As we come to a standstill, I feel her fingers affectionately feathering my wrist with my hands on the wheel. "I can't imagine. You survived, at least."

"Joy."

With the car parked and the engine off, I observe the ranch-style home. I can already tell that the house is well-kept, as the door seems new and the paint is recent. Savannah inhales a deep breath and blows out her exhale. "Okay."

I shift in my seat to get a better view of Savannah and see that she's nervous. A man could easily fear that one is embarrassed to introduce their partner, but in this case, it's Savannah trying to figure out her words.

"I told her that you were passing through town because you had to meet a client out in Lake Spark. She's expecting you. Except not... as, well... she isn't judgmental, but 'oh hey, I'm sleeping with my boss' might cause her to be." Savannah twists the strap of her purse on her lap. "I'm not sure why a person with two degrees can't come up with a plan of action for this, but I can't." She's talking to herself.

It's time for me to take things into my own hands. I quickly lean through the gap in the middle console and grab the bottle of wine from the back before I open my car door with enthusiasm, energetically close it, and round the car to the passenger door. Opening it, I offer Savannah my hand. "Let me deal with this."

When Savannah is eye level with me, I simper. "Come on."

We walk up the front path to the stoop. Ringing the doorbell, we wait, and I again take in my surroundings. I notice a neighbor across the street with a bizarre mailbox, and I tilt my head in a few different ways to try to evaluate what I'm seeing.

"Trust me, I still haven't figured out why they keep their mailbox like that. They used to be neighbors who hated each other and crucified each other's mailboxes. They're married now, but apparently, they like the nostalgia of their passionate outbursts."

"Hmm. Not a crazy idea. Understandable." We can relate, even.

She gives a little wiggle of her fingers in the air to a car slowing down to turn onto a driveway next door.

"Who's that?" I wonder.

She smiles brightly. "That's Elodie's mom. Remember, we grew up as next-door neighbors. She'll probably text Elodie before we even manage to get inside. Something tells me she won't let it go that I'm standing in front of my aunt's house with a man with a sports car who resembles her daughter's boss." She chews on her bottom lip.

The wheels of this day could quickly spin out of control, to be honest. A lot of eyes are on us in this town. It could be a distraction if we're not careful.

23
JULIAN

The door to the house swings open, and our attention turns to the woman I've seen in pictures. Her hair dyed blonde in a natural way, and a smile that I'm not sure ever disappears.

I'm not nervous or feeling a need to impress, but the importance of this introduction and meeting still matters to me.

"You're here." She pushes out the screen door and opens her arms for Savannah.

"Yeah. Had to run around town for a bit." She hugs her aunt. Savannah's eyes divert to me, and she steps to the side of her aunt. "I brought company. My boss, Julian Haven."

Her aunt travels her eyes between Savannah and me. "Wonderful to meet you. Savannah mentioned that you were in the area. Hopefully, she gave you a tour of town."

"She did." I bring my arm from behind my back and reveal the bottle. "And this is for you."

"Oh, you shouldn't have." Her smile remains unchanged as she accepts the dark red. "Come on in."

We follow her, and I instantly notice how clean everything is and the number of photos on the hallway table. I do a quick skim and spot it instantly. "Look at you in your royal glory."

Savannah follows my line of sight and is quick to sweep up the photo of her in a dress and crown, even with a little wand. She was younger, her hair down and curled, makeup a little too much, but a beauty all the same.

"Don't be a pain," she mumbles so only I can hear. It will be hard to do because she's fun to rile up.

We enter the kitchen, and the smell of baked cookies infuses the room. "I baked your favorite," Aunt Bea tells Savannah as we stand around the island.

"Ah, thanks. Does this mean you have an entire stash of sugar cookies that I can take back to the city, too?"

"You betcha." Her aunt sets the bottle down on the counter in passing as she walks to the wire cooling rack on the counter and uses a spatula to scoop cookies onto a plate. "It's interesting that you take a vested interest in where your PA is from, Mr. Haven." This woman might have a heart of gold, as Savannah claims, but she's sneaky. I understood that question clear as day.

"Please, it's Julian, and I don't take any interest in my PA's hometowns, only this one." We both look at Savannah watching from the side.

"She is special, isn't she?" Bea admires her niece.

"She is indeed."

Savannah tucks a loose tendril of hair behind her ear and avoids looking at either of us. She hates the attention on her right now. "Let's focus on other things, shall we? We went by the Riverbell."

Bea continues to scoop the baked cookies. "Thought you would. I stay out of their way for the busy lunch rush."

"My aunt prefers evenings to chat with guests," Savannah adds.

"Well, I'm not a cook and only sometimes good at helping

the wait staff. I stick to playing hostess and doing the books. Come, let's sit down on the back porch."

We take a minute to grab some soft drinks and the plate of cookies and find a home on the screened-porch table that overlooks a garden that backs onto the woods.

Savannah shoves the plate of cookies at me. "Eat it, or she'll cry," she mutters under her breath to me. I'll do as I'm told on this one.

To be fair, I'm not a cookie person. But a flower-shaped cookie with blue icing and pink sprinkles kind of just won me over after one bite.

"These are good," I compliment.

"Thank you. Savannah never wanted to learn the recipe."

"Because only you can make them," she validates.

Her aunt waves her off. "So Julian, what do you think of Everhope? I'm sure it's nothing you're used to."

"Definitely quieter. Tranquil," I admit.

Bea's eyes lock onto me. "It is. It's good for the heart."

"Hopefully, because someone at this table used to say mine was made of stone." I direct my gaze to Savannah.

Bea chuckles. "She can be spirited. And modest, too. She won't even celebrate her accomplishment of getting a master's degree."

Savannah blows out a raspberry. "Is this why you asked me back?"

"It's not crazy to want to celebrate. I want to have a special dinner tomorrow and give a little gift, too."

"Savannah doesn't like gifts, I've observed. Also, I couldn't agree more that she shouldn't be so modest." It's endearing, though.

Savannah shoots us both a warning glare. "Stop talking about me."

"Is it so wrong that I paint you in a positive light in front of your boss?"

I grin and chuckle under my breath. "No need to do such a thing, and the pretense of the boss might need to be shaken while I'm here."

Bea beams. "Oh, imagine that, you are more than a boss," she plainly says because she isn't surprised.

Savannah drops her face into her hands, exhausted and humored by our ruse. "What gave it away?"

"Darling, nobody takes their boss to meet their family for kicks. I also highly doubt Mr. Billionaire here really had business out this way. You also made a reservation at the Schoolhouse. Glenda let me know when I walked by the new donut place in town this morning."

I like this lady a lot. "You're a smart cookie, Bea. Yes, your niece got under my skin, and here we are." I let my hand float over to Savannah's arm to touch her the way a man who has her should—tender yet possessive purely by a touch of the fingers.

Savannah gives me a warm look. "It was unexpected. All of this. He and I. It's new, too. But something chased us together," she reflects.

"The way it should," Bea laments. "I'm going to assume that the reservation isn't for one and you're a grown woman."

"I don't mean to steal her away, but I kind of can't apologize, either. I never take time off."

Bea's face is neutral, unreadable. "You might want to take more time off, then. We lose precious things if time isn't given." That's her warning shot.

A fair one, too.

"I don't lose things that have value," I respond.

"Good." Her mood perks up, and she swings her focus back to Savannah. They quickly dive into a conversation about old photos.

I want to listen intently, but I can't help but observe, as I'm surrounded by two people in the same family, showing every ounce of love, completely invested in one another's words, mementos on the wall, and favorite cookies to be shared.

Everything that is foreign to me.

I only accept success, but I'm feeling uneasy about how I can be any good at this; what's in front of me. I've never had anything that resembles family like this. I'm not even sure I'm jealous because I'm not sure what I've been missing, except that in front of me is the image of honest love.

Savannah deserves everything. I'm not even half that guy. I've never been anywhere near invested in a woman, and here she is bringing me into unknown territories, bringing out parts of me I haven't seen before.

Some men would run away, but I'm determined to do the opposite and succeed, similar to everything else I touch.

Because she's no exception.

24

SAVANNAH

Lying in bed with a sheet wrapped around me, I rest on my side and lean my head against my propped arm, watching as Julian pokes at the fire burning inside the fireplace. The moment we entered his room at the Schoolhouse Inn, clothes were ripped off in record time. Now it is who knows what hour during the night, but we're still awake.

"I could get used to this *Little House on the Prairie* stuff," he remarks as he sets the poker to the side.

I lick my lips as I fight a grin. "Enlighten me."

His hands go out to display the room. "I mean, I have a fire to keep warm at night, and there isn't even a TV in here."

My eyes fall to my hand that brushes along the mattress as my lips slip into a smile. "I think that's what most people would call chic. The pristine wood floors and antique porcelain that they serve breakfast on are hardly screaming 'let's churn butter from the milk we collect from the cows, while I wear a bonnet.'"

Julian's eyes brighten as he walks back in the direction of the bed. "A bonnet, eh?"

I swat his arm as he joins me back in bed. "Don't even joke about that."

His sheepish smile is enough as he mirrors my position, and a blissful silence fills the room. I feel it, the obvious thought and feeling that has blown around me all day.

A fragility hits me as my words begin to form. "Thanks."

"For what?"

"I don't know. Coming here and meeting my aunt. Truthfully, I thought it was something you would fight for a long time. It's not exactly an 'oh let's grab dinner tonight' kind of thing. It's a little more than that. And you initiated it."

His mouth slides to the side, and he seems to deliberate with himself. Maybe he hasn't realized the optics until now. But his fingertips softly touch my arm on the spot below my shoulder that always seems to be the button of assurance.

"I'm not afraid of things."

Instantly, I snicker at the ridiculousness. "I beg to differ. I believe you were afraid of me."

He shushes me with his long finger when it lands on my lips. "I'm not afraid of things, I conquer them. The path to you took a different approach."

I set the palm of my hand on his cheek and give him a saccharine look that'll tell him it's the sweetest thing he could say. I pat his cheek. "Keep telling yourself that." Because deep down, we both knew we were scared of the magnetism we felt toward one another.

His response is to move hastily, and I land flat on my back. "Careful," he warns.

"Oh dear, what will you do? Remember, I need to wake with the roosters and bake the bread for the day," I tease him because of what he said earlier.

It causes him to grin. "There is only one thing you will be waking to." He kisses my neck, but it quickly turns to a slight sharp pain.

"Don't you fucking dare." I stare at the ceiling and giggle ridiculously as he continues his pursuit to mark me. As funny as it is, it's really not, and I begin to push him away. "Seriously, I don't want to go to lunch with my aunt wearing a scarf in 70-degree weather."

Julian pulls back with an understanding grin. "You have a solid point."

He wiggles until his forearms are framing me as they rest on the pillow on each side. This time, the moment of quiet is his own doing. "Savannah…" His sentence drifts away, leaving me to wonder. "We can't keep doing this."

The words hit me like a bolt. Cold and unnerving. Panic flickers in my chest, and I know he sees it. Still, the corner of his mouth lifts, barely, a shadow of something softer under the surface of his control.

"Denying that we're moving toward something," he says, tone deliberate, "and we can't keep ignoring it."

A flicker of relief slides through me, though caution claws at the edges. I'm unsure what he's really saying.

"Talk faster," I murmur. "Because starting with *we can't keep doing this*? Not a great strategy."

He chuckles once before his eyes lock on me—piercing, commanding, yet… raw in a way that catches me off guard.

"True." His tone softens enough to betray the wall he's holding up. "What I mean is… we're something. I don't know the name for it yet, but it's real. And my feelings for you… They keep growing. It's dangerous. More for you than me."

Shimmying against the mattress, I manage to bring my arms up to rest my hands on each side of his back. "Tell me to run," I challenge him.

"No fucking chance."

I smile, satisfied. "Excellent answer, because we have a problem." His eyes squint in curiosity. "I used to despise you. Now I only despise you because you've made me see a side of you that feels like it's only for me. That's a powerful thing because now my feelings for you are stronger than imaginable."

We're trapped in a trance that strikes us. I feel his pulse pick up, and he feels mine. I stare straight into his eyes, and I'm not even lost. It's the clarity of our magnitude. Our lips slowly meld together as our fingers interlace against the mattress. Unlike all the times before, this kiss holds a promise.

―――

Lunch is a struggle. As much as eating a BLT sandwich at the Riverbell, seated outside on this beautiful day, should be pure relaxation, I'm tired. Julian woke early when he began to cough. I'm positive he has a headache, too, but he seems to be in denial. Taking a deep breath, I soak in the sun while I watch the green water of the river, and the pine trees along the shore bring some tranquility as I hear my aunt chatting with Julian in the background.

"This place is packed like yesterday," he comments.

I grab a chip from my plate. "Well, it's Saturday and lunchtime."

"It's a nice casual vibe."

My aunt smiles warmly. "Now. There's a wedding here tonight, a totally different feel. White tablecloths and all."

He sneezes into his arm, and my face puzzles as we seem to be losing him physically. "I can envision a lot of business meetings here."

"Well, I guess people stop by on their way to or from Lake Spark because of the hockey team there. There's a golf course not far, too," she explains. "I've had this place for more than thirty years. There has never been a time when I felt we didn't have enough customers. I tried to change the lunch menu once and got some complaints, so I changed it back. I guess people like the classics. But at night, we do dip our toes into that fancy stuff. Blue cheese and pears seem to get people excited."

I lean to my side to touch her arm. "All the more reason this is so unfair if they sell the docking rights."

She smiles weakly at me, and the disappointment is apparent. "You never know. But I've prepared myself for the most-likely scenario. We'll know in a few weeks when it all comes to a vote. But whoever the investor is, their wallet is too appealing to the county."

Julian jumps in. "Let's see if we can find a loophole. I'll have my guys look into it."

My aunt waves him off. "Don't involve yourself in this. Fate will be fate." I shake my head, but before I can say anything, my aunt squeezes my arm to stop me. "How was the inn? Sleep alright?"

Julian coughs again, and that's when I decide to state the obvious. "Are you sure you're feeling well?"

He grins. "Don't be ridiculous. I never get sick."

"Right. Superman never gets sick." There is little conviction in my tone. "I don't know. You have a different color than normal."

He scoffs at me, as though I'm crazy. "Really. I'm fine. My immune system is as hard as steel. Must be something in the air. I'm probably not used to the clean fresh air."

"Right. Earth-shattering," I say dryly. "Most people who get sick struggle to eat much." I give him a pointed look and draw our attention to his plate, which holds a half-eaten sandwich.

"It was a big sandwich. I'll take the rest as leftovers," he rationalizes.

My aunt looks at me with a closed, knowing smile. Maybe Julian doesn't want to appear weak. I'm not sure, but it kind of irks me. "I'm going to leave you two be. I want to check that everything is set for tonight's event."

"Sure. We'll swing by the house later," I mention.

Julian gives her a little nod in acknowledgment. "See you."

When she's gone, I cross my arms and lean back in the chair as I study him. "Would you like to admit defeat now that you're getting sick?"

He shakes his head and grabs his iced tea to drink. "Savannah," he says, saying my name tightly. "Stop this. I don't get sick. I don't have time to be sick. My daily diet consists of power bars and smoothies with vitamins so I don't get sick."

I raise a finger in the air and sit up. "*Except...* you know, they say once you finally relax, that your body allows itself to get a virus or cold?" I bring my finger to my chin. "I believe you, dear boss, have been relaxed lately. So much so that your body might be in shock and is finally allowing itself to combust."

"Then why don't you have a cold?" he asks flippantly.

"Because I just don't." Maybe he'll pass on his germs. My mind goes through the files of possible scenarios, and it hits me, and I wince.

He notices. "What?"

"You know how marketing dragged you to the daycare for PR?"

"Yes. The cries and toys thrown were my idea of hell."

Casually, I take a bite of another chip. "There's a virus floating around there. Lola got hers from there."

"You were the one who was thrown up on," he states impassively.

"Not my first rodeo of a sick Lola. Anyway, congratulations, Julian Haven, you are officially knocked out." I stand and hold out my hand. "Come on. Let's get you taken care of."

He is struggling to admit defeat, but reluctantly, he follows my lead.

Within two hours, a fever hit Julian. Even a number on a thermometer couldn't end his denial. He said he had emails to catch up on. But it went downhill, and a headache made his 15-minute rest last an hour.

He drags his body up to sitting on the bed as I return to the room after heading out to stock up on supplies.

Julian scrubs his face with his hands. "What is this misery?" he groans in drowsiness.

I really do hate seeing him like this, but I also can't help biting my lip to keep any humor from showing, given his stubbornness today. "What we common people call a virus. You're down for the count." I come to sit on the bed and drop a cloth shopping bag on the duvet. "Here."

He digs out the items in the bag. "Medicine for headaches." He tosses it on the bed. "Medicine for a sore throat." It lands next to the other box of pills. He pulls out a bottle of green liquid. "Nighttime sleep."

I point to that one. "That's a classic and a goody. It'll knock you out all night, and you'll wake feeling refreshed."

"And this?" He holds up a pink bottle.

"Yeah, they were out of the option for fever and only had the kids' bubble gum flavor, so I figured we could just double or triple the advised amount."

A smile breaks out on his face. "Am I supposed to take all of this?"

I shake my head. "Don't be silly. We'll do like three. We needed options. This is all new to you."

He continues examining items in the bag, and his brows furrow when he sees a green glass bottle. "This doesn't even have a label."

I snatch it from his hand and begin to unscrew the cap. "It's from my aunt. She makes it herself. Rosemary and thyme, and a bunch of other things from her garden. Apparently, it's great for sore throats."

"And today we needed muffins, a thermos, and I think a bag of fruit snacks?" He is pleasantly confused.

"My aunt sent over some things, in case you get hungry. I thought I deserved a box of fruit snacks for my nursing skills."

He chuffs a sound and leans back against the headboard. "Your aunt sent over things?"

I shrug before I begin to move the items to the side. "Of course, you're in my life. It's what families do for one another. We take care and help make someone feel better."

His face becomes unreadable. "Family," he whispers. The way he says it makes it feel as though it's a foreign concept to him, far off in the distance.

I get it. The idea of it all is still unnerving for him, and I scoop up his hand in mine. "Yeah. You'll have to get used to that."

The twitch at the corner of his mouth signals that he seems to be succumbing, in little pieces, to the idea, and it warms me to the brim.

As I begin to adjust the blankets, I make it my mission to care for him. "Come on. Let's get you recovered."

His arm swoops to the side and around me, guiding me close until my ear rests against his chest. I feel the heat of his fever through his t-shirt. But when he kisses the top of my head and I peer up to see that his eyes begin to hood closed, I don't care, and I cling to him.

"You are an overbearing nurse that under normal circumstances, I would lose my cool with until they were fired, but with you, I'm lucky," he voices, with lethargy taking over.

The balance of power is how Julian is with most people. And he always wins.

But on the lucky scale, I think *I'm* the luckier one.

25

JULIAN

Looking at Savannah's desk peculiarly, I study the contents as she sets up her desk as if it were a typical day. A circular tin with flowers on it, a bottle that appears to be medicine, and some bizarre pair of knitted socks.

"What the hell is all of this?"

She grabs the tin and presents it to me with her usual cheery morning smile, and I reluctantly accept it. "Elodie went to Everhope over the weekend, and she was sent back with the cookies you like from my aunt, and also, my aunt wanted to ensure you keep your cold away, so there is a natural remedy with rosemary, and the knitted socks..." She brings her finger to her chin. "Well, she thought they would be good to keep your feet warm, but I realize you will look ridiculous in them, so I'm saving you, and they are now mine." She snatches them up and tosses them aside.

I open the tin and grab a cookie. "That was thoughtful of her. Why would she do that?"

Savannah sputters a laugh. "You know the answer. Practice saying it with me. Because that's what people do for family," she articulates, and with her hands, encourages me to say it in sync, which isn't happening. "Since you are attached to me, it means that you're family."

I'm completely out of my realm because this is a benign concept to me, and the only thing I see. Now I'm enriched by the act, and it feels… good. "I'll be sure to send her a message."

"You have her number?"

"Of course, Aunt Bea and I need to conspire to ensure you are happy as a clam," I say so easily.

She laughs in response. "I'm not surprised. Now go, you have a call with the legal department in exactly…" She glances at her watch. "Three minutes."

"Fine. Keeping a tight ship. I'll see you later."

We're doing our best to keep our hands off one another in the office, and for the most part, we succeed. We make up for it in the evenings, and tonight, we're heading to a little Italian place for dinner.

The call drags on, and I've only learned two new facts about a major contract I'll be signing. Hanging up, I blow out an annoyed breath and sink back into my chair, my gaze drifting up to the ceiling. The door to my office opens a second later, and I straighten slightly—surprised to see my sister standing there.

"Caroline?" I sit up. I guess it's a pleasant surprise.

She pauses in the middle of my office, her demeanor cause for concern. "Sorry to stop by unplanned. I needed to speak with you in person."

Slowing, I indicate with my extended arm for us to head to my sofa area. The moment I sit down across from her, I notice that she isn't as composed as usual.

"Your assistant isn't out there, so I let myself in."

My eyes squint at her. "And?"

"You're sleeping with her." There is a tad of judgment in her tone.

My eyes blaze open, as it feels like cold water being thrown at me. "That's not exactly your business."

She groans and pinches the bridge of her nose. "It's why I'm here."

"Enlighten me, because I don't appreciate you coming to my office only to pass judgment."

"Is it serious? Or a fling?"

"Why does this feel like a line of questioning?"

She inhales a deep breath through her nostrils, and her fingers claw the side of the couch. "Because it really does matter."

The way I see her in front of me causes me to believe she isn't judging me at all. There is another angle that I'm struggling to see.

"Julian, someone from the board saw you and her when they were in Everhope a few weeks back."

My face squeezes. "Why would someone be there? I don't see any of those old people on the board thinking Everhope is a weekend getaway over their house in St. Barts."

She sighs and appears to prepare herself. "Julian, Savannah is your assistant, and that's a problem."

Now, I'm beginning to fume. "It's none of your business." I raise my voice.

"Her family is the owner of the Riverbell."

Strange that she knows these details. "Again. None of your business." My tone is sharp and my face indifferent.

"The Riverbell that is about to become history."

Abruptly, I stand, impatient at the lack of clarity in this conversation. I walk straight to my window to see the calming view of the skyline. "What the hell is this interrogation?"

"The board member was in Everhope because of Davenport's interest in the river."

My father's company. The one he stole.

I completely pause mid-pace and spin to look at her at record speed. "Davenport is the silent party?"

She nods her head with effort.

I rub my face and begin to feel sick in my stomach. "Fuck."

"It's worse, Julian."

"Tell me how that can fucking be?" I point to the door. "There is someone on the other side of the door who loves her family and worries day and night over their business."

Caroline stalls for a few seconds before her voice cracks. "You care for her?"

"Yeah... I do."

"More than someone would a friend or colleague?"

My head tilts to the side to grasp that she means another level. "That's what people tend to feel when they're in a relationship." I drag my finger to the corner of my mouth for a beat. "I'm no exception." It's an overwhelming brick inside me that would need to be hammered down.

She shifts, weighing her words. "You know how you let me vote on your behalf at the last meeting?"

Oh no.

I'm already anticipating her following sentence, and my body feels the weight stuck at the bottom of the sea.

She squeezes her eyes shut with remorse. "I voted with your shares to go forward with the plan."

My body completely turns ice-cold, and I begin to feel the cracks in my world. "Are you telling me that I unknowingly voted to ensure that my girlfriend's family business closes?" I grit out.

She stands and seems to panic. "I'm so sorry. It seemed like the right vote, a financial gain for everyone. If I had known, I wouldn't have. I... thought you should know."

"I can't believe this."

"I'll do anything to help. I don't know if it can be fixed, but I'll help," she promises.

Raking my hands through my hair, I'm about to combust. That's probably why I go to my desk and swipe everything off in rage, items landing on the floor. "Fuck." I rub the back of my neck.

"Julian…"

"Get out." I'm not angry at her, because she didn't know, but I'm furious with myself for not paying attention and letting my disdain for my father prevent me from reading the fine details. "Leave me alone."

Caroline doesn't argue and nods numbly before following my request.

Maybe it was the sound of the contents of my desk turning into pieces or Caroline's sympathetic look toward Savannah as she leaves the room, but Savannah enters, worried.

My lips roll in because I'm not sure what to say. I can't hide this from Savannah. But I'm already breaking down because this won't end well, I feel it inside.

"What's going on?" A mix of her confusion and her eyes noticing the floor cause her to race forward to me to inspect me with deep concern.

With my head bowed low, I stand stably in place. "Savannah." It comes out delicate.

She senses that everything is not alright, and she strokes the back of her knuckles along my cheek, and I trap them to ensure we don't lose the touch. I kiss her wrist faintly and keep her hand to the side, our hands interlaced.

"We need to talk."

"You're scaring me. What's going on?"

I do everything but look at her. "Promise me that you trust me when I say I didn't know."

She steps back and snatches her hand away. "What's happening?"

I bite the inside of my cheek, debating my words, but I can't hide behind anything but the facts. "It's my grandmother's—my father's," I correct myself, "company. It's Davenport. They are the silent party trying to buy the permits."

Her eyes grow wide as her face falls into disbelief. "What?"

I swallow because this will be the most painful moment of them all. "I didn't know, but Caroline…"

"That's your sister, right?" she double-checks.

"Yes. She voted with my shares…" Savannah tries to follow my story. "To ensure that Davenport proceeds with their plan."

She steps further back, covers her mouth, and I see the wave of mistrust taking over her body. "Are you telling me that you are partly responsible for this?"

I'm quick to follow my urge to be closer to her, to comfort her, but it's one step forward and two steps back from her. "Please, understand that I didn't realize."

"They're your shares!" she barks out. "Surely, you know what the hell you're voting for. Was this before or after we started to… you know." She's breaking.

"No," I say, adamant. "Believe me, I didn't look at the meeting agenda because I never go, simply to avoid my father."

Tears fill her eyes. "Oh my God…" Her face goes pale. "I shared so much with you. Were you using me to get intel for your horrible profit?"

The moment I'm close, she attempts to pound my chest, but I'm quick to grab her wrists and hold them up to ensure she concentrates when I explain. "No. Absolutely not. I wouldn't do that."

"You also say you only succeed," she cries.

My hands crawl up to hold her face. "Baby, no. This isn't something I would want. Listen to me, if I had been aware, I would have tried to put a stop to it."

She continues to shake her head profusely, her eyes swelling with tears. "This isn't happening," she whispers to herself.

"I'll make this right," I promise, and my entire body is now flooded with adrenaline.

"You can't!" She shakes me away and zips straight to the open door of my office.

"Savannah, please." She's so enraged that it's pointless to have a conversation with her right now.

She points at me, and she's shaking. "Leave me alone. You can't fix this…" She wipes a tear away. "And even if you could, you will always be the man who had a part in ruining my family."

Our eyes meet, and it's cold, tense, no sign of hope.

"Don't follow me," she bites out and walks away.

"But I'll still find you," I call out, completely insistent.

I never understood how a heart could beat entirely for someone else. Most would say, including myself, that I don't even have a heart.

But today simply proved how I have one, because it just completely broke, and I feel every single shard.

26

SAVANNAH

Attempting to cover the deep circles under my eyes has proven to be an obstacle. Lack of sleep and crying can really test your concealer. Still, I continue my pursuit of looking refreshed and unaffected as I stare into my bedroom mirror.

"Why don't you give it a few days?" Elodie sits on the edge of my bed as she outstretches her arm to ensure Lola doesn't fall off my bed while she plays with an old blush brush.

I grab the shade of red lipstick that screams F-you and begin to apply. "No. My mind is made up. I'm already in misery, and I won't give Julian the satisfaction of thinking he can salvage this."

"So, you just show up and quit? You really think he'll let it be so easy?"

I pause for a second before applying it to my bottom lip. "I'm sure he won't. But he doesn't have much choice. He hurt me."

In the mirror, I can see that my best friend has a strained look. "Maybe he's telling the truth, he didn't know. You really think he would go so far as to take you both on some whirlwind romance only to gather information to hurt you?"

Turning around, I give her an incisive look. "It happens all the time to people, and unfortunately, I'm part of the general population that is at risk, and I wasn't immune."

She sighs, and I'm still a little confused as to why she isn't as spiteful as I am. Julian hurt her best friend, yet it almost feels like she's on his team. "I think you shouldn't act so irrationally yet. Let things cool off, then approach him in a clear way."

"Why are you giving him so much grace?"

"Because you can lose something and never get it back. Those things happen when we think irrationally. I'm speaking from experience." Her glance at Lola says it all. The reference is to the one night that led to her daughter.

"I'm going to choose to ignore your advice right now, but I still love you." I begin to fluff my hair when I spot a random necklace on the jewelry holder that reminds me that he got me one, which I gave back. A new cry bubbles inside of me, and the sadness hurts my chest. For a second, I question if maybe she's right. But Julian, attempting to reach me with messages and calls I don't answer, won't help me right now.

"I'm going to quit." I don't sound as confident as I did a minute ago; it's soft because my eyes can't tear away from a necklace. A thoughtful gift, even if the presentation was poorly done, makes the corner of my mouth tick up at the memory.

"Fine," she says. I glance over my shoulder and see that my friend is watching me, and her facial expression is set to neutral. "Whatever you do, I will support."

I smile dimly as I face her again. "Thank you."

"And your aunt?"

"She hasn't said much. Soaked in the information and told me to make my own decisions on how to handle Julian. I would be a lot more furious than she is."

Elodie seems taken aback by my aunt's response. "Do you think she already gave up on the Riverbell a while ago?"

My foot slides into the black stiletto that I picked out to match my blue fitted dress. "That would be silly."

"Did she ever like Julian?"

"Yeah. So we can add another layer of how his charm is a conning gift."

She picks up her daughter, who makes an undefined sound that might be an attempt at a word. "Is it charm? Because with everyone else, he normally demands, he doesn't need to charm people. He has no reason to. He has it all. But you? Your family? It's a different side of him, he finally has to put in the effort to impress. And he is only like that… for you."

I shudder from the thought that she's correct. "Thinking like that is dangerous. Distance is what I need. I'm too angry to be close to him."

She stands with her daughter on her hip. "Okay. You sure he'll be in the office at 5?"

"Yeah, I have his calendar memorized as well… I was his assistant."

"Oh yeah. Well…" She walks to me and gives me a side hug on her childless side. "Good luck. You can come straight to my place afterward and relax in pajamas for a movie. Have another cry if we need to."

I touch her arm in appreciation. "I'll take you up on that. Tomorrow, I'm escaping the city and heading straight to Everhope."

It's time to leave, and the confidence I thought I had begins to crumble slowly.

THE MOMENT I step off the elevator, my nerves have me bursting at the seams. A deep breath only steadies me for a second.

Julian's office door is closed, and I take the opportunity to go to my desk, fury only intensifying because there is a bouquet of pink roses.

As if that's going to fix it. He's a smart man, he's trying to get under my skin. He hated flowers, then gave me one, and now a bouquet is supposed to show me how much he cares. I'm so close to ripping them all off from their stems, but deranged isn't the angle I'm going for right now. The rest of my desk is untouched, except for a new box of fruit snacks. That boils me, though; as if a four-dollar box of gummies could solve our situation. Even if they are my favorites, and to a normal person walking by, it would seem like a sweet gesture.

I grumble and begin to toss a few items into my oversized purse. Good luck to whoever finds a new residence here. It's a place where many have been, and they've all left scorched.

My breath gets caught in my throat when I hear Julian's voice booming to what seems to be someone on the phone. He isn't in the best of moods, but neither am I. I'm not going to wait to rip this bandage off, and I give myself a second before the sound of my heels pattering on the floor leads me straight to his office door which I barge open.

He instantly stalls in his seat behind his desk when he sees me, maybe in disbelief, or perhaps he was expecting me. "I gotta go." He doesn't wait for a response, and his thumb hits the screen as his phone slides down the side of his face. His jaw has stubble, and he seems to be lacking sleep, too.

"Savannah," he says softly and takes a deep breath as he slowly stands.

With purpose, I sway to the middle of the office, my face hardened. "Don't come closer, Julian," I warn, mostly because feeling him near my body will completely weaken my resolve.

To my surprise, he obliges and slowly sits back down. "I've been out of my mind trying to reach for you, waiting for you. I need to know that you're alright."

Scoffing a sound, I shake my head once. "No. I'm not alright," I mock him. "You... you made me feel things, so many things, only to obliterate them because you lied—"

Quickly, he interrupts, and his palm flies up. "It's not a lie. A lie is when you understand what you're hiding."

"Still, by association, you're part of the problem. You helped try to ruin my aunt's business, a small town, everything I hold dear."

He shakes his head fervently. "I can fix this." His adamancy is almost laughable.

"You..." My confidence falls to zero, and the emotions I've been trying to control now show as a silent weep creeps up. "Why did you have to let this happen? Why? Not everything can be a game to you," I choke out.

He hops up, and as he is about to follow the circuit around his desk, he stops, still wanting to respect my boundaries. "I honestly had no idea. If I did, I would have ensured this never happened. We can move past this, we can." He swallows, and his eyes are full of sorrow. "Space? Is that what you need?" He struggles to say it, but he does.

"No. I need you to accept that you ruined a good thing. I'm not something broken that you can fix."

His splayed fingers tap on the side of his desk, while he glances down briefly and thinks for a moment. "Then we'll create something new," he replies softly when he looks up.

We both stare at one another, pain enthralling us, our eyes locked in a standoff, his side yearning and mine full of anger and sadness.

"How do I know you weren't using me?"

That sets him off. "You know you just asked a ridiculous question, because do you believe that?" he challenges. "Actually, really believe that?" Returning to his chair, he grumbles and ensures we don't see eye to eye.

Deep down, I don't think I do. Did I say it as an excuse to

belittle our relationship, making this process easier? It doesn't help. I see that now.

My head bows down. "No. I don't," I admit honestly.

Julian is relieved, and the stiff silence in the room taunts me, causing me to consider my two choices right now. Either walk straight into his arms and let him comfort me with his hope that we can brush past this, while he's convinced he has fixed the issue. Or do what I came for and make it clear that he can't expect everyone to forgive him and sweep things under the rug.

"I should never have agreed to be your assistant."

"But you did."

My feet move a few strides closer to his desk, thankful it's between us. "You wanted me gone, though."

"Back then I did." His voice grates. "Now? Not so much."

I continue to move, on a prowl that leads to only one source. "I can admit that we were not smart people. We ignored boundaries, and now there is a path of destruction."

"Savannah." There is an edge in his tone, and he drills his gaze straight into me.

"I'm fucking miserable. Not the kind that has anything to do with work, but it still has to do with you."

Standing, he doesn't break our eye contact, and he hovers behind his throne. He wants to be on the same level as me.

"What are you saying?"

My lips tremble, and I bite my lip.

Composure. You can do it. You only need a few seconds.

"We crossed lines, Julian. God…" I comb my hand through my hair until my hand claws the back of my head. "I worried that I was a secret but had to be because I too have a career. It turns out that wasn't the issue to fear at all. I was never sure whether I saw a side of you that nobody has, or whether you have changed. I want to believe both. But one thing I am 100% certain of is that one thing hasn't changed."

"I'm struggling right now to respect the distance, but I'm a moment away from snapping and kissing you until you find logic."

I chuff a bitter laugh. "You always made assistants run away. You didn't want me to be the exception when I started. But congratulations… I quit," I snipe before I pivot on my feet and quickly leave. I can't bear to give him another glance, it could cause me to crumble weakly in front of him.

He broke my heart and my determination to succeed.

All I hear is him behind me slamming his fist onto his desk before he calls out. "I'll chase you until you're mine again."

27

JULIAN

"You look like hell," my sister remarks honestly as she sits down to occupy the vacant stool next to me at the bar.

Nursing my second whiskey, I can't disagree. Failure is hard to swallow. It's what I've led myself into.

"I'm getting a glimpse of hell, thank you very much, Caroline." I ignore her and look forward at the row of expensive bottles against the wall of this chic club where members conduct afternoon business meetings with alcohol on the side. Today, the meeting is just me.

In the corner of my eye, she indicates to the barman for the same drink. "I figured you might be here. We may not be close, but the few times we've run into one another unplanned, it's usually here. Although under better circumstances."

Lifting my glass in the air for a lazy cheer, I highlight the obvious. "Are you here out of guilt?" My gaze swings to her with loathing.

Her face falls, with guilt written plainly all over it. "Yes." The candor surprises me. "This possible scenario never crossed my mind. How was I supposed to know who your assistant was?

We don't speak often. I definitely had no clue that you're in a relationship with her," she explains.

"*Was*. Was in a relationship with her. Something tells me ruining her aunt's life kind of put a dart into that chance of a relationship." Misery floods my tone, and I set my empty glass down on the napkin.

I'm a man who judges choices for successful gain, it's second nature to me. Even when intuition poked me, I failed at listening. The warning was always present. Hell, I even warned Savannah that I'm not a man capable of a relationship. Lo and behold, it didn't take long for me to destroy everything into smithereens because I misstepped, stuck in my thirst for her to notice the finer details. I didn't protect her, and I'm not worthy of her.

All along, we knew the risk.

Still, my body feels hollow.

Caroline gently touches my elbow. "Despite this situation, where did you see yourself going with her?"

"The question of the hour." I've been here for one, and my mind fixates on a vision of what a future with her would be. "We weren't ready to end." Was I always only going to see the present?

"The world has only ever known you as a man who dates. That isn't the same as a relationship. It's a first for you."

"Aren't you observant," I say, cynical. "I'm older than Savannah yet lack the experience of being a man who gives it all to someone."

She thanks the bartender softly for delivering her drink and continues our conversation. "What are you going to do? Let her go?"

"I said I would look for her until she's mine again, but now I'm wondering if I will only end up hurting her more."

My sister shakes her head fervently in disagreement. "You

always figure it out. There has to be a way to win her back... if that's what you want."

Remaining silent, I give her an astute look. As much as I've been wallowing, I have weighed the pros and cons. Running away is tempting and easy. Chasing her as I promised? A battle that I have to be ready to conquer.

I answer her honestly. "I feel terrible, and I will say sorry a thousand times."

"I'll do whatever I can to help. That's why I'm here, actually."

"Humor me."

"I can attempt to convince the board to kill any possible deal, but it won't be easy. There has to be something more than business logic. They think in money and publicity."

A button is pressed in my brain. "Publicity."

She nods. "Bring me something to deliver to the board. I can't think of what, but it needs to create a rift."

Chuckling deep in my throat, a sinister thought comes to mind that definitely isn't on the straight and narrow. "Blackmail, perhaps?" I'm only half-joking.

Judging by Caroline's face, she doesn't find it funny, nor is she showing distaste. "You're serious?" She shrugs and lets out an audible breath. "Someone on that board must have skeletons in the closet."

"Of course they do. What person with a seven-figure bank account doesn't?" I pause as a theory begins to brew in my head. I tap the bar top as I consider the option. "But they don't air their dirty laundry."

"Exactly."

I sure as hell can find it. There are questionable methods that are aboveboard but still devious all the same.

"Find it, and I'll deliver it to them... only if you want. I mean, you really want to be with Savannah."

We circle back to the root issue. Being with Savannah, or am

I really a broken person unable to be in a relationship and give her a future?

Is missing her already a sign? Or is it the loss of lust? The unbearable feeling to want to end her pain? It's overwhelming, because everything I've been doing lately is because I'm out of my depth, because my feelings are stronger than I ever planned, and I haven't experienced it before, either.

It's love.

This has to be it. It's the only explanation.

I told her that I would chase her because my heart spoke before my mind could clear.

The only reason I would chase her is that there's a future for us.

"You need something to solve this? Consider it done."

―――

Rubbing the back of my neck, it makes a slight cracking noise, which isn't the best sign that my stress or deep fear is getting any less. I'm pacing by the window with my cell phone lying on my desk on speaker and listening to the man on the other end of the line. I vaguely hear his explanation as I look out on the cloudy late afternoon.

"Listen," I say. "I don't particularly care how low we need to go on this. I need to ensure we get this done. You have my full permission to go in any direction that will help solve this issue. If I need to throw money at it, no problem. If I need to rip someone to shreds, consider it already done. But speed this up because a lot is on the line," I remind the independent investigator who better be worth his salt to help dig into any possible hole that could solve Savannah running away.

"I'll need a bit of time. There are a few avenues we can possibly go, but it could get ugly."

"I don't fucking care. Get it done," I growl before I jab the end button on my screen.

I'm still in misery and despair. Even when my dad made a power move to ruin a company that was supposed to be mine, it was something else: fury. This is not the same. One is utter disappointment and bitterness, and the other has me clinging to hope and fear.

It's still no surprise that every message to Savannah and every attempted call has gone unanswered. I decided yesterday that the best course of action was to stop trying. After tossing and turning all night and considering my talk with Caroline, one possible solution to this mess came to me. Now, I need to get the wheels turning on it.

Space, they say, can help solve situations. But right now? I need to know Savannah is okay, to touch her to make sure she won't break, and to remind her that, deep down, she has to believe that my intentions are pure.

My fingers thrum on my desk that I tower over with my hands firmly planted. My mind isn't racing because my body is numb. It's different from a fine whiskey winding you down; this numb is purely heavy and dark.

It hits me, one way to solve a mystery. I check the time, and it's approaching five. Immediately, I swing my suit jacket off the back of my chair and slide it on as I walk to my office door, briefly taking in the scene of an empty desk where Savannah should be on my rush to the elevator.

Three minutes later, I find myself where I never would have thought to be. Awkwardly, I stand to the side outside the daycare and wince when I see a screaming toddler being carried in his father's arms, followed by a mom holding her daughter's hand and explaining that dinner will be fish sticks. Both parents seem very invested in preventing further meltdowns, so they don't even see me. It's not every day that their CEO shows up unannounced here.

Yeah. The company daycare was not on my list of places to voluntarily visit.

As confirmed when Elodie exits the daycare, carrying her daughter, and she instantly squinches her face when she notices me.

"Elodie, I need to talk to you."

She approaches me with caution. "What are you doing here?"

"Stuck in anguish due to my predicament," I state the obvious.

She side-eyes me. "Clearly. You are voluntarily showing up at the company daycare."

I tilt my head to the side. "True." Glancing around us, the after-work pickup is a zoo. "Can we go somewhere to talk?"

Elodie looks at her daughter, who she bounces on her hip. Admittedly, the kid seems to be the calmest of all of them. Elodie sighs. "Fine. But not for long. Lola will get cranky if she doesn't have dinner soon."

"Perfect. The café next door? We can get her a snack or something."

Reluctantly, she agrees, and we walk together but say little. It must appear odd to some to see us together. We have no connection to one another in terms of work.

When we settle in a booth next door, Elodie excuses herself real quick to change Lola's diaper. I order us a few things, all while my knee bounces under the table with nerves. This plan has to get me somewhere.

Elodie returns and still appraises me strangely as she sits Lola in the highchair, and she slides herself into the booth and hands Lola a book from her bag.

The waitress in an apron appears, sets down a piece of chocolate cake and two iced teas, and leaves.

Elodie swings her gaze to me and seems unimpressed. "Please tell me that you are not trying to feed my two-year-old chocolate cake two hours before her bedtime."

"I mean, why not?"

She rubs her temples. "Oh my God, you are doomed if you ever have kids."

"Well, that's not going to happen if you don't tell me how Savannah is doing."

I swear I see sympathy shadowing her face. "I shouldn't be here. But I am here to listen because nobody wants to see two people apart if they fit."

"Obviously, you think something."

She puffs out a breath and slides the plate of cake to Lola. "Go ahead, kid. This evening has already gone downhill." I'm waiting for a morsel of insight. "Julian, she's miserable. I don't think I've ever seen her this way. That's probably why... and you can't repeat this. But maybe... she can't see every detail of this situation."

"I've guessed that. What should I do? You know her best."

Taking a fork, she takes a giant bite of the cake for herself, probably to delay continuing this conversation. "Maybe time. Maybe it isn't meant to be. I don't have an answer. I've never seen her with someone, and it's intense."

"Why is it intense?"

She gives me a you-already-know look. "From day one of her becoming your assistant, you have both been heavily in one another's orbits. When you two went a step further, it's like lust took over, and you two went full swing. It wasn't slow, but it seems to be the only way you two would be. I can't imagine another way. So yeah, I can't help you much."

Everything she says is on point, but I don't know how to be anything but determined, and not quietly either.

"Fine. Tell me where she is. I need to see her."

She plays with a fork and watches Lola smoosh cake between her fingers.

"Did you mean what you said about the child thing, that it

can't happen without her? Does that mean you see something long into the future with her?"

I think for a moment, because only now do I realize what I said. Second nature, perhaps, and everything I never imagined, either. "I-I... Maybe so. This isn't a fling."

She smacks her lips together and debates with herself for a few seconds. "So, a longstanding kind of relationship?"

"Yes." It bursts out of my mouth without hesitation and catches even me off guard.

"Well, if you're so confident that you and she are meant to be and you know her so well, the answer to where she is should be pretty obvious, no?"

Multiple thoughts travel in my brain waves. My mind finds the page in my head, causing me to close my eyes and curse to myself. I was hoping she had locked herself in her apartment to decompress, but if I had stepped back from my panic, then I always knew. "She went back to Everhope."

Elodie nods. "Escaping you, the city, waiting in a coffee shop on Main Street and driving herself crazy staring at the Riverbell."

"I'll go to her."

"I'm not sure it's the best idea."

I shake my head. "I don't particularly care. I'll try anything at this point."

"Figured you would say that... Be careful. Savannah is delicate right now, and she deserves happiness."

"You think I don't know that? But I swear I'll make her happy if she lets me." I stand and tuck my hand into my pocket, pull out my wallet, take out some twenties, and toss them on the table. "I have to go. There's somewhere I need to be."

She rests her elbow on the table and rubs her forehead as Lola looks at her chocolate-covered hands. "This could go so wrong," she groans to herself.

"I'll take the chance." I grab my suit jacket. "I ordered nuggets, I'm not a complete idiot," I add before I leave.

I'll give myself the night to think through this, the best approach, and arrange a few things.

I'll surprise her whether she wants me to or not.

Probably not right now.

But I'll change her mind.

EVEN THOUGH I'M aware that there are only so many roads in this county, and I don't need the GPS, the lack of GPS is frustrating. It keeps telling me I'm on Country Road One when I'm positive it's two. When I see the barn up ahead, with a sign for a large antique store, I decide to stop. Julian Haven doesn't get nerves, but right now, apparently, I was wrong. Maybe I'm buying myself a few extra minutes before I just show up in front of Savannah.

Turning off and pulling up to the gravel parking lot, I notice two other cars. When I get out of my car, I slide off my sunglasses and look out to the other side of the road, where I see more cornfields, the sky clear and sunny.

Maybe I feel out of place, with my expensive car and crisp dark shirt, my sleeves rolled up, but I remember that Lake Spark is in the other direction, which is the town of luxury and hockey. Everhope is this way, which is by no means struggling either, with a few undercover millionaires.

Walking into the store, setting off the bell hanging over the door, I smell old wood and see everything from old furniture to knick-knacks.

The older man behind the counter, with his hands set on his glass counter, notices me. "Hello there, sir."

"Hello." I approach him and notice a woman in one corner examining old plates and the modest couple with a bonnet on her head, setting down a rocking chair that seems to be the man's recent craftsmanship yet suits the store. My eyes swing to focus on the store owner. "Crazy question, but I'm trying to get to Everhope, and the GPS seems to be throwing me off."

He chuckles at me. "You're not the first. Those things haven't been updated. They redrew the lines. Half a mile more, and you'll see the sign that points you in the right direction. What's sending you that way?"

"A problem. I mean, something I need to fix. My girlfriend isn't too pleased with me right now. I'm not sure she even wants that title anymore, so I'm going to have to go out. I would say getting us a room at the inn and locking the door all weeke—" In the corner of my eye, I see the couple quietly listening with a neutral look. "I…" It drags out of my mouth. "I mean, communicating with the woman that I'm courting in a very appropriate way, with the door unlocked and discussing the pie competition because we are obviously waiting for our wedding night to use the key." I cover my almost slip of inappropriate proclamation of being locked in a bedroom all weekend, doing very indecent things.

The woman in the other corner turns slightly and looks at me strangely, and the room falls into an awkward silence.

The man behind the counter clears his throat. "No need for that," he quietly advises me.

I shrug. "I don't know. I'm from the city."

"Since you're heading that way, who are you seeing? We all know one another."

"Savannah May."

He steps back. "Really? Well, that is handy."

"Why?"

He turns around, walks a few steps, and searches the counter. When he spots the package he needs, he picks it up and returns to me. "You can take this with you. She must have forgotten to pick it up." He sets the box down.

"She was here?" That surprises me.

"Yeah. Twice. Once to pick up an old pack of cards and the other time to ask if I could find someone who she could order another pack of cards from."

My eyes narrow and zone in on the box. "As in playing cards?"

"Yes, sir. Not every day that I have someone requesting that. Actually, never. By chance, I had some on hand the first time, and last time she asked for something special. Nothing in particular, only that it should be unusual and would make someone smile. She was over the moon when a contact up in Geneva had a pack supposedly from the 20s and Al Capone's circle. I thought she would pick them up when she was back in town."

My heart is getting poked. They're for me. She did this for me. Because she possesses every little way to make me happy, I can't let this be the end of us. I won't let it be. She'll crack her resolve, I'll make it happen.

I pick up the small package. "I'll make sure she gets it."

"Thank you. I don't like having things lying around."

"I don't like having things unsettled, so perhaps we're alike. Anyhow, I have to get going. Thanks for this." I hold up the box.

When I'm back in my car, I press the button to have the top down. The breeze will be good for me, and maybe I have a little confidence boost with the knowledge that Savannah did this for me. On a mission, I rev the engine, and when I'm back on the road, my tires screech as I pick up speed.

AFTER CHECKING in at the inn, I decide my best bet is to walk around town. I could show up at Aunt Bea's house, but that feels a little daunting, and I'm not sure her aunt would appreciate the effort. After all, I'm the guy who is ruining her business and breaking her niece's heart. But it's a beautiful day, and I'm taking my chances that Savannah might be somewhere on Main Street. It's near lunchtime, so she could be at the Riverbell or grabbing something from Foxy Rox. The Riverbell most definitely isn't an option to check out, as stepping anywhere in that radius would have me slaughtered, most likely.

Deciding to sit on a bench up ahead, I'll wait for any sign that she's nearby. Ten minutes pass, an hour passes, and after an hour and a half, I feel her behind me. I don't need to look, she's here. I've learned to sense her body, both in my arms and in proximity. The way she breathes is imprinted in my mind, too. My body tightens because I hold a breath, everything inside of me is for her, and I'm toeing a delicate line.

"Julian." Her voice is emotionless, but when I stand and slowly turn to face her, she's not surprised, only exhausted. She's wearing a light blue sundress, but nothing in her face is bright to match. Dry cleaning is hanging off her finger, and I hate that she's had enough time to send something off to the dry cleaner while she's been here. Savannah should be back in the city by now, with me.

"I'm not leaving until you hear me out." She shakes her head gingerly. "You obviously feel for me the way I feel for you… The cards are special. I was at the antique store by chance." Her head perks up, surprised. "They were ready for you to pick up. My guess is you ordered them before…"

She crosses her arms, ready for the offence. "Yes. Keep them, I have no use for them. And there is nothing more to say."

"Oh, there is." I step forward, and my voice grows persistent, demanding. Everything that I'm positive she was attracted to in the first place.

"Go back to Chicago." She hasn't blinked once.

I dart my arm out and touch her elbow, the connection enough for both of us to take a second while the electricity zaps between us. "Savannah." My voice scrapes, and my throat feels thick.

Her eyes are dull and somber. I want to wrap my arms around her, but I need to follow her cues on this. "I have a room at the inn. I'm staying there, and even if I have to go back to the city, I'll keep the room." I smirk slightly to myself. "They appreciate my business."

Her eyes bug out. "You are seriously keeping a bedroom at the bed-and-breakfast for eternity?" Her voice rises.

"It won't be eternity," I swear, and my tone matches hers, yet a little cockiness comes through.

The familiar need to bicker, at least, returns to us.

"You're unbelievable."

"I'm not. I'm standing right here waiting."

She grumbles to herself and stares up at the sky before dropping her gaze back to me. "I can't do this right now."

"You know where to find me."

"Who the hell does this?" she says to herself, frustrated.

The back of my finger slides down her face. "The man who will chase you until you have nowhere to go."

You would think it would be her to walk away in this moment, but it's me.

Leaving her to contemplate.

28

SAVANNAH

Warily, I knock on Julian's bedroom door at the inn. It's been a few days, and my body has a constant swirl of emotions. Anger that he let this happen, disappointment that he ruined a good thing, and, admittedly, sadness that a big piece of me is broken because I miss him, and in this moment, I can't deny the tiny flick of excitement that jabs my heart to see him again.

When he opens the door, his eyes immediately drill into me with the lightness of his eyes, pleasantly surprised. Hell, I'm amazed I'm here.

"Savannah." It's hushed in disbelief.

"Hi," I say softly and press my lips tightly together.

He steps back and holds the door open. "Come in."

I walk in with a sigh, and I hear the door behind me close. Stopping in the middle of the room between the desk that barely fits his laptop and the four-poster bed, this isn't a smart move. The worst, actually. It's evening, and he has the fireplace on, probably to add to the ambience with his tumbler of whiskey next to his work.

"You're here."

Slowly, I turn to face him. "Trust me, I'm as shocked as you are. But you are annoying the hell out of me, and probably this town, so if coming here means you'll go, then here I am."

The corner of his mouth lifts into a devilish smirk, and he tuts a sound. "Not everyone is thrilled that I'm around, considering..." He strides my way with a smolder that I wish he didn't have. "But the coffee place knows my order to a T. And a time or two, I've even talked shop with the owner of the hardware store who smiles at me."

Damn it. It's all true. Despite everyone else, he has a talent for winning people over.

But I'll highlight the issue. "Will you take away his business too?" I snipe.

His smirk disperses, and the subtle shade of pain appears because I'm aware I stabbed him again with my anger. "Savannah, I can repeat myself a thousand times if I need to. I didn't know."

My chin begins to quiver, and being emotional around him comes naturally. That's what happens when two people are pieces that fit, right? You're able to be vulnerable without thought.

"It doesn't change the fact that you will always be connected to it. Whether you want it or not, the association can't be shaken from my head. When you have family, you become fiercely protective of them, you want them to have only the best, and when someone so deserving is thrown that obstacle, it means you ache with them. I'm not sure you'll ever understand. You didn't ever have that."

That last sentence hangs in the air, and I bunch the side of my dress in my fisted hands. We have issues, but neither of us stoops to bitter words.

His face is incomprehensible, but I see the bob of his throat as he steps forward with his arms outstretched and takes hold of my shoulders. "You're wrong. Very wrong." His eyes laser into me, and I wait for something to snap, but all I get is the ability to hold me captive both physically and emotionally. "I do understand. Ask me why?"

"Why?" I whisper.

"Because I feel the same way about you. I'm flooded with thoughts of every way that I can make your pain less. It's an instinct to protect you that even I can't control. Everything about you is extreme, Savannah. The way I ache, the way I yearn for you, the way every time I close my eyes, you're there. Right now, I'm touching you, and I'm struggling not to take you into my arms before every inch of you gets attention. I'm too far gone that I can't rein it in even if I tried."

Parts of me open up and accept what he's feeling. He's a mirror to me. A reflection that we share. Everything between us is mutual, but right now, not united.

I'm weakening, I can't tear my sight away, nor can I run. My feet being unable to move is the opportunity he has been waiting for, because he closes our space with a simple step, and his hands on my arms turn into his arms wrapping around me. I fist his shirt, doing my best to hang on, to hold tight, and remember why I'm here.

"I came to tell you that you should leave Everhope. It's pointless to stay. I'm not going to change my mind, and seeing you around town only hurts me more. I don't need the reminder…"

He nuzzles into my hair, and his breath cascades down my cheek. "Of what?"

"Of what happened."

Julian doesn't seem fazed because he brings his mouth close to my ear, nipping once while one hand cradles the other side of my head, his fingers fisting some hair. I'm familiar with him when he's like this. Persistent in his pursuit.

"Or of us?" He scrapes his teeth beneath my ear.

A cold chill runs through my body, and sensitive parts of me become affected. "I should go."

His mouth travels along my jawline, and when I think he's about to touch the corner of my mouth, he diverts, and his lips follow the curve of my neck instead. "But you're here." He hums against my skin.

A line could be crossed if I don't try harder to claw away.

He presses a kiss on the side of my neck, and both of his hands firmly frame my face with a fervent insistence that I listen. "Because part of you believes me that I would never hurt you."

The only sign that his words are affecting me is the visible movement of my chest as my breathing changes.

"Because you believe in us."

I attempt to shake my head, but he presses a kiss on my collarbone, and I'm not yet immune to his touch. Instead, I'm now fighting an urge to burst into tears in his hold and be cured by having him inside me.

"Julian, please leave and go back to the city," I attempt to plead, but my voice is barely a whisper.

Our eyes meet, with great tenacity in his. "No. I'm staying until you're mine again," he reminds me.

Arguing to make my case is useless. His eyes aren't wild, they're certain.

My eyes hood closed once, only to open with a tear escaping the corner of my eye. "Julian." I'm no longer saying his name to request or warn him; instead, I'm saying his name in the hope of comfort to calm me. "It's not that easy." It's my last-ditch effort, but my voice is too uneven.

He brings his mouth to hover over mine. Hot, close, teasing, and making me desperate for his kiss. "I accept the challenge, Savannah." His whisper is mixed with his lips ghosting mine.

I was adamant that I would come tonight not even to hear him out, only to request that he give up. For the first time, our age difference plays a factor, because I was terribly naïve.

And maybe that's my excuse as to why I give in when our lips feather, only to lead to his mouth claiming mine with a kiss. A demanding and overwhelming kiss that I have no power over. Nor am I fighting it. Instead, I hungrily take more.

I'm so lost in this moment of misjudgment and weakness that I fail to register that he walked us backward while his tongue stroked mine. The back of my knees hit the mattress. Everything in the room slows, and he hypnotizes me as I slowly lower onto the bed. First sitting, but when he lowers his body, I lie back. Something flickers between us when our eyes connect. Maybe guilt on his part, and longing from mine. He doesn't deserve me, right? But deep down, my body screams that I'm wrong, which is why I reach for him.

His response is to kiss me tenderly, his forearms framing each side of my head.

"Let me show you how I would never hurt you," Julian whispers, the words brushing against my skin, voice firm and edged and undeniably seductive. A single, unhurried kiss presses into my neck, deliberate and reverent. "All I want to do is protect you." Another soft kiss follows, trailing along my skin, every movement unrushed—intentional.

The heat of his hip rubs against my thigh, and I've entered uncharted territory again, yet he is still somehow my anchor.

His hand floats up my thigh, dragging my summer skirt with it. He doesn't move in haste; he is deliberate and delicate in his touches.

But I want to be lost even sooner. Squeezing his arms, indicating that I want more, we meet for a kiss as my fingers search for the bottom of his shirt to lift. We speed up when the urge between us to be naked and connected takes over.

"This isn't me forgiving you," I clarify with a single pant.

His sinister eyes beg to differ, but I'm already too breathless and unraveling to continue to argue.

Clothes are thrown, and we find home when he holds me

rooted to the mattress. I open my thighs and reach for his cock, guiding him to my opening. He sinks into me, slowly. Taking a moment for our eyes to hold as he moves, and my walls tighten around him. Gently, he pulls out, only to rock back in, every time faster and more deliberate.

I've missed this.

Adjusting my body, I lean back on my forearms to watch the view of him inside my pussy. He could take this moment to say something filthy, but instead, his hand finds the back of my neck to gently tilt my head forward to kiss me, long and hard. Parting, our foreheads remain touching as our eyes lock.

My thighs clutch around his waist, eager to get more from him.

"I'm yours. You have me," he whispers the reminder.

Our bodies fit together. Everything in this moment is overwhelming me, but one thing that I'm sure of is that I want to be in the moment with him without any thought. He leans down to kiss me again, and I moan into his mouth as I feel him buried inside me. Pulling him closer, I tighten my legs around him. Sinking into the mattress, we are so lost in one another that I'm not sure if there is any place we don't touch. Julian moves deep inside of me, and my toes leaving a print on his ass only encourages him to fill me to the hilt.

His face pulls back slightly to ensure it's clear that I understand I'm with him right now and I have him. He's waiting for me and will continue to do so.

I ignore the whole reason that I'm here. "Don't stop."

He releases a half-smirk. "I won't, baby. I'll never stop." He isn't only talking about now, and my emotions take over my body. Our lips find one another again as we desperately move.

The realization that we're making love overcomes me to the point that I teeter on the edge of an orgasm.

I slip my gaze to the side to see our hands interlaced against the mattress, and I don't want to come. I want it to be at the same time with him, as one.

I'm so far gone that I don't even realize that our deep kisses are now to cover the sound of our moans and grunts.

We get there. Together.

It's heavenly and heavy at the same time.

We stay in an embrace as he stays inside of me, our eyes latching, and we lie there for minutes and say nothing.

———

THE WARMTH SURROUNDING my body is from Julian and his naked body spooning me. I glance over my shoulder to see that he's sleeping. We must have fallen asleep. Except it took effort to get under the covers and use pillows, which means I knew what I was doing. But our silence continued, and Julian, to my surprise, didn't press to convince me that this was a reunion. It wasn't.

Taking the opportunity, I gently lift the duvet on my side and slip out of bed. My clothes are scattered haphazardously on the floor, and I collect my skirt.

Was this a mistake or a goodbye? I can't process my thoughts right now, only panic to escape. He did it once. The first night we slept together, he was gone when I woke up. Now, I'm doing it in return, which by no means is revenge. That's why I spotted the pad of paper on the desk and a pen. Tiptoeing to the desk, I pick up the paper and jot down a note:

You need to go back.

I return to the bed and set it on my now-empty pillow before pattering on my toes to the door and leave.

29

JULIAN

The coffee is strong for a filtered drip. That's fine. I was up late working and taking calls, as I don't have the luxury of my office, and working remotely can have its drawbacks. But I'll take it if it means I'm a step closer to reclaiming Savannah, and I can't seem to think of another way of looking at it. The other week, she was gone before the sheets even cooled. She's running away, but I'm certain, deep down, she believes we can overcome this obstacle; it's just taking her a while to get there.

I take a longer sip before setting the mug down on the antique dark wood table. Today's breakfast is a plate of scrambled eggs, bacon, and a lone pancake because I can't handle any more full-on breakfasts complete with cinnamon rolls and sausage. This is considered light, and I didn't want to offend Glenda, the inn owner. The sun seeps through the lace curtains, and I'm debating whether to make my not-so-casual walk along Main Street and face Savannah on the other side of the street, throwing me a token glare, or to continue working from my room, hoping she shows up to talk.

Other guests haven't bothered me. They come and go, and I

usually have my breakfast before or after they all leave. I have been going back and forth to the city for the last two weeks. The other day, I felt it. Her glare softened, and yesterday her eyes lingered on me a few seconds longer than usual.

"More coffee?" Glenda comes through the swinging door from the kitchen carrying a porcelain pot with an overdone yet honest smile. She's in her sixties, and this place is her love and joy.

"No, thank you." I glance at the front page of the local newspaper on the table. I chuckle to myself. Not an ounce of world news, only a picture of the local high school graduation and a column about the upcoming festival. That sends a wave of fondness through me.

Maybe Glenda notices. "Everyone is excited that Savannah will be back to fulfill the queen's duties. It's a big deal."

"I can get that. She is queen material." My queen, to be exact. The sound of a ping indicates that I got a message, and I quickly flip my phone over on the table to see that a message came in from the investigator I hired.

Got what you needed. Sent digital. The physical docs were couriered to you.

That's a relief, as he was a day away from being fired because this has been taking too long. I need something to help me solve the problem that pushed Savannah away in the first place.

"By any chance did I receive something?"

Her body bounces from the reminder. "Oh, I almost forgot." She sets the pot of coffee down on a hot plate on the high side table against the wall, where there's a basket with a napkin and donuts. "This came for you. A delivery man bright and early. I was busy in the kitchen but noticed him lurking outside, and he seemed harmless enough." She slides a big manila envelope off the table and hands it to me. "Seemed important."

I accept it and quickly break the seal.

"I'll let you be. The oven timer is about to go off."

My eyes do a quick appraisal of the room, and I squinch my face at her. "More food? Breakfast is a little overboard today."

She scoffs at me. "Not for breakfast, silly. I'm making a new batch of cookies for tea today," she tells me in passing.

I grin to myself because that lady is pure hospitality, and she keeps to the preservation of the inn and spirit. She offers afternoon tea to guests. Typically, I take a pass. I'm not a tea drinker, but she leaves me cookies just in case.

All alone in the dining room yet again, I lift the seal and pull out the document. Instantly, my mood has been lifted, and a sly line forms on my mouth. I'm positive that I appear to be a man right now who received victory, and not by any means aboveboard either.

"Bull's eye." I sort through the photos and receipts, looking for everything I need to get me closer to where my life should be.

I LIFT my sunglasses as I slide onto the booth bench directly across from my father at a diner, a town over from Everhope. I feel the lack of emotion for the man, except satisfaction that I'll land on top, especially with the envelope by my side.

He ditched the tie today, and his unemotional facial expression has a glint of curiosity in his eyes. I don't see anything of myself in him except a similar chin people say we have.

"Julian." He's curt. "Long time. Care to enlighten me as to why I find myself at a diner where there are grilled cheese sandwiches on the menu?"

"Too lowly for you?" I smile cheekily, only to let it fall. "It was easy for you, as you have a driver, I'm sure. And like a real man, I have my Jag to drive myself." I'm surprised he agreed to meet me here. I didn't want to head back to the city, nor did I want to have this conversation in Everhope, either. Luckily, Lake Spark County has options. I guess when you say to your dad that it's important and it's been years since we've spoken, then his interest is piqued, and he would drive anywhere without question.

"Shall we cut to the chase? You don't bother with any holidays, any board meetings, and you don't even send a hello to your old man every now and then. So why the sudden need to see me urgently?" He glances briefly at the waitress who sets down a coffee for him, and I indicate for her to get me one too.

I let out an audible breath. "No need to pretend that we have a happy family. We let that go years ago when you showed your true colors. However…" I hold my finger up. "Some things never change. For example, your lack of commitment."

He scoots closer to the table. "You're the one who didn't want a relationship," he bitterly reminds me.

I quirk my lips out and hum a slight sound. "Hmm. Was there even a relationship after you backstabbed your own family?"

"Cut the crap and grow up."

"Oh, I have. You know, Haven Crossroads has been named one of the top companies in the country, and I must have missed it, but I didn't see yours there. Either way, let's not play a game and get right to it, shall we?"

With pleasure, I toss the manila envelope onto the table, and it lands with a thud.

"What's this?"

"A present." I offer him a cunning smile.

He hesitates for a moment, looks at me skeptically, then grabs the envelope and begins pulling out photos.

"I guess old habits are hard to break. How does wife number three feel about that?" I pretend to think as his face turns pale. "Oh. She doesn't know, does she?"

My father's sight is set on the photos of him and his bikini-clad twenty-year-old intern, who is a board member's daughter, in a compromising position on a beach in the Bahamas.

"Really failed on discretion there. Then again, you prefer indiscretions, right?"

He zooms his gaze to me, and he isn't impressed with today's antics. His jaw tightens, and his silence says a thousand words because he doesn't have the upper hand, but a concerning-to-me sly smirk forms on his face.

"Pot kettle, no? You've done a shitty job of hiding the fact that you're screwing your assistant."

My body tightens from a protective instinct that he is dragging Savannah into this, and a bit of anger that he's trying to compare me to him. I don't want us to have any resemblance, and deep within, he might have stung me with partial truth. I keep my face unfazed because I don't want him to see an ounce of unease.

"No need for such language. We might have met while working together, but Savannah and I are more than that. I'm not afraid for the world to find out about Savannah, and I know it's clearer than ever that we most certainly aren't a fling. Besides, I don't have a wife that I'm cheating on, let alone sleeping with the daughter of the board member who has a sole interest in making money off a river."

"The owner of that restaurant, isn't she related to your girlfriend?" he counters, and it's evident that he is trying to spin this.

"Not the same. Wanting to preserve a perfectly established location is the opposite of greed."

"Well, Son, you were not so smart letting your sister use your vote."

I lift my shoulders, still unnerved. "Unlike you, we live, and we learn. Oomph, I hope that pre-nup of yours is strong."

"Anything else? Throwing this at me is the oldest trick in the book." He's agitated; I'm breaking him down.

"I mean, I would say ensure the deal doesn't happen and the photos will be burned. One problem with that…" I slip out of my seat and stand, taking pleasure in the fact that I'm towering over him. "The photos were already sent to the board, and yikes, apparently, the investigator found a video of you two. I'd say you might want to call your wife, but that might have already been done." I hold my hands up in surrender. "That one wasn't me. You can thank one of the women on the board for reaching out to her in your wife's time of need. Of course, there is the optics of why you are pushing such deals." I cluck my tongue. "*Yeah*, nobody wants to be involved in the mess of an agenda getting pushed, all because of the owner's shitty behavior. And oops, a few decided even to leave the company because they disapprove of the morals. They're expecting your resignation as a parting gift."

My father shuts his eyes, then opens them, his teeth grinding. His downfall all happened in one minute with me.

I set my hands down on the table and stare him straight in the eye. "Getting the rug pulled from under you doesn't feel so great, does it? This is how it's going to go. Enjoy your resignation, take whoever the hell you want on a long holiday, and stay the fuck away from Savannah. You so much as go near her, and I'll find another way to ruin you," I threaten.

It clicks in a moment of pure protectiveness. Savannah is the only thing that matters. The future is her. She'll take me back, and one day she'll be my wife.

I can hang onto a cliff about to fall, holding on to whatever tiny piece I can to stay alive. But I come to the conclusion that I need more stability, something long-standing, strong, and that grips me so hard that I can't go anywhere. And I don't want to go anywhere because she is actually someone who gives me all of those things.

It's her.

My dad stifles a chuckle. "You'll screw up somewhere. Love and marriage are the biggest bullshit they feed us."

A gruff sound comes from deep in my throat. "I guess you and I are looking at two different menus. Stay away. I don't ever want to see you or hear from you," I warn with almost a snarl. Straightening my posture, a tiny smile of gratification forms. "You can keep those. I have copies. We all do." Smirking, I turn around and walk away.

Knocking that domino down, I need to reach my ending.

30

SAVANNAH

"You don't have to make that face," Aunt Bea says gently, not looking up from her mug of coffee as we sit at her kitchen counter. "I know what you're thinking." She has a familiar softness in her voice.

I exhale through my nose because I don't believe that she does. Anger consumes me, and I still wilted into his open arms. Sometimes at night, I touch the pillow next to me, wishing he were there. But then I remember why he's not.

"I shouldn't have gotten involved with my boss. I probably blew up my career," I quietly note.

"That's not what is really bothering you." My throat is dry, and I save my words. "Savannah." She waits for my gaze, and when she receives it, the half-line on her mouth is comforting. "It's fate. The Riverbell, I'll remember only great years, including you working there in the summers as a teenager and messing up many orders." She bubbles a laugh. "But maybe it's time."

My chest tightens. "Julian didn't let fate happen," I say. "He tried to take the Riverbell away from you. The place with rave reviews because people love it."

"I know it appears that way," she says calmly. "And I also know it isn't as black and white as that."

The thought that she's right scares me.

She reaches across the counter and covers my hand with hers, her grip grounding. "People make mistakes when they're used to winning. Doesn't mean they're incapable of doing the right thing when it matters."

I swallow. "You're telling me to forgive him." My voice rises in surprise.

"I'm telling you I don't blame him," she replies.

My eyes burn, with a tear forming because I can't hold it in any longer. "You didn't have to take me in," I say quietly. "You could've said no."

Her grip tightens a little. "But I didn't."

"And sometimes it feels like I owe you," I admit as the words rush out. "Protecting this place. Protecting you. If I let Julian be part of my life—really part of it—it feels like I'm a traitor for being with someone connected to this all."

Aunt Bea studies me for a long moment. "Oh, Savannah, I would never think that. I also believe that you're afraid of loving someone new." She sighs. "Perhaps you're afraid that it will feel like you're abandoning me. But do you know why that is?"

I shake my head in loss, and she squeezes my hand. "You're allowed to have more than one family. Having a future with him, well, somewhere in the back of your mind, you are aware that you could be creating a small one with him. With kids or no kids, but he would be your family if you two are serious."

The word family echoes in my chest, and for once, it's terrifying. Julian's world has always been different. Big, flashy, and a family background that many would consider cold and stale. It's not that I'm afraid of any of that. It's more, I'm scared he will break my heart when it already feels like I'm abandoning my aunt.

"Everything inside of me aches," I admit.

"You just need to wrap your head around a few things."

Sadly, I attempt to smile. "When I started working for him, he looked at me as though I was replaceable. No different from the others. Now? He looks at me like I'm *irreplaceable*."

"That's a perfect sign that his intentions are true."

I nod slowly, holding onto her hand like an anchor, even as part of me knows I won't always need her to be one because there is someone else who might fill the role.

TRUTHFULLY, I'm aware that my smile appears forced. Still, I do my best to put on a brave face as I walk slowly along the tables of pie under the white tents. The last place that I want to be is judging a pie competition with a crown on my head. Alas, a commitment is a commitment, at least in this situation. When it comes to relationships, I'm not sure where I stand. Everything I imagined has come undone. You're supposed to stay together through thick and thin, but here I am with a hollow heart that might break into a thousand pieces at any moment.

The lady of retirement age looks at me with bright eyes as I approach her table filled with lemon meringue pie.

"Not too tart or sweet," she says and hands me a fork.

"Similar to people," I say mundanely because it's a reminder of Julian's personality that drew me to him until I was so glued that I really did have to be ripped away when everything imploded. I shake my head to remind myself that now isn't about my sorrows. "I mean, a good balance."

Gladly, I accept the fork and dig into the piece that she cut. It does feel awkward when everyone around me watches as I taste. The instant zing that hits my taste buds is a pleasant kick that brings my focus to the moment. "Mmm, that is good. The graham cracker crust is a nice complement to the taste. Better than a normal pie crust."

She brings her hand to her heart, covered in an apron. "I do think so myself. And lemon meringue is by far better than an easy blueberry pie." She scowls at the next stall and returns her gaze to me with a bright smile.

"We shall see." I begin to stroll to the next and find myself in front of a neighbor from my street. Esme is a little older than Julian and is by no means a professional baker, but she hands out homemade pies on Everhope Road to everybody's delight.

"A classic blueberry pie. Simple yet pronounced. Even picked the berries myself," she proudly explains.

"I hope they're not poisonous," I joke, and she chuckles as she hands me a piece of her pie and a fork. I'm not sure how much more I can do of this. One bite of eight different pies is going to kill me on the sugar front. Then again, it's all comfort food, right? The taste of her pie hits right. It would go perfectly with whipped cream, but the competition rules state that only the pie is allowed on the plate. "Yum. It's fresh."

"I did my best, considering I have whining children at home and a husband whom I could throttle daily." She smiles while she holds her palm up. "Lovingly, of course."

I inhale a deep breath and feel the fragility in me retaking the stage inside me. Bickering can be fun. Or was it always a sign?

"Still, you managed to make a pie."

She's in a good mood. I don't think she's taking the competition all too seriously, or rather, just having fun.

"Savannah." Julian's voice flips all of my feelings inside of me. My focus is lost as I accept that he's here. But I don't turn around; instead, I stand, staring at the pie, feeling motionless because my entire body is tight with tension. I don't even say a word. The air feels sucked out of my surroundings.

"Savannah, look at me," he pleads.

Esme picks up her whole pie and aims. "Do I need to throw this at him?" she asks me and is dead serious. "Because I *will* do it." Ah, fudge, everyone knows my misery lately is because of

Julian. My lack of an answer actually causes her to raise the pie a little higher to prepare.

"Don't do that. It's a good pie," I tell her weakly. My eyes pinch together, as though hiding in darkness could protect me, because I can feel him so near, and everything inside me is sinking to the floor, as I'm heavy.

"Please, hear me out." There is desperation laced in his tone.

Everything around us goes silent, and I decide that I can't remain like this forever. Slowly, I open my eyes and turn to see Julian smoldering in dark blue jeans and a light blue shirt, the expensive watch a reminder that money does things to people. A need for power, mostly. Still, his stubble is a few days old, and his eyes show he hasn't slept, and there is one thing about them that has me feeling that magnet preventing me from running away. They're flooded with deep anguish because he honestly yearns.

"You shouldn't be here," I hiss. Briefly, I see my aunt and Elodie to the side. Both give me a sign to hear him out, purely with a reassuring look.

"No, I should. I've been waiting for you, and I will continue to do so. Except, you're too far, and I need you closer. I'm dying here." He steps forward, but there's still distance between us, and if I'm honest with myself, I hate the distance. "I've been miserable."

"Yeah, everyone at the office has noticed," Elodie comments, causing Julian to shoot his gaze at her because we forgot we had an audience. She clears her throat. "I mean, so I've heard or something." She tries to save herself before looking away.

He only gives her a quick blank glance. "Please," he returns to begging me. "I swear, I will get on my knees and beg every day until you listen."

That's bold. And yet...

"Julian, I've said it already. I want zero connection to—"

He cuts me off. "Even if I fixed it? Because I have."

I shake my head. "You can't fix this."

"Yes, I can. And I have."

I stare at him, unwilling to speak but intrigued to listen. Stepping forward, I yank his arm in passing, towing him behind me and leading us away from the tents in a hurry to a place of quiet near the park's gazebo. Dropping his arm, I create space again.

"Savannah, I meant it when I said I didn't know about the Riverbell. You believe me, I see it that you do. If I could go back to not being an idiot and missing the fine details, I would, but I can't. I've given all of my shares up. I want zero connection to Davenport."

It piques my interest and creases my forehead because his connection to his grandmother matters to him, he has held onto it, always. It's the closest thing that resembles family to him in his world. "You cherish your grandmother, and holding onto a piece of her empire is important to you."

"But she wouldn't want any of this either. My father tarnished her company too far, and I don't want to deal with the mess. If she were alive, she would tell me that it's okay to run away because I have someone to love, and I won't let anything happen to that person or the people around her."

A wave of softness goes through my body, of hope. But the waves constantly crash. "It doesn't change the fact of what is going to happen to the Riverbell." I somberly drop my view to the ground.

"Listen to me, you're wrong. The board has already been flipped, and I went even further to find a way to force my father to resign."

I give all of my attention to him. "What do you mean?"

He steps closer and swoops up my hands. His touch keeps me grounded, and it also sends me a message of optimism. "When I discovered that Davenport was trying to take the Riverbell, I went through a thousand scenarios of how to fix it. The solution was found, but I needed time."

My face contorts into complete confusion. "You're not making sense."

He scans the area around us, and we see everyone's eyes watching us, including my aunt, who is standing next to Elodie. My aunt gives a gentle nod, indicating that I should listen. Julian moves to ensure there is barely any air between us, and he quickly places a delicate kiss on my forehead before he moves his mouth closer to my ear. His breath along my skin tingles every nerve, awakening the power within me, and I am unable to deny him.

"I managed to flip the board because I had someone following my dad." His voice is low and quiet so that nobody can hear it outside our little bubble.

"And?"

His deep chuckle under his breath feels steeped with confidence, but it's sinister. "Let's just say there's a video with a woman in a compromising position that isn't his current wife."

I jut my chin up. "*So*, you blackmailed him?" I'm neither surprised nor impressed. This should be a red flag, but selfishly and oddly, I grasp that it's how he does protectiveness, and when it comes to his dad, I would never expect the situation to be clean.

Julian bobbles his head side to side, unfazed. "I mean, when you state it like that, I guess that is how you could label it."

I rub my temples. "I'm trying to follow. You sold your shares and have zero connection to your grandmother's company anymore, you blackmailed your own father, and flipped the board to kill the deal?"

"Yep. Your aunt no longer needs to worry. *You* no longer need to worry."

All I do is gingerly shake my head to myself and begin to grasp the facts. The balloon of concern I've been carrying around for my aunt begins to deflate, and I do feel my smile appear because of it. But it doesn't grow, because on the other side of the equation is Julian, standing right before me.

He searches my eyes, and I have to admit it uplifts me, and I can't push the hope for us away.

It's a lot of overwhelming emotions. He's intoxicating. Takes over my heart and controls my breath, and it's all because of a simple fact, and it causes me to step aside and begin to walk away.

"Savannah, I love you in every way that I'm supposed to love someone. We bicker, you invade every part of my body, you see inside of me the way nobody else can. Hell, you keep me in check and call me out because you believe I am a better version of myself. I'm only ever going to have this with one person, and it's you."

My cheeks grow tight, and my throat cracks, and a tear fills the corner of my eye, threatening to drop. Every word is true because I feel it, too.

Turning to face him, I meet his eyes. "You love me?"

"Yes."

That three-letter word tips me, and the tear falls as everything inside of me gushes open into the air, and I feel light. There are still, however, a few bricks on my wall.

"Everything with you has been one game after another. Compromising positions, withholding information, blackmail, blowing up my career, and ooh, a bonus, you made my life miserable at the start, and I've been pretty miserable lately. Did I mention blackmail? Because that was mentioned again today as a tactic. I'm not a game."

Instantly, he pulls me close, his hands frame my face, with his thumbprints stamped on my cheeks, our eyes locked. "You are not. You were an intriguing thrill until you became someone I care for, want to protect, and keep you as mine, all because I want you happy, and I believe I'm the man for that. I love you, and I'm well aware I need to learn how to do it all better. But you make me a better person. And you have me. Let me love you."

His thumb swipes away my tear droplet. "We're doing this while I'm in a crown and sash," I weep humorously and briefly look away.

His grin is wickedly sexy. "Even better."

Giving myself a long pause, I double-check with myself what my mind has decided and what my heart feels.

I give up because it's right.

"I love you, too," I admit.

"You asked me once about my company name. We reach crossroads in life when you have to make a decision to lead to the right path. You are my crossroad. Changing my direction straight to everything I need and want. I won't need any other way."

Another tear slides down my cheek because it's poetic and defines where we are together. Incredibly cheesy, too. My smile grows, as I bring out that side of him.

He sweeps my hand up and rests it under his palm on his heart. "I was about to tear the world apart because I need you, Savannah."

I recall the last few weeks, and without him, it was the true cause of my misery. "Me too."

It happens, like my body knows before my mind catches up. One second we're staring at each other, disbelief and relief tangled between us, and the next my mouth is finally on his again. The world shrinks, and so does the ache in my chest. Everything was lost and now found again. A kiss can be an apology, and I'll take it instead of words. Our lips continue to press until we pull back.

He kisses my forehead one last time and creates space between us.

In the depths within me, it finally releases the simple fact; distance never really stood a chance between us.

He dips his hand into his pocket, and for a second, I panic because if he does what I think he's about to do, then it's too soon. Instead, he smirks and presents me with the box with the necklace.

"It's been waiting for you. You lost your necklace once because you were meant to have only a key from me. Take it."

I playfully slap his shoulder, amused. "Did you practice that line in the car? It's smooth."

"It's true and will have to do until I slip a ring on your finger one day. Apparently, push presents are a thing, so if I get you pregnant, you'll get one of those, too."

He's thinking the long game.

I loop my arms around his middle, and he jerks me tight to him. I've missed the way his fingers brush strands of my hair behind my ear.

"Big plans, Mr. Haven." I can't stop beaming because my emotions have returned to the peaceful state they were in before this whole situation happened. "What happens now?" I wonder. Do we pick up where we left off?

"We'll find a way to make it work in the office." His face strains. "I should probably tell you that the blackmail material kind of had to do with my dad and his intern at his office."

I roll my eyes. "Great. Now you probably have to enter therapy because of the similarities," I say, sarcastic.

"Nah. I'm okay," he grins comfortably, then turns serious. "We'll go at whatever pace you want. I will be a better man because of you. I hope you realize that."

I'm confident when I say, "I do." Another moment is lost between us as we soak one another in. Extending this moment between us as we enter a new phase of our relationship.

He examines me differently this time, his face breaking the seriousness. "The crown and Miss Everhope sash... do you get to keep it?" His eyes flash with complete innuendo.

"If I say yes, I have a feeling you will throw me over your shoulder, and I actually need to pick a pie winner."

"Fine." He exaggerates his sigh. "I'll wait to make up for lost time."

I smile, and we kiss once more before I shake him away.

Clicking my tongue, I hitch my thumb over my shoulder. "Gotta go. Responsibilities and all."

I begin to walk away, but he catches my fingers, reeling me back in. "I'll be waiting. I'll go check out the state cow winner. And only you would ever cause me to say that sentence."

I sputter a laugh. "City boy."

"I'll enjoy it because I love you."

I take a second and let out a serene breath. "I like hearing that."

He lets me go, and I begin to continue my task of the day. I notice my aunt knowingly smiling at me. She quickly joins me and gives me a hard side-hug.

"He came to see me this morning."

Does that surprise me? No. Julian will take any means necessary to get what he wants.

"You found someone," she says.

"I did."

And finally, I feel safe for the long road ahead.

With him.

WE WALK into his room at the inn, hand in hand. I'm surprised Julian didn't yank me in. Instead, he's letting me lead the way. We talked on our walk from the festival, and I get to set the pace even if we both agree that what's between us is real and the future.

With the door closed, we finally meet for a kiss that nobody can see. A kiss for us. It's endearing and soft, then deeper.

"I love you," he whispers again as his mouth trails along my jawline.

"And I love you. I believe we have to make up properly." My fingers begin to claw at his chest near his buttons.

"Couldn't agree more." His hands travel between us, and the click of his belt triggers a thought in my mind.

Julian isn't the man I imagined when I was summoned to work for him. Nor am I the woman I was. My confidence never left me, but my desire for his control only grew.

"Julian," I purr as his lips kiss the corner of my mouth.

"Yes."

"Your belt. Let's use it." His head retreats in surprise. "You tied me with a ribbon, but a belt is stronger." I step forward to close our space, and my fingers find the clasp of his belt.

His face floods with understanding. "And I'll never let you escape from me again."

"And I wouldn't want you to let me go."

This is sentimental in our own way.

"If you're sure."

I nod as I thread his belt out of the loops with firmness and confidence. Walking backward, the back of my knees hit the edge of the bed, and I sink down, our eyes staying intact. I quickly discard my dress while he undresses. We meet right by the headboard.

Slowly with purpose, I lie down and stretch my arms over my head against the pillow. He loops the belt around the bars of the headboard, bringing it through to bind me tightly, and I flinch slightly.

We hold our gaze and get lost in one another's eyes.

"Safe word," he reminds me.

"I trust you."

His thumb does that thing where he caresses my cheek, so delicately, reminding me of the soft side of him that is overflowing with care.

"You may be tied up right now, but I want to make love to you long and slow."

My heart blooms from his wish. I thought for sure he would take the opportunity to fuck me hard for lost time.

"Deep, too," I add with a half-smile, and he has a crooked grin. I want him to make me come undone. He has the power to do that.

He kisses me again before he plants his forearm on the mattress next to my head, and his other hand travels along my body, moving lower. "Whatever you desire, you get."

His heart.

That's what I desired.

And it's what I already have.

31
SAVANNAH

I'm not sure I appreciate that Julian is trying not to sputter a laugh as I stand before him in his office. As silly as it may be, I want to do it my way, even if it is only mental gratification.

He leans casually against his desk with his arms crossed and his closed mouth stretched to one side. It's that swagger in him that displays he is waiting for me to take the lead.

I glare at him to get it together, ignoring any temptation to veer off course.

"Mr. Haven, I respectfully *resign*. That is not the same as quitting."

"Right. It's the classy way of quitting, basically." Is he doing this to rile me, or is this Julian being serious? For once, I'm not sure of his humor level of the day.

"Well, I'm a classy lady." My palm flies up to stop him as his mouth is about to open. "Except quitting that one time, which does it count? Because there were extenuating circumstances." My voice entwines with a question. "Anyway, I resign, which means you will need to find a replacement for me, and I will no longer be reporting to you."

"No. You'll be under me," he retorts.

I roll my eyes, but I feel the droll smile on my mouth.

He pushes away from his desk and takes a few steps in my direction. Always a dangerous move. Only made worse when his hands lightly take hold of my upper arms. "I don't accept your resignation."

"You have to. We can't maintain our professional dynamic this way. Too many gray areas, and I really don't want to be in a foul mood when I'm cooking you bacon for breakfast, all because you forgot to read your very organized calendar."

The corner of his mouth turns up into a soft, comforting smile. "You are staying in your role, and I'm promoting you."

My body sinks into exhaustion. "No. No. No, you are not. That makes it even worse. That screams that I'm sleeping with the boss and got my role. So not a solution."

"It would be to a different department. Away from me. Back to Charles's area and whoever takes his role," he tries to bring reason, but it fails.

I shake my head but smile affectionately at him for his effort. "You know, I've been thinking about it, and it's really important that I have no ties to Haven, other than you. It's better for us. Also, I found something that I think I could enjoy, and it's been playing in my head. Recruitment for finding the perfect personal assistants. High-end and a boutique style."

"Might want to rephrase the high-end part. Some men can take that in a different direction." I continue to hold my smile. He tips his nose up and studies me. "But I could see that career suiting you."

I splay my hands out. "Problem solved."

He takes hold of my hand with his and gives me a chaste kiss on the back of it, almost tongue and cheek. "I guess so. But only if you're not making this decision because you feel you need to."

I push my lips out and nod. I'm positive. The last few days, it has danced in my mind, and I might as well take the jump.

The step closer that he takes brings our bodies tightly entwined. "You are going to have to hire someone," I point out.

He hisses a breath. "Don't remind me. I mean, my last assistant was a pain in my ass, so I'm sure anyone will be a step up," he jokes, and my response is to pinch his arm, and he fakes pain. "Okay, she wasn't that much of a pain. Still, kind of irreplaceable."

"Maybe it never worked with anybody because you were cranky, and it was because your personal life was in shambles, but now you have me and you're a bit more chipper these days, so you'll be a great boss."

He stares blankly at me. "Let's not use the word chipper."

I giggle at his counter-reply. "I promise. You still need to find someone to replace Charles. That's turning into a dire situation. I heard him mention he wants to join a pickleball team, but he needs his Tuesday afternoons back."

"All I need is a signature on paper, and it's solved, but enough logistics chat. There is one thing I'm not sure you realize." He begins to smirk slyly, and his eyes dance with mine. "We have no reason to keep it professional within these walls anymore. That means only one thing…"

"Which would be?" I coo.

In one swift move, his hands move to my waist, and he hoists me up. "I can finally have you on my desk."

I laugh, and my head falls back as I smile. "One-track mind."

He sets me down on his desk and slides items to the other side near his laptop, ensuring nothing falls to the floor. His haste increases, and I fall back and rest on my elbows as I watch him loosen his tie. I'm very happy that I wore a skirt today.

"Still highly inappropriate," I chide.

Julian raises his brows, intent on calling me out. "Yet, in a few seconds, when I touch your pussy, it will only prove that you're along for the ride."

I shake my head but take hold of his loose tie and wrap it around my knuckles to pull him closer until he hangs over me. "Please, shut up and kiss me."

"Say no more. We'll have to make this quick if we want to beat the afternoon traffic out of the city to Everhope."

I titter a laugh. "You really want to go?"

The way he shrugs like I'm crazy is cute, but I'll never tell him that. "Why not? Plus, maybe we should look at some properties. I want to buy something as an investment. Make things easier when we want to escape this place."

Everything inside me melts because everything he says is deeply earnest and with a depth of care that I never imagined he had. And I get to experience all of it—every morning, afternoon, evening, and in between.

Which is exactly why I yank him to me and crash my lips onto his.

At ease with the direction of where we're heading.

It's promising and right.

Most of all, our hearts used to clash in a tug-of-war of dislike before they crashed, and all the pieces are ours, only we get to touch.

That's what we are.

And it makes sense.

Only to us.

EPILOGUE: JULIAN

4 MONTHS LATER

The wheat field blows gently with the breeze while the sun shines in the pristine blue sky. It's tranquil out here. It started out as our weekend home, the perfect escape from the city. A house in Everhope was a surprise I casually sprung on Savannah when she moved into my place in the city. We still have it, as we do need to be at the office. If it weren't for the company office, we would be here most of the time. For now, I enjoy walking down Main Street and grabbing a cup of coffee in the morning. There's always someone talking about the high school's upcoming Friday-night game; they're good this year.

Savannah beams as she surveys the patio, clearly impressed by the organization. "Wow, the purple and silver balloons are a nice touch."

"Your replacement arranged them." Because it pained both of us to admit that Savannah and I were right, that working together isn't for us. We want to keep ourselves separate; plus, she has gone freelance with recruiting PAs for companies. Still, the new assistant doesn't have the same sense of sass to keep my day moving, but she is organized.

I survey the beer on ice over on a table near the pool and BBQ area. There's comfort in the simplicity. No need for overpriced champagne bottles; instead, classic bottles of beer and pitchers of iced tea. It's not going to be too big a gathering, but still large enough. It's Savannah's birthday, and I had to persuade her that we should do something. It could be anything. All she wanted was modest, similar to what she would have with her family.

"My aunt is bringing the cake. Elodie has a salad. And you are going to impress us with your grilling skills," she goads me.

I snake my arm around her middle, pulling her against me with a playful grin. "Hey, don't be like that. I've improved on that. I even took a grilling class," I remind her.

She chuckles. "That was a good present, wasn't it?" She smirks. For my birthday, she sent me to a grilling class since that skill needed some tips. I was a little offended, but she made up for it two minutes later when she revealed present number two underneath her dress.

"I do believe, however, I win on the present front," I challenge her as she drapes her arms around my neck and gives me a beaming smile.

"Oh yeah. *That*," she teases me as she raises her hand and appraises the new diamond on her ring finger. We've been moving fast. Somehow it feels like our speed, though. "I won myself a fiancé during a match of Go Fish last night."

It wasn't a plan—just a sudden burning need. I'd kept the box, heavy with hope, hidden in my pocket, expecting to propose today, surrounded by those we love. Yet, when she asked for sixes, and I was stuck holding nines, the impulse seized me. Her laughter at my blurted proposal loosened every nerve, and when she crashed into my arms to kiss me hard, joy burst through me like fireworks.

"Everyone is going to flip," she notes.

My face squinches. "Will they?" I feign doubt. "Because I'm positive they have a betting pool going on."

"Very true," she agrees matter-of-factly.

She pulls back so my hands can frame her beautiful face. Our eyes meet, and every time, I'm reminded how lucky I am. Half her mouth stretches; she's probably reading my mind.

"Yes. You're lucky. I'm lucky," she informs me. Point proven.

I shake my head side to side, amused, before diving in for a kiss, one that allows my tongue to slip in. She murmurs from the power of the kiss. Not exactly chaste for a family festivity, but luckily, we're still alone while the sound of cars pulling up to the house is in the background. We reluctantly part, only to snag one more quick kiss.

"Tell me something to kill the dirty thoughts in my head," I beg her in a whisper.

A bright smile appears. "No can do. I keep revisiting myself naked with only your ring on last night. *However*, for the sake of trying to remember that you have to bless us all with your grilling? No pressure or anything. Ooh, and someone is bringing an ambrosia salad." She pats my chest.

I step back, putting some space between us as I cringe. "I thought they outlawed that in the 1970s."

She starts to walk away, then glances over her shoulder and points at me. "Remember, no refined personal-chef palate. We're doing family style, and don't pretend you hate it. Betty down the street told me the lie you fed."

"Fine. Only if she ditches the tangerines for pineapple."

Savannah continues her stride toward the open sliding doors to our renovated kitchen. "Start the grill," she orders aloud. "I need to find the juice boxes for Lola."

"Bossy," I call out.

A few minutes later, I'm successful at preparing the grill and checking my seasoning inventory next to the plate of burgers. The backyard is now bustling as people arrive. Hugs. More hugs. And if in doubt, just hug. I'm mentally preparing for what happens when we share the engagement news.

I tip my head up when Hayes arrives. He grabs two bottles of beer from the bucket and beelines straight to me.

"Look what the cows dragged in." I grin as he hands me a drink.

"Only for you did my navigation send me through corn fields to get to your weekend chalet."

I take the bottle, line it up on the edge of the cooking station counter, press down to pop the cap off, then hand it back.

We clink our beers. "It'll grow on you. Just wait. Thanks for coming. Nothing's better than having a friend and new COO at my backyard BBQ for Savannah's birthday." I've finally won him over. He's in Illinois, finding a place before we announce his new role next week.

He studies me, and he looks funny. "All you need is an apron with some ridiculous phrase, and we're all set."

"Har-har."

"Where is the birthday girl? Contemplating her birthday wish and whether it should involve you or not?" He's sarcastic.

I hold out my bottle, waiting to accept a toast. "It does, as we are getting married."

Hayes grows a wide grin. "Ah, congrats." We clink bottles. "You're settling down. Next thing you know, there will be a little one and a Labrador running around."

"We'll wait. Unless I get a little demanding on the honeymoon." And I have no problem being persuasive.

He shrugs. "Marriage and having a kid are two different things. Anyhow, where is the bride-to-be?" He begins to search the yard.

I follow Hayes's gaze and spot Savannah walking out of the kitchen carrying a tray of veggies. Elodie walks beside her, holding a bowl of dip.

Hayes does a double-take, and his face is perplexed. "Why is she here?"

I swing my gaze between him and his target, Elodie. Huh, they haven't met yet. "Elodie? She's Savannah's best friend and also works at the office."

His eyes go wide. "You mean Ellie?"

"I mean, Elodie," I repeat.

He begins to laugh cynically to himself. "Of course, we used different names." He can't look away, following her movement.

I'm completely puzzled as we watch them set items on the buffet table. "You know her?"

He whistles to himself. "You can say that again. Kind of a one-night thing about three years ago."

Surprise hits me like a wave of thunder. "That's her?"

Hayes is a composed man, but he seems a little lost right now and even takes a deep breath. "I didn't think I would see her again. I'm kind of caught off guard right now."

My head tips to the side, as I begin to run with an idea in my brain. "Wait... did you say about three years ago?"

He shrugs a shoulder and takes a swig from his beer. "Yeah, why? Do you know her through Savannah or does she work for you? Tell me she doesn't work for you."

That's the least of his worries.

The sound of a little girl giggling as she wobbles in her run makes his gaze snap to her. He sees a smiling Lola racing straight to Elodie, who lifts her up and tickles her daughter's belly.

He looks at me, and lines form on his head. "She has a kid?"

I'd rather not get involved. I want to throw a calculator in the field and avoid speculation. But Hayes is my friend, so I just state the facts.

I take a larger swig of beer, maybe for courage. "Uh, yeah. Lola turned two in the spring, so plus nine months is... math, right?" My voice shakes; my smile is weak.

Hayes swings his gaze to Elodie and Lola.

And it happens.

Hayes and Elodie's eyes meet.

BONUS: SAVANNAH

3 YEARS LATER

Ugh, the reminder causes me to roll my eyes. Every time I visit Julian at his office, I see his assistant with new flowers on her desk from her husband. Why? Because I broke Julian Haven, and he abolished the "no flowers on his assistant's desk" rule. Samantha should consider herself lucky that I played a role in getting her a kind boss.

I smile at her as I walk past her desk. "I'm assuming my husband is in there, probably cutting someone in half through the phone line?"

"Very true, Mrs. Haven." The woman who's my age, wearing a beige sweater, gives me a knowing look.

Not stopping for chitchat, I continue on, and when I quietly open Julian's door, he notices me right away and stops mid-pace by his window of the city. His eyes flick up as he continues talking on his phone, but he quickly wraps it up.

"Gotta go. You have a deadline of 5 PM. I'm not budging." I hear someone on the other end talking, but Julian just hangs up and prowls my way with a sexy smirk forming.

"I'm late," I say point blank.

He glances at his watch. "No, you're not. We weren't going to meet until six at that new little Greek restaurant." His arms find me when he stops in front of me, and he pulls me close to him.

"I'm late," I repeat, wondering how many times it's going to take for him to catch on. My face is stoic, and my eyes are big as I wait patiently.

His facial expression shades to a mix of realization and surprise. "Ah... that kind of late."

I nod my head.

Julian lets me go and swipes his hands through his hair as he steps back, his cheeks puff from a breath. He doesn't seem thrilled.

"I know we weren't planning on this at all. It wasn't on my agenda for the year, either. I mean, I'm still young, and you're—" I decide not to finish that sentence when Julian's brows rise.

"Yeah, let's not finish that sentence," he agrees. Scratching his cheek, he seems to be searching in his head for words. "You say late. As in you aren't completely sure?" I nod.

"Do I need to send my assistant to run out and get us a test?"

My mouth gapes open, and I shove his shoulder. "Are you kidding me? That's something you would have her do?"

He shrugs a shoulder as though I'm the one who's crazy. "Why not?"

Now I shake my head once to the side. "Because that just crosses the line of all the things she probably already knows about us."

"Fair enough."

I shove my hand into my bag and fish out a test. "I've come prepared."

His eyes drop to the box, and reality hits him. "Right. You could be pregnant." He's speaking to himself more than to me.

"Well, you think about that a little more while I use your bathroom," I tell him and leave him to ponder.

While peeing on a stick, it hits me with an obvious feeling that I didn't get until now. I'm not nervous. Nor scared. Maybe even excited.

I choose not to look at the stick and decide to wait.

Returning to Julian's office, I find him with his hands tucked in his pocket, and he looks out on the horizon through the glass.

"*So,* a baby." He doesn't turn around, and he's still unreadable.

"I haven't looked yet."

He turns slowly, his face almost solemn, and my stomach sinks. He isn't happy, I guess.

Disheartened, I decide not to make a big thing about it and flip the stick, only to see a negative and hold it up. "Well, false alarm." I hear the somberness in my voice.

"*Oh*, no baby." My head perks up because his voice catches me off guard. He sounds the same, nor does he look like a man relieved. "I think I'm kind of disappointed about that."

"Really?" Optimism hits me.

He approaches me with a warm smile, scooping up my hands to hold in his. "I am. I guess I don't want to wait anymore. No, I *really* don't want to wait anymore."

My entire body relaxes, and I feel my smile bloom. "Me neither."

Ah fuck, he's doing that "bringing my hand to his mouth for a kiss" move. Charming as always.

"I don't need to persuade you to let me put a baby inside of you, do I?" His cunning look is trouble.

I drag his arms to wrap around me. "You don't need to persuade me," I promise.

"Good. I would like to get started on this right away, if you don't mind?" His suave grin is making me melt, especially as his fingers begin to feather my lower back.

"Have I just unleashed a new side of you?"

His lips quirk out, and he bobbles his head side to side. "Nah, I'll just keep you tied to the bed a little longer to ensure my cum stays inside you, and we need to be thorough."

I scoff a laugh. "There are people walking in the halls here."

"And I've fucked you on my desk before, so we're good." He walks me back to his desk, slowly, sinfully, until my ass sits on the edge. "I would say to add every date we have a better chance into my calendar so I can cancel meetings, but I'll fuck you every day all the same."

I bring my finger to his lips. "Cancel the meetings anyway."

Julian catches my finger between his teeth. "Let's get out of here."

"It's not 6 PM yet," I deadpan.

"Who the fuck cares. I need to make love to you in our bed."

Leaning in for a kiss, it doesn't faze me that I'm extremely lucky. "I love you," I murmur against his lips.

"Good, because if you think I'm possessive of you now, wait until you're pregnant with my baby."

And that's exactly what I'd expect him to say.

www.ingramcontent.com/pod-product-compliance
Lightning Source LLC
LaVergne TN
LVHW021336080526
838202LV00004B/198